ADVANCE ACCLAIM FOR *SNOW ON THE TULIPS*

"A splendid debut novel! With a tender romance, a gripping plot, and a well-researched setting, *Snow on the Tulips* drew me in to the harrowing uncertainty of life in the Netherlands under Nazi rule. Liz Tolsma's beautiful story kept me up at night—not just wondering what would happen to her endearing characters, but wondering what I would do in similar circumstances. Do not miss this book!"

—SARAH SUNDIN, AWARD-WINNING AUTHOR OF *WITH EVERY LETTER*

"Being widowed at a young age, I once again felt the pain and joy during those days as Cornelia fights her own feelings for Gerrit. The guilt of loving again, the desire to be wanted, set against the backdrop of the Nazi-infested Netherlands brings joy and heartache to the reader. New author Liz Tolsma brings her fresh writing to a tragic time in history. Her use of engaging characters and description should not be missed."

—DIANA LESIRE BRANDMEYER, AUTHOR OF *MIND OF HER OWN* AND *WE'RE NOT BLENDED, WE'RE PUREED: A SURVIVOR'S GUIDE TO BLENDED FAMILIES*

"*Snow on the Tulips* is richly layered with courage, faith, and love. It reminded me of all the things I loved with Bodie Thoene's Zion Covenant series: characters doing more than they thought possible, wrestling with how to live lives of faith in time of war, and history that comes to life on each page. It is a compelling story that will delight readers."

—CARA PUTMAN, AWARD-WINNING AUTHOR OF *STARS IN THE NIGHT* AND *A WEDDING TRANSPIRES ON MACKINAC ISLAND*

SNOW ON THE TULIPS

LIZ TOLSMA

THOMAS NELSON
Since 1798

NASHVILLE   DALLAS   MEXICO CITY   RIO DE JANEIRO

Published in Nashville, Tennessee, by Thomas Nelson. Thomas Nelson is a registered trademark of Thomas Nelson, Inc.

Thomas Nelson, Inc., titles may be purchased in bulk for educational, business, fund-raising, or sales promotional use. For information, please e-mail SpecialMarkets@ThomasNelson.com.

Publisher's Note: This novel is a work of fiction. Names, characters, places, and incidents are either products of the author's imagination or used fictitiously. All characters are fictional, and any similarity to people living or dead is purely coincidental.

Unless otherwise noted, Scripture quotations are taken from the King James Version.

Library of Congress Cataloging-in-Publication Data

Tolsma, Liz, 1966-
  Snow on the tulips / Liz Tolsma.
     pages cm
  ISBN 978-1-4016-8910-0 (trade paper)
  1. World War, 1939-1945--Underground movements--Netherlands--Fiction. 2. Netherlands--History--German occupation, 1940-1945--Fiction. 3. Historical fiction. 4. Christian fiction. I. Title.
  PS3620.O329S66 2013
  813'.6--dc23

                                2013006376

Printed in the United States of America

13 14 15 16 17 RRD 6 5 4 3 2 1

In memory of Heinrich Harder, Dirk DeJong, Hendrick Jan DeJong, Jan Nieuwland, Henry Joseph Spoelstra, Douwe Tuinstra, Egbert Mark Wierda, Hyltje Wierda, Klaas Wierda, Sijbrandus van Dam, and Ruurd Kooistra—the Dutch Resistance workers who gave their lives on April 11, 1945, in Dronrijp, Friesland.

In memory of Gerard DeJong, who survived that day.

*"God is our refuge and strength, a very present help in trouble.
Therefore will not we fear, though the earth be removed, and
though the mountains be carried into the midst of the sea;
Though the waters thereof roar and be troubled, though
the mountains shake with the swelling thereof. Selah."*

PSALM 46:1–3

*"You ask, what is our aim? I can answer in one word.
It is victory, victory at all costs, victory in spite of all
terror, victory, however long and hard the road may
be; for without victory, there is no survival."*

WINSTON CHURCHILL

"For the dead and the living, we must bear witness."

ELIE WIESEL, NOBEL PRIZE–WINNING AUTHOR

GLOSSARY OF FOREIGN WORDS

DUTCH

BANKET: almond-flavored pastry

BEDANKT: thank you

BEDSTEE: a bed, usually a double, hidden inside a cupboard, most often found in the front room of the house. The doors would be closed during the day to hide the bed.

DEEL: large, sloped barn, often attached to the house by a breezeway

ELFSTEDENTOCHT: an almost 200-kilometer skating event held on the canals in Friesland. It is typically held in January or February and only when the ice is at least fifteen centimeters thick. It may be held on consecutive years or may skip many years, depending on the ice conditions.

HAGELSLAG: chocolate sprinkles

HEEL HARTELIJK BEDANKT: heartfelt thanks

HONGERWINTER: the especially long winter of 1944–1945, during which over eighteen thousand Dutch people starved. In September of 1944, the Dutch government-in-exile ordered a railway strike in the Netherlands, and as retaliation, the Germans blockaded the western part of the country, including the important cities of Amsterdam, Rotterdam, and the Hague. Because Friesland is an agricultural center, the food situation wasn't nearly as dire there, and many women came from those blockaded cities looking for food for their starving families, often bartering anything they had of value.

HUTSPOT: a Dutch dish consisting of mashed potatoes and mashed carrots, as well as meat, all mixed together

JUDEN: Jews

KLOMPEN: wooden shoes

NEDERLANDERS: Dutch people

NSB: the Dutch police who worked in collaboration with the German occupiers

OLLIEBOLLEN: powdered-sugar-covered donut holes

ONDERDUIKER: literally an "under diver." Dutch men hiding to avoid being sent away to a German work detail.

RADIO ORANJE: Radio Orange, the Dutch language program broadcast by the BBC and listened to in secret by many Dutch. Orange is the Dutch royal color, and the queen often broadcast messages to her subjects as she spent the duration of the war exiled in Britain.

RAZZIA: a plundering raid

SLOTEN: a ditch around a farm field, usually filled with water

SNERT: pea soup

VRIENDELIJK BEDANKT: friendly thanks

FRISIAN

(You may see these same words spelled differently elsewhere. Frisian is mostly a spoken language and spellings can vary greatly. There are at least four spellings for the Frisian words for "thank you." In Friesland, Frisian is spoken in the home and Dutch in the schools and for business.)

BEPPE: grandmother

DOMINEE: preacher

FIERLJEPPEN: (lit. far-leaping) ditch or canal pole vaulting, a traditional Frisian sport. Still today, there are competitions held around Friesland.

FROU: Mrs.

HEAR: Mr.

HEIT: father

JA: yes

LEAFDE: love

MEM: mother

NEE: no

PAKE: grandfather

TSJERKE: church

UMPKA: uncle

GERMAN

AUSWEIS: a paper exempting a man from a German work detail because of a job he holds

DANKE: thank you

FRÄULEIN: miss

IIERR: mister

HEIL: hail; carries connotations of well-being and health

MUTTI: mom

NEIN: no

REICHSMARKS: the standard monetary unit in Germany from the mid-20s until 1948

SCHNELL: fast

SOLDBUCH: pay book

UNTEROFFIZIER: an under officer or sergeant

CHAPTER 1

THE PROVINCE OF FRIESLAND, NETHERLANDS

February 1945

chnell, *schnell!"* A German soldier jammed the cold, hard barrel of his rifle into Gerrit Laninga's back.

Gerrit's heart throbbed against his ribs like waves in a squall against a dike. Any minute now, it would burst through his chest, splitting open as it flopped to the ground.

He scrambled to keep pace with the nine other Dutch Resistance workers in front of him. If he fell behind, the Germans would shoot him on the spot. Not that it mattered one way or the other.

Gerrit was on his way to his execution.

"Be merciful unto me, O God: for man would swallow me up." The words of Psalm 56 that he had memorized long ago became his prayer. *I know, Father, what awaits me on the other side of the bullet. But if it be Your will, let this cup pass from me.*

The smell of boiled cabbage wafted on the early evening air as people finished their suppers. He sensed their pitying stares as they hid behind their lace curtains, peeping out to spy on the men marching to their deaths. Behind closed doors, these people

1

whispered, wondering what crimes the men had committed to be executed in this way. Tomorrow morning they would talk about it around their breakfast tables.

He would not be here in the morning.

Behind one of the house's brick facades, a child shrieked in laughter. The Gestapo officer jabbed his weapon between Gerrit's kidneys.

"What time I am afraid, I will trust in thee." Please let it happen quickly. No pain, no suffering, Lord, please. But spare me, Father. *"When I cry unto thee, then shall mine enemies turn back: this I know; for God is for me."*

He'd had many close calls during the war, like the time the Nazis searched every nook and cranny of the house where he had been hiding. They failed to move the rug that covered the trapdoor to the cellar where he was concealed. Or the time he had seen some soldiers on the road when he'd been delivering ration cards. He was able to hide in a ditch before he was caught.

I trust my life to You, sovereign Lord.

Peace filled him, a sweet taste of the heaven that awaited him.

No matter what happened, God was in control.

The men in front of him watched their feet as they moved forward, their backs hunched, their shoulders slumped.

Gerrit held his head high. He refused to let the Germans think they had him conquered. Death was not defeat. Death was victory.

His hands were tied in front of him. He clasped them together, tighter and tighter as death approached.

His ankle turned and he stumbled on the uneven street. The butt of the rifle slammed into his back.

With his wrists bound, he couldn't balance himself. He fell to his knees. His breath caught in his throat. Any second now, a bullet would pierce his skull.

The Gestapo officer grabbed him by his upper arm, placed him on his feet, and shoved him. Gerrit spoke his thanks with a smile. If he could earn the sympathy of the soldier, maybe somehow he could find a way out.

The man stared at Gerrit with frosty blue eyes. Then he frowned and turned away.

Escape slipped out of his grasp.

A cold chill wrapped itself around him.

The death march continued to the canal. A squat house stood sentry at the water's edge, its two first-floor windows like eyes, watching, recording, memorizing these events. The setting sun's rays reflected off the still water.

Visions of Mies and Dorathee flashed across his mind. One woman had broken his heart. His heart broke for the other. He did this so they could be free.

The Germans forced the condemned down the icy canal bank beside the bridge. The early evening frost made the grass slippery. Gerrit and the other prisoners slid and skidded down the small hill. The Gestapo officers shouted at them while jabbing them with their guns. "Get up, get up. *Schnell*. Now line up here."

This was the end.

Gerrit righted himself and faced the officers. The men who were slow to stand were kicked and dragged to their feet.

A neat line formed.

Silence filled the air.

He stood tall. He couldn't think.

"Ready? Aim."

He fixed his gaze on the cobalt-blue eyes of his executioner. "Fire."

Into Thy hands I commit my spirit.

A white-hot pain seared through Gerrit's body.

He crumpled to the ground.

CHAPTER 2

Cornelia de Vries sat in her rocking chair, alone in the small front room with its out-of-date red brocade wallpaper, the heat from the black cast-iron stove warming her cold feet. Twittering birds serenaded her as she sewed the fraying hem of her silky green Sunday dress. Glancing at the picture of Hans on the wall, pain nibbled at the edge of her heart.

The skirt's material cascaded over the arm of the faded blue davenport beside the rocker as she laid aside her mending. She rose, watched the pendulum swing in the schoolhouse clock on the wall, stared at Hans's picture, then went to the long front window. Parting the lacy curtains, she peered out to watch the birds on the bare, brown branches of the bush. The sky, often filled with droning Allied planes on their way to Germany, remained serene. The sun cast its dying rays over the canal, a thousand lights playing on the water's surface.

The birds blended in with branches, but when one of them hopped from twig to twig or flitted to another bush, she caught glimpses of their black and brown feathers.

Then a different kind of movement on the other side of the

water caught her attention. Not the cheerful, bouncy action of birds, but the movement of men. A plodding motion. She parted the curtains farther for a better view.

A number of men, maybe a dozen or so, marched toward the steep canal bank. Five or six German soldiers, armed with rifles, surrounded the men and shouted at them. If they were trying to reach the edge of the canal, it would have been easier to do so about fifty or sixty meters from the bridge where the land once again became even with the water level.

What was happening?

The answer came as soon as the thought crossed her mind. From her vantage point, she watched as the soldiers forced the men to scramble down the bank, though their hands were tied in front of them. The Germans kicked many of them as they slid and fell.

Cornelia dropped the curtain.

She closed her eyes because she couldn't watch.

She covered her ears because she couldn't listen.

She sank to the floor because she couldn't stand.

Memories of that horrible night more than four years ago knocked at her consciousness. Denying them entry, she pushed her hands harder against her ears and scrunched into a ball.

Pop. Pop. Pop.

She had hoped and prayed to never hear that sound again, but the reverberations echoed in her head. The past mingled with the present.

Pop. Pop. Pop.

All fell silent. The birds ceased their chirping.

Five or ten minutes passed as she sat on the floor, her entire body shaking. The floorboards creaked under the unmistakable bounce of her brother's footsteps on the stairs. She opened her eyes. He moved down the hall and passed the front room to the door.

She rose to her feet. "Johan?"

5

He stopped, frozen by her call.

"Johan?"

"I am going out."

"Nee," she screeched. "Nee. The Nazis just executed a dozen men. There is no way you are going to step foot outside this house."

He stood several centimeters taller than her and he used his height to his advantage, peering down at her. "I want to see the men they shot. Maybe we know some of them."

She stepped in front of the door. "They will arrest you on the spot, you know."

Her brother ran a hand through his tousled sand-colored hair. "They are gone now and I'll be careful. I promise."

"I won't let you go." She stood with her hands on her hips, something she had seen *Mem* do a thousand times. With their mother no longer here, she was the caregiver to her brother.

"You can't forbid me. I'm an adult."

"Only a fool would go out there now."

"Maybe I'm a fool, then. I am going anyway."

"What will happen to you if you get caught? Working in German factories with all the other young men who have never returned—is that what you really want?"

"Nothing will happen to me, because I'll be careful."

"What do you plan to do out there?"

"That is none of your business." He tried to push past her.

She stood her ground. "You are my business. And my responsibility. You're not going anywhere."

"Yes, I am."

Holding to what Mem always did, Cornelia stopped arguing and glared at Johan. She wouldn't let him out the door. Not when it meant an almost-certain death sentence. A few moments later he shrugged his broad shoulders, sighed, and turned up the stairs.

She won the battle. This time.

GERRIT BREATHED IN and out. Pain arced through his body.

Pain. He was still in pain.

He wasn't dead.

German voices floated around him. The soldiers who had attempted to execute him remained here. If he moved at all, he would be dead. The rise and fall of his chest, the twitch of his eyelids, a swallow would mean a bullet in his head.

The Gestapo spoke among themselves. "Give each of them a good kick. Let's make sure we got them all."

What would happen to him when a jackboot met his side? The pain would be unbearable, but he couldn't cry out, not even a whimper, no matter how great his agony.

He heard them as they made their way down the line, reassuring themselves that all of their prisoners were dead. *Thud. Thud. Thud.* A boot met each body. Each of his friends. Each of his fellow Resistance laborers.

He gritted his teeth. Forcing himself to go limp, holding his breath, Gerrit lay motionless.

Lord, please, spare me.

The soldiers moved closer. They stood right next to him.

"This one is dead. I hit him squarely. Come on, let's go. Leave the bodies here to teach these people a good lesson about what happens to those who resist."

With that, the sound of the German voices, the clacking of their weapons, and the heavy thunk of their boots faded.

How could the officer be so sure he was dead? Gerrit didn't believe his acting skills were quite that convincing. Did his executioner hold himself in such high regard that he believed he couldn't miss? Or when Gerrit locked eyes with him, did he unnerve the man enough to cause the shot to go astray?

One thing he didn't doubt—he needed to be gone from this place before the soldiers came back. No need to put his theatrical abilities to the test again. He also had to be cautious not to leave too soon. They may look this way, spy movement, and come back to finish the job.

He lay without moving for as long as he dared. Around him, nothing stirred. No one moved about.

When he convinced himself that the Gestapo had left the area, when he hadn't heard their voices for many minutes, Gerrit moved. Pain shuddered through his right shoulder when he lifted his head. He looked down and bile bubbled in his throat. The bullet had torn away his skin, and blood spurted from the wound. He needed help.

Forbidding the anguish in his shoulder to register in his brain, he rolled to his left side. He pulled himself to a sitting position with the greatest of care.

The world careened, then crashed to a halt.

He sat without moving for a minute, not daring to look at the broken bodies of his comrades. His chest tightened.

The brown brick house at the top of the bank beckoned.

He sucked in his breath, then pulled his feet underneath himself. Pushing off with his uninjured arm, he stood. Or attempted to stand.

He couldn't bring himself upright. The world kept moving. Dusk had fallen. A sense of urgency pulled him along.

The light in the house's window winked at him. The occupants had yet to draw the blackout curtains. Biting his lip, tasting the saltiness of his blood, he rose to his knees, tucking his injured arm close to his body to keep it from jostling.

He crawled like a baby, edging his way along. He couldn't climb the bank. Instead, he needed to get to the place where the land flattened. Each movement sent a searing heat through his shoulder. Each movement brought him that much closer to safety.

Centimeter by centimeter, he fought his way to level ground.

He lay panting for a moment, drenched in sweat, though the cold breath of a North Sea breeze touched the late winter evening.

He didn't have time to rest. Any moment those German soldiers could return. Gritting his teeth, he continued his excruciating crawl toward the house at the top of the bank.

The green door lay a few meters in front of him now. Hand, knee, knee; hand, knee, knee. Then it stood within arm's length. He reached up, knocked, then collapsed to the ground.

Rustling came from behind the solid wood door before it opened. Gerrit peered into the soft, round face of a dark-haired woman. She glanced around and, not noticing him lying in front of her, began to shut the door.

"Please, help me," Gerrit's voice rasped.

She turned her gaze downward. Her mouth fell open into a small O, but she didn't utter a sound.

A man came behind her, gray tingeing his hair. "Who is here, Maria?"

She pointed to Gerrit. "What are we going to do about him?" she whispered.

"Help me get him inside. Then close the door and bolt it."

They grabbed Gerrit by the shoulders and he groaned.

Maria released her grip while the man clinched him around the waist, dragging him to his feet. "Get that door closed. I'll bring him to the *bedstee.*"

Blackness closed in on Gerrit, but he fought it. He needed to stay alert. These people might be collaborators.

The man half carried, half dragged Gerrit to the front room and deposited him on the bedstee, a bed in a cupboard with doors that could be opened or closed. Oh, the joy not to be moving, not to be jostled, to have a few minutes to let the throbbing in his right shoulder calm a little.

"Who are you?" the man asked.

"Jan Aartsma." One of his many false identities.

"We heard the shots. What did you do?"

Was the man curious, or did he have another agenda? "Last night I was arrested. They caught me out after curfew."

The man pulled Gerrit's shirt away from his wound with jerky actions. The fabric tugged on the raw edges of his flesh and Gerrit tensed.

Maria examined the hole in his shoulder then turned to the man. They held a brief, hushed conversation. Gerrit couldn't hear what they said, but the woman shook her head. The man nodded, taking her in his arms. He brushed her dark hair from her face and kissed her forehead.

He glanced over her shoulder at the entryway, then leaned above Gerrit, the long-forgotten odor of pipe tobacco clinging to his clothes. "Why were you out after curfew?"

He asked enough questions, questions Gerrit didn't want to answer. So he told the man what he had first told the Gestapo. "I had a meeting with a woman. A married woman. In the fields."

A blush crept into Maria's pale cheeks and the man took a step back. Good. Maybe they wouldn't question him further. The occupiers may be ruthless, but they didn't shoot men for clandestine meetings. They must know there was more to his story than he was willing to share, but the less they knew, the better for them. The less he told them, the better for him.

Maria handed a bottle of something to the man, whom Gerrit assumed to be her husband. Her hands shook. "You'll have to clean and dress the wound. The sight of it makes me sick to my stomach." She ambled out of the room.

Gerrit bit his lower lip as the man poured the pungent peroxide over his bloody shoulder. Millions of little needles pricked his wound. Darkness crept over him and he wanted to embrace it. But he couldn't. Not until he determined what kind of people these were, until he could be sure they wouldn't turn him over to the Germans. They had to know he had fabricated his story like a woman knitted socks.

He cried out in agony as the man patted his wound dry and when he positioned Gerrit to dress his shoulder. The rough cotton he used to cover the injury rubbed and chafed until tears came to Gerrit's eyes.

The man finished his work and stepped back, pacing four or five meters from one end of the small, bright room to the other, pausing for a moment before repeating his circuit. "You have to leave here." Maria returned to the man's side and he rubbed her shoulder while she wrung her hands.

His voice rose in intensity. "The Germans will come back to bury the bodies. When they count them and know one is missing, where do you think they'll look? Our house is the closest to the bridge, and they won't hesitate to turn this place over and shake it until they find you. And then they will arrest us for helping you." Fervor filled his words. "I have to protect my family, and having you here will mean we will all end up in prison. I'm sorry. You have to leave. Now."

Gerrit tugged on his hair. The man wanted to guard his young, beautiful wife. Maybe he had children who slept upstairs. He refused to help. He would sit by and let others do the work.

He would let others give their lives.

Gerrit wanted to shake people like this.

"I'll leave," he told Maria and her husband.

He would leave, but he didn't know where he would go.

CHAPTER 3

Only the drip, drip, drip of the water from the tip of the rowboat oars broke the stillness of the night. Johan Kooistra dipped the paddles into the water without making a sound, pulled back, and lifted them. A chilly breeze seeped through his thin clothes. The weather had warmed since the blizzard last month, enough to thaw the canal, but winter had not yet gasped its last breath.

He counted on absolute silence. Needed it. He couldn't be caught out at night. He couldn't be caught out at all. At twenty years old, Johan might get picked up at any minute by the Gestapo or the NSB—the dreaded collaborating Dutch police—and shipped off to work in the German factories.

His sister Cornelia caught him the first time he tried to leave the house, forcing him to wait until she got busy out back. She wouldn't understand his aching desire to be outside. He loved her, but this war changed her into a different person. Most of the time she acted more like his mother than his sister. He couldn't talk to her and have her understand his feelings like she did before.

While he had been working and hiding on his *umpka's* farm in the country, he had the freedom to go outside every day and breathe fresh air. He liked staying with his father's brother and his cousin. Then a few months ago they had been betrayed and the situation became dangerous there. Not having anywhere else to go, Johan returned home to his sister.

He wished she didn't watch every move he made.

He had heard the gunshots by the canal bank. Like a child who runs to the schoolhouse window to watch the first snowfall, he needed to see up close what had happened. So he snuck away in the dim light and pushed their rowboat onto the canal.

He took a deep breath of the crisp evening air, and liberty filled his lungs. The risk was worth this moment of freedom.

He had found some orange fabric in Mem's sewing basket. He didn't know what she had intended to do with it. Sometimes mothers bought material and never used it. She died in the second year of the war, so he couldn't ask her, but he didn't think Cornelia would mind if he took it. He wanted to cover one of the bodies of the executed men with it. Displaying the color of the Dutch royal house would be his show of resistance to the occupiers. He had heard tales of others doing the same.

A rush of adrenaline surged through him. He couldn't fight since the Germans had dismantled the woefully unprepared Dutch army. He couldn't join the Underground because Cornelia kept such a thumb on him. But this he could do. The tips of his fingers tingled.

He turned the boat to shore and, within a few strokes, beached it on the grass. Though death happened all the time on a farm, he hadn't prepared himself for the sight in front of him. All these men, shot in the head. He turned away from the gruesome scene while the small dinner his sister prepared burned in the base of his throat, threatening to erupt. He inhaled, then walked down the line of men. At the ninth and last man Johan stopped, pulled the orange fabric from inside his jacket, and laid it over the body.

His chest swelled. He had done a brave and noble thing.

Then he detected movement from the corner of his eye. Something—or someone—stirred at the end of the bridge.

Johan fell to the cold, hard ground and flattened himself. The hair on his arms bristled. *Just breathe.* He listened for the thudding of jackboots on the pavement but heard none, nor the clack of *klompen*.

Cautious or daring—he didn't know which he was—he lifted his head. Whoever moved before now lay still.

Lay. Not stood.

Johan scrambled to his feet but kept low as he climbed the bank toward the figure. A man lay crumpled on his side near the end of the bridge. A moan escaped him. He tried to move but winced in pain. "Help me."

"What happened?" Johan crouched but couldn't see much in the gathering dark. All of the blackout curtains had been drawn and for almost five years the streetlights had been dark. Only a sliver of the moon illuminated the scene. A ring of blood stained the man's right shoulder, like he'd been shot.

One of the executed men?

"Help me."

Johan didn't miss the pleading in the man's voice. "Where do you live?"

"Nee. Help me."

What should he do? He couldn't leave the man here. His sister Anki was a nurse, but she didn't know he had returned. His family didn't trust her husband.

He could take the man home. Cornelia wouldn't like the arrangement, but he couldn't think of anywhere else to go. "Can you walk at all? We have to get to my boat." He couldn't leave their rowboat on the opposite shore. It would raise too many questions with the Nazis about how it got there.

The man reached with his left hand and Johan pulled him to his feet. He held the injured man around the waist while he flung his good arm over Johan's shoulder. Together, with the man leaning much of his weight on him, they made their way to the canal bank. Though sloped, it was shorter than going to the flatter ground. The wounded fellow distributed more of his mass Johan's way.

"Don't pass out on me."

"I won't. I don't think I will."

Lifting milk pails and working around the farm made Johan strong, but they still struggled down the bank, slipping and sliding. All the while, his heart kept time with his legs. They could get caught at any moment, so exposed they were out here. He wanted to hurry but the man couldn't.

Please stay conscious. He wouldn't be able to lift him if he passed out.

Johan tried not to jostle his patient, but it proved to be impossible as they slid down the icy bank. The man cried out in pain.

"Hush or both of us will end up dead."

The man nodded.

They reached the boat and now Johan faced another difficulty—how to get the man in.

"I can do it." The injured man managed to sling one leg into the boat. The vessel wobbled, then stilled. Carefully, he leaned one arm on the boat's edge, then pulled the other leg in. He slunk in the seat.

Johan pushed the boat away from shore, then hopped in, picked up the oars, and headed for the little house on the far shore. When he left home tonight, he wanted adventure. He sure got it. More than he planned.

They didn't talk, the need for silence absolute. Where had the man come from? He had been shot, that wasn't in doubt. But how? He couldn't be one of those executed, could he?

No one survived his own execution. The Nazis weren't that sloppy. Johan had no other explanation, though.

Wouldn't his sister be surprised when she saw what he brought home?

CORNELIA RELAXED IN her rocking chair, enjoying the peace and quiet of the darkness. Right now, no planes flew overhead on their way to bomb Germany—a rare occasion these days. Silence enveloped her. Johan must have fallen asleep upstairs because all remained still. Since her parents had died and her sister, Anki, had married, the job of caring for her younger brother had fallen to her.

Three years ago, when he was seventeen, he had received notice that he had to register for service in Germany. They promised good meals and a salary. Right away, Cornelia didn't trust it. Since Hitler broke his pledge to respect the Netherlands' neutrality, she didn't trust anything that man or his compatriots said. After a lengthy talk with her umpka, they agreed that Johan should go into hiding at his farm. He could work there and earn his keep. Umpka Kees had plenty of places to hide, and his own son, their cousin Niek, would hide there too.

Two months ago they had been betrayed. Someone must have seen the boys working outside as they often did. Both of them managed to get into the hiding spot in the hay mow, but she and her umpka agreed it was too dangerous there now. Niek had gone to another farm while she and Umpka Kees constructed a hiding place here so Johan could come home.

She sighed and her black-and-white short-hair cat, Pepper, stirred at her feet. She wanted to stroke his head but didn't want him to jump up and find another place to sleep, so she resisted.

This war had a way of turning everything upside down, like

a jigsaw puzzle whose pieces didn't fit together. They had lost so much. Too much.

She rubbed her temples, erasing all of these musings. She didn't want to think about the past. Or the present. She gathered Pepper in her arms and nuzzled his soft neck. "Come on now, time for bed, though you have slept all day today, haven't you?"

He answered her with a lick on her cheek with his rough, bumpy tongue. A gurgle of laughter bubbled inside her, the rare treat sweeter than chocolate.

A knock at the door tightened her throat and her pulse rate kicked up a few notches. Who would come unannounced at such an hour? No one would dare venture out after curfew. Only the Gestapo and a few audacious Resistance workers roamed the streets at this time.

Whoever was outside now pounded on the door. Could it be the police? You never knew when the Gestapo or the NSB would show up. She had to warn her brother and get him into his hiding place before they broke down the door.

She squeezed Pepper so hard he screeched and jumped from her arms.

The pounding continued. "Cornelia, open up."

Her mind whirled. That sounded like Johan. But wasn't he upstairs?

"Open the door. Now."

She cracked open the door.

Johan stood on the clean-swept step, another man draped over his shoulder.

Behind her, Pepper scampered away. She drew the door open a sliver wider. "What is going on?"

"This man has been shot. Help me get him to the bedstee."

The man reeked of danger.

"Corrie, help me."

She clung to the doorknob.

"Let us in."

"I can't."

"Help me." The man took a labored breath.

"He will die if we don't aid him. You have to open the door. Please."

What if this had been Hans? What if he had knocked on someone's door, desperate for help? She knew what he would have wanted her to do.

She opened the door and stepped to the side.

The man must weigh almost twice as much as she did, and Johan struggled to half drag him to the front room.

She walked beside them, studying the man, his handsome face pallid, his lips tinged with blue. He smelled of filth, his wavy, sandy-colored hair matted, his clothes caked in mud. Then she saw his shoulder, blood seeping through a crude bandage, and the metallic taste of bile bit her tongue.

"Shut the door." The man's voice, though weak, held an air of authority. "Lock it."

Cornelia scurried to the front and obeyed. Why would he need the door locked?

Johan went to the front room and crossed to the two sets of double doors. The built-in cupboards were painted yellow with green trim. Behind one was a bedstee. Behind the other was storage. Cornelia scooted in front of them and flung open one of the bedstee's doors. No one had slept here in a while since she and Johan each had rooms upstairs, but clean red-and-white-checked sheets stood at the ready.

Johan eased the man's torso across the mattress, then swung up his feet.

She stood beside him but turned to her brother. "Where did you find him?"

"On the road, near the bridge."

"Do you know what happened to him?"

Johan shook his head and the man remained silent.

"Let me look at your shoulder." Taking great care not to hurt him in any way, she pulled aside his ripped shirt and lifted a crude dressing. Red oozed from a gaping hole. Her stomach recoiled and she dropped the bandage in place as she turned away. "What happened to you?"

"The Gestapo tried to execute me. They missed."

Johan gasped. "You. You were one of them. The men by the canal."

"*Ja.*"

Cornelia touched the bandage. "Who took care of you?"

"Your neighbors across the canal treated me, but they turned me out. They were too afraid to let me stay."

Her neighbors had done the right thing. A current of panic shot through Cornelia. She had been wrong to allow him in her house. The Gestapo would arrive to search for him, and when they found him, she and Johan would be shipped to a prison camp.

"You have to let me stay."

"I—I—I don't know." Was he dangerous? What was the right thing to do?

Again she asked herself, what if this had been Hans?

Her brother leaned against the door of the storage cupboard. "If we turn him out, he will die for sure."

She twisted her damp hands together as she looked at the man. His eyes, as clear and blue as the big Frisian sky, spoke of kindness. But if she was wrong about him . . . "If you want me to let you stay here, you must tell me what you did."

"I was out after curfew."

"Doing what?"

"Meeting a woman. A married woman."

Nazis didn't shoot people for meeting a woman. They shot people for many reasons and sometimes for no reason at all, but this was an execution. An execution of men who had done something awful.

"You're lying to me. I will throw you on the street unless you tell me the truth." And she might turn him out even if he confessed.

The man sank into the bed, grimacing in pain. His blond, arched eyebrows lowered, a muscle jumping in his square jaw. He hesitated for a full minute or two. "I work for the Resistance in Leeuwarden and was arrested there. They found contraband on me. For your own protection—and mine—I refuse to tell you more."

Cornelia clasped her hands to her chest. Contraband. Resistance. Her safe, quiet life shattered.

A pulse of excitement radiated from her brother beside her. "This man is a hero. We have to take care of him."

"Not a hero, just a man doing what I have to do."

His humility didn't move her.

The circle of crimson on his shirt had grown in the few minutes he'd been here. Without immediate aid, he would die.

"Inasmuch as ye have done it unto one of the least of these my brethren, ye have done it unto me."

For Hans's sake, she had to help him. Her gut twisted. What would she do, what would she say, where would she hide him when the Nazis came searching?

"What is your name?"

"Wim vander Zee."

"Another lie."

Johan tugged on her arm, a little child wanting his way. "You have to get Anki. He needs medical care, but *Doktor* Boukma might not be trustworthy. He might turn in Wim. With her nursing background, Anki can help."

"You want me to go out after curfew?" She would be arrested.

They all would be. The possibility became more and more a reality with each passing second.

Wim reached out and grasped her wrist, squeezing it hard. He hissed at her, "You can't go for this Anki. Nobody can know about me. No one at all. Do you understand?"

She nodded, unable to breathe.

He relaxed his grip. "You will have to take care of me."

Cornelia found her voice and the words tumbled out. "I have no training and I hate the sight of blood, so what happens if I pass out? If I do it wrong, you will die. Having me nurse you is not the way to stay alive."

"Five years we have been occupied and you have never had your abilities tried?"

Wim was testing her. Was she one of those who watched from the sidelines or would she participate in the game?

"Please, Cornelia." Her brother didn't want her to sit by idly.

His pleading gripped her. But she would have a talk with him later about bringing strangers into the house. And about being out of the house in the first place.

She rose and padded across the cold floors to the tiny bathroom to gather everything she needed to doctor him, including an old, almost-empty bottle of hydrogen peroxide and a few cotton balls.

Was she one who watched from the sidelines? Yes, she was.

And what was so wrong with that? The Netherlands was a small country. Their army—which didn't exist anymore—had ridden bicycles, aging rifles slung over their shoulders. Over four and a half years ago, they had been no match for the German tanks. She retrieved a needle and some thread from her sewing basket.

Every Sunday she went twice to the *tsjerke* and prayed that the Allies would come soon and free them. All of her friends chatted about it. Some had wireless sets and listened to *Radio Oranje* on the BBC in secret. The Allies would be here soon, and then it would all be over. Why risk their lives now when before long help would come and they would be free?

She brought her supplies and dumped them on the end of the bed. Trying not to hurt him any further, she peeled off the rough cotton dressing, her eyes turned away. Wim didn't make a sound, not even when she pulled the bandage from his skin. He lay with his eyes closed.

She looked at Johan's wide face. "Did he pass out?"

He nodded.

Good. He had fainted—from blood loss or pain, she didn't care, as long as he stayed unconscious for a while.

Covering her mouth, she swabbed the wound, cleaning it. Then she spied the bullet still lodged in his shoulder. Waves of nausea rolled across her middle. "He needs a doktor."

"Wim told us not to get Anki."

"What if he dies? He's unconscious now, so we can get Anki here to treat him without his even knowing. Whom can we trust if not our own sister?"

"What about Piet?"

Anki's husband did pose a problem. He wasn't a collaborator, but his complacent attitude toward the occupiers made her nervous. "We will make her promise not to tell him. Remember when we were little? She was always the best at keeping secrets."

Johan shrugged. "Fine. I will go get her."

"Nee, not you. What were you thinking when you left before? Do you know you could have gotten yourself arrested? Or killed?"

He opened his mouth and drew in a breath, but she lost interest in his defense.

"Never mind, time is slipping away. I have to get her." If her trembling legs would carry her that far. They had no other choice.

CHAPTER 4

Anki Dykstra had no energy these days to do the most basic of chores. She pulled the blackout shades over the long windows in the front room of her home and sank into the overstuffed brown chair, grateful for the chance to rest and put up her feet. Plates and silverware clanked together as Piet finished the dishes, the lingering smell of *hutspot*, rich with the odors of carrots and potatoes, permeating the house.

She rubbed her still-flat stomach. It wouldn't be that way for long. Inside she harbored a secret, the longed-for answer to many years of fervent prayers. Piet didn't know yet. She wanted to be sure there were no problems before she shared her surprise. They had waited and waited for a child. He would be so surprised and happy. At least she hoped so.

He came from the kitchen and perched on the chair's arm, his long legs splayed to the side. He kissed her on top of her head. "Are you feeling any better? Can I get you anything?"

She held his hand. "*Bedankt* for cleaning up the kitchen."

"You should see Doktor Boukma." He squeezed her hand. "This has been going on far too long."

"It will pass. If we had milk, a warm glass would be good."

He released her hand and stood. "We are not going to go over this yet another time. I refuse to steal milk from the plant. Not only could I lose my job, but it would be breaking both the civil law and God's law."

He was right. She didn't want to rehash this topic. Soon enough she would be able to obtain milk because of her pregnancy. "How about we go to bed? A good night's rest would be nice." She went to her husband, and arm in arm they headed out of the room and to the hall for the stairs.

Before she could place her foot on the first step, someone pounded on the door. Piet squeezed her shoulder. "You go on up while I answer the door."

He had no more than opened it a crack when her sister, Corrie, pushed her way inside. "Is Anki around?"

"Right here." She retraced her steps to the front of the house. "What is it?"

"Umm . . ." Corrie hesitated, pushing back the stray strand of long auburn hair that had escaped its clip. "I need to speak to you alone, about a, well, a woman thing, you know?"

Piet shut the door. "You two have your chat. Come up soon, Anki. Good to see you, Cornelia." He nodded his blond head in Corrie's direction, then disappeared up the stairs.

"I need you to come with me. We have an emergency. Get your coat and let's go." Corrie tugged on her sister's arm.

Anki pulled away. "Are you crazy? Why would you take me out after curfew?"

"Hush." Corrie lowered her voice. "No one can know, not even Piet."

No one in her family trusted Piet because of his unbending convictions. They kept many secrets from her.

"Johan brought a man home tonight. The Gestapo botched his execution. They shot him in the shoulder and the bullet is still in there. There is so much blood I have no idea what to do."

Anki's pulse tripped over itself. Johan was home? And what about this mysterious patient? She couldn't say no. Her nursing training, dormant since her marriage, woke up and kicked in.

"Just wait a minute. I have to tell Piet something and gather a few things. Start praying that the Nazis will not catch us out after curfew."

"I already am. Just hurry. This man is very weak."

Anki flew up the steps and into the bedroom she shared with her husband. He was slipping off his dark blue button-down shirt as she entered the room. For a moment, she forgot everything except why she married him.

He turned to face her. "What did Cornelia want?"

"She has a sick friend who requires some medical assistance."

"What about the doktor?"

That was a good question she had forgotten to ask. "He must be out on another call."

"What friend?"

"Just a friend of Corrie's."

"You are breaking the Germans' law by going out now. You will do that for a stranger?"

"Curfew means nothing when a person is sick. Maybe even dying."

"Is it that serious?"

Anki nodded. "Ja."

"You know how I feel about this."

"I know, but it would be wrong to let someone die because of a curfew."

"God would find a way to heal the person, if it be His will."

"Tonight I am that way."

"Anki . . ."

"Please. I want to be a submissive wife, but this is something I have to do."

Piet put his hands in his pockets. "You know you are risking your life."

And their child's. "I have to go. That is what my nursing training was all about."

"And what if I forbid you?"

"Forbid me?" In their four years of marriage, he had never spoken like this. "Please, please understand and let me go." If Corrie
spoke the truth about the man's condition, they didn't have a minute to argue. "A human life hangs in the balance and precious time
is wasting away."

"You should let God take care of things." Piet sighed. "You
know how I feel, but if you have to go, then go."

"This will take awhile and so it will be morning at least before
I get home. Hopefully before you go to work." She stood on her
tiptoes beside her husband and kissed him. "I love you."

He rubbed her shoulder. "I will be praying for you."

"Bedankt." If she had to sneak out after curfew and remove a
bullet from the shoulder of a wanted man, she would need those
prayers. She gathered a few things and placed them in her rucksack
along with her identification papers. Piet's sat beside hers on the
little night table. She fingered them, then, shielding his view of the
table with her body, slid his into the bag.

Within minutes, she and Corrie pedaled through the chilly
night. All the world, clothed in darkness, slept. The church bells,
which would have rung out the hour, had been confiscated by the
Nazis and melted down as part of the war effort.

Not a word passed between the two sisters. No need to draw
any attention to themselves. A soldier might be lurking around any
corner. They crossed the bridge across the canal, and Anki breathed
a sigh when they arrived at the house without incident.

Her brother met them at the door and she hugged him. "Oh,
I have missed you." She stood back and examined him, his broad
shoulders and work-roughened hands. "You grew quite a bit."

He laughed. "Corrie said that too."

So he hadn't been with their sister the entire time. Maybe they would tell her everything when the war ended.

She didn't come here to talk to her brother, though. She dropped her medical instruments into a pot of boiling water. God bless her sister for always putting on the pot to boil if someone was sick or hurt.

After scrubbing her hands with lye soap, Anki went to the bedstee. Johan joined her. "He passed out soon after I brought him here."

"Corrie told me you were outside."

"Don't worry. She already gave me the you'd-better-watch-out-or-you're-going-to-get-in-trouble speech. And she has a superb one."

"Unconscious. Good. No need for a sedative." Anki lifted the bandage and observed the wound.

"This bullet will have to come out. Get me the supplies in the pot on the stove. Make sure you wash your hands before you touch them."

While he was gone, she stretched her arms and shoulders and formulated a plan. She would have to be meticulous not to nick any other blood vessels.

Johan returned with the sterilized instruments. "Can I watch? Or maybe even help?"

"Ja, I need you to hand me what I ask for." She glanced at him, a grin stretched across his wide face.

The bullet had cut a clean path into the man's shoulder. Johan assisted her. Holding her breath, she managed to remove it without causing further injury. She exhaled and relaxed her shoulders.

With peroxide, she cleaned the wound. Infection could be deadlier than the bullet damage. That they would have to guard against. She wasn't a surgeon, but in the end, she was pleased with how she closed the wound. Not bad for a needle and thread.

Johan leaned over and inspected her work. "Can I keep the bullet?"

"That is disgusting." And very typical of her brother.

When they completed their work, they joined Corrie in the kitchen. "I stitched his wound closed and that should stop the bleeding. He will need to be still until it heals. Clean it every day and watch for any signs of infection. He was one of the men shot near the canal?"

Johan stood straighter. "Can you believe that? I found him lying on the bank, begging for help."

Anki looked between her siblings. "What have you gotten your-selves into?" She couldn't believe her sister had become entwined in this.

Corrie hugged herself.

"You two have to get him out of here before the Germans find out. Do you hear me?"

Johan stepped farther into the light. "He has nowhere else to go, and when the Nazis come back and count the bodies, they are sure to search for him."

"Therein lies the problem. The Gestapo will be here. Not only do you have this man here, but you have Johan to protect."

"He has a place to hide, but we have to figure out a plan for Wim. The hiding place is too small for two, and his shoulder would prevent him from making it in there, you know?"

"Where is it?"

Even in the dim room, Anki could see her brother's baby blue eyes light up. "Under the house. I crawl into it from the storage area next to the bedstee. Corrie puts the potatoes back and no one even knows it is there."

The more she heard of this, the less she liked it.

Corrie tented her fingers. "He'll leave as soon as he is better. Please promise me you won't let out even a squeak of this. Promise me."

Anki sat next to her sister at the smooth dining room table that had once belonged to their parents. "You are in so much danger."

"We'll be in far more if anyone finds out Wim is here."

"What about Piet? I told him you had a friend with an emergency and you couldn't reach the doktor. I could say that much without telling a lie."

"You can't tell him the truth. Not ever. Even if he asks you a direct question about this. And don't tell any of your neighbors or your girlfriends or anyone from church. You must keep this secret. Do you promise?"

Anki folded her hands in front of her. "I promise, Corrie. I promise."

She didn't like it, but she would keep her word.

LOUD, INSISTENT BANGING at the door jolted Cornelia. The thumping, the shouting came straight out of her restless, nightmare-drenched sleep. In her dream, she rode a stuffy, crowded train due east. Sweat covered her body and she shivered.

Guttural German voices filled the dark night air. "Open the door. Now. Let us in."

She came fully awake.

They pounded without stopping while she roused herself. She had slept in her clothes, knowing this would happen. The Gestapo had arrived, searching for Wim. And here he lay, unconscious, in her very own home.

All of the years of the occupation, she had lived in apprehension of this. For some reason, the Nazis would come for her, would arrest her, would take her away and she would never come back. That happened to people. They vanished off the streets one day and were never seen again.

And now she had Johan to shelter.

He appeared as if she had conjured him. "Quick, help me in."

With shaking hands, she slid the false panel out of place in the storage cupboard. He slithered in and wriggled into the tiny space under the floor. She slid the panel back.

Umpka Kees helped them construct this when Johan first came home. They told her it was not quite a meter high, and about two and a half meters wide and long. She had not gone down to check the dimensions for herself.

After she handed him Anki's supplies, she plunked the potatoes back in place and closed the cupboard door. Wim stirred in the bed. She leaned over and whispered in his ear, "Quiet now, be quiet. The Gestapo are here looking for you. Just play along with us." She prayed he heard her.

The pounding on the door continued, as did the commands to open up.

Everything inside her turned to water. Her mouth went dry as she ordered her legs to carry her to the front door.

Anki met her in the hall. "Do you remember what to do?"

She nodded, only her sheer will holding her upright. Her sister left her side to put their plan into motion.

She prayed Anki's theatrics would convince the Germans.

CHAPTER 5

The pounding of the German soldiers on her door matched the painful pulses in Cornelia's head. She straightened her skirt. "I'm coming, I'm coming," she called in Dutch, though fluent in German. Her small act of resistance.

She pulled the door toward her a few centimeters, giving her sister more time to prepare. Five Gestapo stood on her front step, their green canvas topped truck idling in the street, waiting to haul them to prison. She forced her words to be calm and sure. "What is going on? What do you want? It's the middle of the night."

The men pushed the door open wide and marched inside, shoving her away. "I want every centimeter of this house combed. A thorough search. Don't miss a thing. Schnell, schnell."

One of the soldiers, a wiry man with a mustache like Hitler's, spoke Dutch. "We are looking for an escaped prisoner. He has been shot and is very dangerous. Goes by the name Jan Aartsma. Have you seen him?"

Cornelia shook her head.

Wim had been lying about his identity.

The man left her to do his investigating while Cornelia stood by the door, a cold sweat drenching her. She hugged herself. *Oh Lord, oh Lord, oh Lord*. She could manage nothing more.

One of the Nazis opened the yellow-painted door of the bedstee where Wim lay on his side, his back to the room. Anki, lying beside him, rubbed her eyes and sat up, pulling the blanket to her neck. "What do you want? Why are you here?"

The soldier who spoke Dutch took charge. "Out of bed, both of you."

"We can't. My husband had a wee bit too much to drink last night." Anki put on a great acting show, even slurring her words. Cornelia prayed they wouldn't realize that Wim and Anki didn't reek of alcohol. "He's out passed. No, no, that's not right." She giggled. "He's passed out. Out passed."

"You then, get up."

"But, *Herr* Hitler, you don't want to see me in my altogether." She flopped back on the mattress, pulled the blanket over her head, and engaged in peals of laughter.

The Nazi was not amused. He jabbed Wim with the butt of his gun. Not a flinch. Unconsciousness had claimed him.

The clamor her blood made as it coursed through Cornelia's ears almost drowned out their words. "Drunk. We aren't going to get anything out of them."

Another answered, "What about this other one? She must know something."

The one Anki called Herr Hitler faced Cornelia. "What about you? Did you see the execution earlier?"

Out of the corner of her eye, she spied the rest of the soldiers continuing with their search. Some of them went outside to investigate the yard.

Her examiner shifted his weight and leaned in farther. "Did you watch the execution?"

She faced him and stared straight into his blue-black eyes.

"Nee, I was at my front room window and I saw you march the soldiers out, but when I knew what would happen, I turned away from the window and covered my ears."

"One of the bodies is missing. What happened to it?"

Cornelia couldn't keep the tremor from her words. "Missing? I would never touch a dead body."

"Did you see someone come and take it?"

"I never looked out my window again the rest of the evening."

Herr Hitler leaned toward her, his hot breath reeking of sauerkraut. He tapped his finger against her chest. "That man is alive and here. Where is he?"

Cornelia shrank back. "I don't know. Perhaps a family member came and took his body. All I can tell you is that no man named Jan is here."

"What about her?" He pointed to Anki, now quiet under the blanket. "Who is she? Did she see anything?"

"My sister. They got married a few weeks ago. They live with me because, well, they drink. A lot. I take care of them, try to keep them sober enough to work every day, you know." The story slid off Cornelia's tongue like a skater down the frozen canal.

The German stood back. "Identifications. I want to see everyone's papers. Right now."

What would they do? They hadn't thought about that. Cornelia had hers and assumed Anki grabbed hers when she came. But what about Wim? The Gestapo must have confiscated his when they arrested him. And they couldn't use Johan's because of his age and lack of an *ausweis*, a special work permit. Their little play was about to have the curtains pulled shut.

If only she could think of some reason why Wim wouldn't have an identification card. Had he lost it somewhere during his supposed drinking binge? Would the Gestapo believe her, or would they want to take him until they could verify the story?

Trying to give herself time to concoct a believable tale, Cornelia dug through her handbag as if the identification had sunk to the bottom, pushing aside her ration coupons, an empty tube of lipstick, and her identification. She stretched out her rummaging for as long as she dared before she produced the little booklet and handed it to Herr Hitler. He ummed and ahhed, then slapped it shut but didn't hand it back.

"Your sister and brother-in-law. I have to see theirs too."

She went to Anki and nudged her. "They need to see your papers. Both of yours."

Anki's head peeped from under the blanket. "Hmm? What?"

Cornelia had never seen a motion picture, but the actresses in them couldn't be as good as her own sister. Even her medium-length, always-perfect auburn hair fell into her eyes.

"Both papers. Where are they?"

Anki handed them to her. "Now leave me alone." She dove under the covers once more.

Cornelia dragged her feet as she made her way back to the officer. Her throat closed. In prison they tortured you and left you in a cramped, filthy cell to die. They starved you. If you made one wrong move or said one wrong word, they beat you. And if they thought you did something like hiding *Juden*—or escaped prisoners—they killed you without a second thought. Perhaps they would shoot her right in her own home.

To top it all off, she had gotten Anki involved.

Taking a deep breath, she fingered the paper book. Nee, two paper books. Anki had given her two sets of identification. She didn't understand. Whom did the second card belong to?

Her fingers shook so much she had a difficult time holding them. With knots in her stomach, she handed them to her interrogator.

Please, Lord, please.

All of her thoughts fled from her brain. If they questioned

her about either of the identifications, she didn't know how she'd answer.

Please, Lord, please.

More hemming and hawing from the German. The soldiers who searched the backyard returned. Herr Hitler questioned them. "What did you find?"

"Nothing, sir. No sign of anything."

Herr Hitler handed the paper books back to Cornelia. "Everything is in order. We didn't find anyone, but you watch out. This man is very dangerous. We think he is alive and someone is hiding him. If you see him or hear anything about him, you must let us know at once. Do you understand?"

Cornelia nodded.

"We will hunt him down. We will make sure he is eliminated." Goose bumps covered her arms at the man's words. "We cannot allow him to continue his evil ways. This is very important."

Again she nodded. She understood. From now on, she would be under surveillance. She would have to live under their attentive eyes, and Johan would have to be more careful than ever.

The soldiers left. As soon as the last boot crossed the threshold, she ran and bolted the door, leaning against it, her legs unable to hold her upright anymore. Only once before in her life had she been so terrified. That time things hadn't turned out so well. And maybe they wouldn't this time either. Two wanted men lay under her roof.

Once they had released Johan from his hiding place, the three siblings retired to the kitchen and sat at the table. Cornelia's curiosity overtook her. How could it be that Anki had two identification papers? The top one belonged to her, then came her sister's. The bottom booklet was her brother-in-law's.

She shook her head. "You brought Piet's card with you. Why?"

Johan leaned over Cornelia's shoulder. "You really did grab it."

"I don't know why I did. Somewhere deep inside I had this

inkling I might need it. I didn't even think much about it. I just grabbed it from the nightstand as I left our bedroom. He is going to want an explanation from me if he finds out I took it, and he will need it when he goes to work in the morning. I have to get it back to him as soon as possible."

Cornelia stared at her brother-in-law's picture on his identification. He and the wounded man had similar sandy-blond hair. That's where the resemblance ended. Wim sported angular features and a square, cleft chin. Piet's face was long and thin. They had been smart to turn Wim toward the wall. If the Gestapo had gotten a good look at him, they would have figured out that the identification didn't belong to the man in the bedstee. She and Anki and Wim would all be on their way to prison at this moment.

"You can slip out at first light. If Piet notices it missing, you will have to tell him some story or another. You always were the best of us at devising them."

Johan laughed. "Ja, remember when Anki broke Mem's vase? She blamed it on the cat and Mem believed her."

"We have a bigger difficulty." Cornelia rubbed her forehead. "What do we do when the Gestapo return? Wim can't be passed out in bed all the time. They will grow suspicious."

Anki traced an imaginary pattern on the table with her long finger. "Since the incident with the vase, I have matured. Don't you remember, Mem uncovered my falsehood and, after a long talk about telling truth, punished me by making me sweep the floors every day for a month? I learned my lesson. I hate that I had to lie to save that man. Let's pray God will keep them away."

Would He? God hadn't taken care of Hans. He hadn't watched over her and kept her from becoming a bride and a widow on the same night. Cornelia didn't know if she could trust Him.

CHAPTER 6

Light and darkness warred for Gerrit's consciousness. He struggled to lift his eyelids, but the blessed relief of oblivion fought back. He forced himself closer to the daylight on the other side of his closed eyes.

Trying to roll onto his right side brought a rush of pain. He moaned from the effort but couldn't speak.

"Wim." The soft word lilted in a most feminine way. "Are you waking up? Let me bring you some broth."

He heard the muffled footfalls of her stocking feet as she scurried away. The banging of a pot lid, the scraping of a ladle prevented him from returning to sleep.

Vague memories danced at the corners of his mind. He had slept in so many places in the past months and years, he had to work to recall each morning where he had laid his body the night before.

The flaming pain in his shoulder informed him that last night and this morning were different.

Then the blast of gunshots echoed in his head.

He remembered.

He wanted the woman to come back. Last night a haze had

clouded her face. He had battled so hard to stay aware that he did not get a good look at her. Or didn't recall. She smelled of potatoes and carrots and it reminded him of home.

He hadn't been there in a long time.

This time he refused to give in to oblivion and pried open his eyes. He lay in a cupboard, a bedstee, facing the wall decorated with fancy red paper. A clock, the queen's picture, and a picture of a young man hung there. He turned his head to the doorway, toward the clanking of dishes. A vision swam before him, a slender young woman, her shoulder-length hair the color of fall leaves, the sides rolled, framing her heart-shaped face.

She strolled toward him, carrying a blue-and-white Delft bowl of something hot, the steam curling around her. She raised her pale eyebrows and hooked her mouth into a small smile.

Gerrit's breath whooshed from his lungs—whether from his pain or her beauty, he didn't know.

"You are awake." Her cheeks turned as pink as a North Sea sunset. "How do you feel this morning?" The bowl clattered on the plate.

"You put me back together?" Even such a short sentence winded him.

Her color heightened and a full minute passed before she answered him. "I helped you."

"Your name?"

"Cornelia de Vries. And I'm telling the truth. After you eat a little broth, you can tell me your name."

Ah, she did possess a spark of life.

"I have vegetable soup. You need to get your strength back."

He heard the directive in her voice. Get strong so you can leave. "I'm not hungry." The odor of the soup turned his gut.

"You have to put something in your stomach."

"The pain is too bad."

"I wish you would. Please."

He was a windmill, helpless against the breeze, unable to refuse her pleading hazel eyes. "You will have to help me."

She nodded and scraped a rocking chair to the bed. With his head propped on several pillows, he managed to swallow three or four spoonfuls of the tasty, salty broth to please her, but he couldn't force down more.

She set the bowl on the floor and leaned forward in the chair, her long, white fingers splayed across the seat. "You have to tell me your name. Your real name. Are you Wim vander Zee or Jan Aartsma? Or something altogether different?"

The Gestapo confiscated his identification when they arrested him. The only way she would know his alias would be if he'd been delirious and blurted it out. Or if they'd been here. "When did they come?"

"About one or two this morning."

"Then why are we still here? They didn't arrest you? Us?" He battled to keep his eyes open. He wouldn't be able to carry on the conversation much longer.

"Johan scurried to his hiding place with the old dressing. When they found you in the bed, I told them you had become very drunk and had passed out. And that you were someone else."

"And they believed you?"

"Ja."

He yawned and his weighted eyelids fluttered shut. "You should join the Resistance."

SEEKING COMFORT IN her morning routine, Cornelia stepped onto her front porch with her broom. Not far to her left arched the bridge that carried bicyclists, pedestrians, and the rare German car or truck into town. The road in front of her house ran perpendicular to the canal, a narrow strip of grass separating the street from the collection of small houses. All the while, a sentry patrolled the bridge. She tingled.

With the sweeping finished, she shifted to her laundry. She tied an apron around her old blue-gray dress, then heated a large pot of water on the woodstove and shaved off a thin slice of lye soap. It didn't produce the suds of normal laundry soap, but she had nothing else. Another thing they lived without these days. At least it made the clothes and sheets smell fresh and clean.

If only Johan could help as she lugged the hot water to fill the washer tub that sat in their small back garden. A hedge surrounded the yard where a riot of blooms would erupt in a few short weeks. But even as she ran the clothes through the wringer and hung them on the line, the heat of the gray-clad soldier's stare bored into her. She would string her brother's items on a line in the kitchen.

As she reached for the line to pin her dark green A-line skirt, shouting came from down the street. Not the shouting of children at play, but the screaming of men and women in anguish, the screaming of taskmasters driving their charges forward.

The damp skirt dropped from her cold hand into her wicker laundry basket, and the wood clothespins she clutched scattered on the ground. She scampered to the front and peered down the narrow street. Soldiers surrounded a red house with a happy azure-painted front door. The Boersma home.

Leaning against the rough brick facade of her home, she watched as the Germans dragged Jap Boersma, their son, a year or two younger than Johan, from the home. *Dear God, nee.* If the soldiers hadn't been in the area searching for Wim, they never would have found Jap. He would be safe at home with his parents, not headed to almost certain death in a German factory.

What had she done by taking in this man? She had endangered

her entire neighborhood, sacrificing the lives of—how many?—to save one.

Hear and *Frou* Boersma stood in the doorway, shrieking at the soldiers who hauled their tall, thin son away. "Don't, don't, please, he is our only boy. God, please do not take him."

Cornelia closed her eyes. Her hands balled into fists as she hugged her chest. Her own words echoed in her head. *"Please, Hans, please don't go."* They were as ineffective as the Boersmas' pleas.

"I love you, Jap. God will watch over you and bring you home soon." The tears in Frou Boersma's voice crushed Cornelia's heart. Perhaps it would be better if she turned Wim over to the Germans.

How many more young men would be torn from their families because of her actions? The chances of Jap ever coming home were small. Almost too small to matter.

When the truck gunned its engine and pulled away from the Boersma home, the acrid smell of diesel fuel contaminating the air, Cornelia dared to open her eyes. The soldiers hadn't left the area but had moved farther down the road.

She studied her hands, expecting to find blood on them. Intent on examining her fingers, she didn't notice her neighbor from across the canal, Maria Wierda, until she stood in front of her. The woman's dark eyes were round. Cornelia dropped her gaze and studied Maria's brown oxford shoes.

"Did you see that?"

"Everyone saw that."

"Do you know what that was about? Do you know why they are here searching the houses?"

Cornelia remained silent.

The neighbor lady leaned closer and whispered in Cornelia's ear, "They are looking for the missing body from the canal yesterday. They shot a group of resisters from Leeuwarden, but when they came back, one of the bodies was not there. Frou Tuinstra said she heard the soldiers talking that they would keep looking until they find it."

An icy jolt shot through Cornelia's body. They would find him. Sooner or later, they would find him. And if they located him at her house, she would be arrested for sure. Maybe Johan too.

Wim had to go.

Hear and Frou Boersma sat on their front step. He had his arm around her and pulled her close. Even from this distance, Cornelia could see the woman's shoulder shake, weeping as if she would never be consoled.

The block of ice in Cornelia's stomach doubled in size. She remembered that feeling.

The green canvas-topped truck rumbled farther down the street.

Maria pulled her to sit on the front step and continued to whisper. "Last evening a man came to our door. One of the men who the Gestapo shot by the canal."

Cornelia sucked in her breath, hoping to appear shocked and surprised.

"I know. Unbelievable. Lucas insisted we help him, but once we had the wound dressed, we made him leave. During the night, the Gestapo knocked on the door. They were rough and rude and searched the house so well they would have found the man if we had been hiding him. I am so glad Lucas made me clean up the mess before we went to bed. If they had found it, they would have known the man had been there."

"They were here too."

Maria paled. "Did they find anything?"

Cornelia gave her head a vigorous shake, maybe overplaying the part a little too much. "Of course not. We have nothing to hide."

The color of Maria's complexion concerned Cornelia. "Are you feeling ill?"

She nodded. "Yes, a little. All this talk, it makes me woozy."

"Let me get you a glass of water." Cornelia rose and went inside, surprised when Maria followed on her heels. She hadn't invited her neighbor in. Johan could be sitting in the kitchen or Wim could be making noise. She raised her voice so the men would hear that the woman had come inside. "Are you sure you don't want to sit outside in the fresh air, Maria? It might help you to feel better."

"Nee. I don't want to hear the screaming and crying. It's too hard." That, Cornelia agreed with. Until last night, she had treasured the peace and security of her little home.

Lord, let them stay quiet.

Maria followed Cornelia into the kitchen where she retrieved a glass and filled it with water before handing it to her neighbor. The young, dark-haired woman, her hair done in two rolls at the top of her head, wrapped her long fingers around the cup and took a lengthy drink. Then she sat on the straight-backed chair. Fine lines radiated from her tight lips, though she couldn't be more than twenty-two.

Cornelia wiped imaginary crumbs from the counter, then leaned against the whitewashed cabinets, hoping to appear calm and unconcerned. Her large pot sat on the small stove, water warming for her wash.

Johan had already strung the clothesline across the kitchen to hang the laundry. If Maria spied that, she would wonder why Cornelia hung half of her clothes outside and the other half in the kitchen.

Maria glanced at the pot on the stove. "Oh, you were in the middle of laundry, weren't you?"

Cornelia nodded.

"With all of the commotion, I didn't realize that. I apologize. There are things I need to take care of too." She scraped the chair from the table over the worn wood floor and came to her feet. "Bedankt for the water."

Cornelia led the way down the hall, past the front room to the door. "You're welcome. I hope you feel better soon."

Cornelia went to turn the brass knob.

A rustling of sheets came from the front room.

Wim must be awake and restless. She pleaded with the Lord to prevent him from calling for her.

Maria turned toward the front room and took a step in that direction. "What was that? Who's here?"

Cornelia's breathing came in short spurts. She didn't know how to answer.

Their secret was about to be discovered.

CHAPTER 7

Cornelia's mind raced, her heart beating out a rapid tempo. The rustling of sheets stilled, but Maria peered into the front room and took a second step in that direction. Wim lay in the bedstee. A few more steps and she would see him there. For now, the open door blocked Maria's view of him.

Thank goodness her neighbor didn't move fast. Cornelia sprinted ahead of her, slammed shut the bedstee doors, and stood with her back against them, almost gasping for air. At least words formed on her tongue now, rapid and uncensored. "I apologize for my mess. My mem would be disappointed in how I keep house. My cat likes to sleep in there, for whatever reason, so I keep the doors open. I should train him better."

"I know I heard a noise from in here."

At that moment, Pepper popped out from behind the blue davenport, chasing a little black rubber ball, pouncing on it, watching it roll away again. "See, Pepper can make a racket, but he's good company for me."

Maria turned on her heel to leave. She lowered her voice. "I am sure one of our neighbors is hiding this man. With how badly he was injured, he couldn't get far. Please be careful, Frou de Vries."

Cornelia tugged her knit cardigan tighter and shuddered. Hiding Wim just became more dangerous.

And getting rid of him more urgent.

THE NEXT TIME Gerrit woke, full consciousness came easier. He opened his eyes, or thought he did, but darkness reigned. Only a few slits of light filtered in through the cracks of the cupboard door.

The dark wrapped its hands around his neck and squeezed. He had to get out of here. Now.

Then he heard a female voice, not Cornelia's, but familiar in a way. "Be careful of this Jan Aartsma. Look at the bad things going on because of him. I don't want anything to happen to you."

Gerrit took quick, uneven breaths in and out. Cornelia wanted to get rid of him already. This woman might make her frightened enough that she would push him out of the door today.

"Bedankt, Maria. Thank you for the warning."

"This man will get us all in trouble, not only Jap. I'm going to be watching for him and if I see him again, I am going to tell the Nazis. We don't need that kind of mess here."

Maria left but, even though sweat covered his body, Gerrit didn't cry out to have the doors opened. There might be other people in the room.

All remained quiet for a time before he heard footsteps approaching. When Cornelia opened the doors, he gulped in the fresh, light air. "Don't close the doors."

"Giving orders? You must be feeling better." A light smile teased her lips.

Gerrit's stomach refused to stop its oddly familiar fluttering.

Like it had when Mies had been around. "I can't breathe when you do that." He didn't know if he meant her closing the doors or smiling at him like that.

The moment of brightness passed and the sunshine left her face. "Did you hear the commotion on the street?"

He shook his head, the movement sending pain slicing through his shoulder.

"The Germans are entering and ransacking my neighbors' homes. They arrested one young man I grew up with." Her soft voice broke and she paused a moment, perhaps composing herself. "He'll die in Germany sooner or later. Another house they searched is the home of two boys Johan's age."

He rubbed his forehead with his left hand. What could he do? "I'm sorry about living and causing you and your neighbors this trouble."

She leaned over him. "What kind of contraband were you caught with? Were you carrying weapons?" Fire burned in her shimmering hazel eyes.

"The less I tell you, the better. If you don't know, you won't reveal any secrets."

"I can keep a secret, especially one like this. Trust me."

Was she like Mies? Would she turn him in the first chance she got? "If the Germans arrest you, they will torture you until you confess everything."

She quivered as she sat with a thunk in the chair beside him, but his warning didn't deter her like he thought it would. "Let's start with an easy question. What is your name? Your real name, the one your mem and *heit* call you."

If he gave her a little bit of information, perhaps she would cease her pestering. "My name isn't Jan Aartsma or Wim vander Zee. The Gestapo have been looking for me under my real name for years, so I had to get an alias. Several of them. The way things are going, I might need another."

"Maybe I don't want to know."

"Many of my colleagues don't have this information."

She clutched the edge of her chair for a few moments, then stood and turned toward the door. "Are you ready for some more broth?"

"Gerrit. My name is Gerrit Laninga."

CORNELIA FUSSED WITH the scalloped hem of her white apron, acting as if his revelation didn't affect her.

In truth, it stopped her as if she had run smack into him.

Now that she had the information, she wished she didn't. Her heart quaked. She didn't want to be arrested or tortured. She wanted this nightmare to end.

"Why did you tell me?"

He paused for a long moment. "I hope I can trust you. I need you to trust me."

"I don't know if I can or if I even want to."

"You want me to leave." He didn't ask a question.

She answered him anyway, turning to face him. "Ja."

His blond eyebrows rose and that sandy lock of hair fell in his eyes again. "But I can't."

"Not now, but soon, very soon. There is room for only one in the hiding spot and it belongs to Johan. Sooner or later, the Gestapo or NSB will be back, and I don't know if I can concoct another story or continue the one I spun the first time they were here. See? I don't even know what to do." Her hands shook.

"I disagree." He struggled to sit and she went to help him recline.

"I can't have them come here again."

He covered his face with his left hand. "I have to trust you, Cornelia, because you have to do something for me."

He was going to ask her to shave him or maybe even bathe him.

Those gestures were too intimate. Already the aroma of his manliness reminded her too much of Hans. She would refuse. Let Johan do it.

"There are people who need to know I'm alive. I have things to tell them and they need to be informed. You have to make contact."

"Nee." She didn't have to take even a second to consider Gerrit's proposal. "I can't do it. I refuse to let you suck me in any further. If you want your cohorts contacted, get out of that bed and do it yourself." She swallowed despite the constriction in her throat.

He shifted and his blue eyes dug into her middle. "You can't do it? Or you won't do it?"

"Can't. Won't. What difference does it make? People get hurt and killed when they defy the authorities. The Allies will be here soon."

"What if the entire world sat back and waited for someone else to free us? Where would we be then? God uses men as His instruments to fulfill His purposes."

"Not always. He used storms and fire and angels of death to defeat Israel's enemies."

"He also used a boy with a rock and a sling. I'm that boy, Cornelia, and my contraband is my rock and sling. I'm fighting for the children of Israel, the same as David did, for the Juden and the *onderduikers*."

Gerrit used his left hand to push himself higher on his pillows, a grimace marring his fair, rawboned face. "We didn't have a chance when the Nazis invaded. They betrayed us and we weren't ready. This is our way of fighting for our country and our queen. God will use us to defeat the occupiers, and the more the Dutch people resist, the faster we will be rid of them. We need to be free of them before more people are hurt or die."

Cornelia's head spun. In the Bible, God stepped in from time to time and saved His people with great wonders, but He also used small boys like David and weak men like Gideon to accomplish His work. How did you know when to step aside and let God do

His work and when to act on His behalf? She had a feeling that if she did this one task, she would end up getting more and more involved. That, she did not want.

Gerrit reached across his body and clasped Cornelia's hand. His was warm and soft and she suddenly knew she would believe whatever he told her. "You have to help. Do you know what the Nazis are doing to people? How many lives they have snuffed out? You saw it for yourself today. Because of them, thousands of *Nederlanders* are suffering."

She ripped her hand from his grasp. "I know what those soldiers do and all about the innocent lives they've taken. I am not as naive as you believe I am, Hear Laninga. I have suffered greatly because of them, from the moment they stepped foot in the Netherlands, you know. I am sorrowing today and will every day for the rest of my life—all because of them."

The creases between his blond brows deepened. "Of course you have suffered. We all have."

She refused to be mollified. "You don't understand what this war has cost me. And I am not giving the Germans any more. I am done."

"Use your anger. Use it to be rid of them."

"What kind of Christian talk is that? I had the idea you were a God-fearing man, but you are bent on revenge. And you are trying to talk me into taking my own revenge."

"Maybe revenge, maybe not. I am asking you to quit acting like a tulip covered in snow. Don't hide in this house until the Allies free you. They may not come for a while."

JOHAN COULDN'T STAND in the doorway and listen to his sister argue with the man any longer. Mem would have had his hide for eavesdropping, which was why he didn't come forward earlier, but he listened to everything Gerrit Laninga said.

He stepped into the room. "I will go."

They both flicked their gazes to him, mouths wide open. His sister got up from her chair and reached him in three strides. "How long have you been listening?"

"I heard everything Gerrit said, and I sure want to contact the Underground."

"Nee." She didn't even take time to think about it.

Gerrit inched up on his pillow. "How old are you, Johan?"

"Twenty."

"Old enough, then, to make your own decisions."

Cornelia spun around to face Gerrit. "He is an onderduiker. I have worked for years to protect him. I won't allow him to go out onto the streets. Especially not after what happened today."

"You can't forbid me. I mean, I'm an adult and can make my own decisions." He stepped next to her.

"How could I stand it if anything happened to you? I promised our parents before they died that I would look after you. They arrested Jap Boersma a little while ago. I can't even think about what they will do to him. I can't keep my promise to Mem and Heit if you put yourself in danger, you know."

Most of the time, because she was older, he backed down, but not this time. "We have to help. If you won't go, then I will. What choice do we have?"

Cornelia sat in her chair and shifted her feet back and forth across the dark red painted wood floor.

"You could go." Gerrit spoke softly.

She shrank back. "Nee."

"What happened before isn't going to happen to me." Johan knelt next to her. The fresh, clean scent of the outdoors wafted from her. He wanted to smell the air himself.

"You can't make promises like that."

"She's right, Johan. Just walking on the street puts you in danger of being snatched and sent away to Germany or to the southern fortifications."

Why did everyone treat him like a child? Gerrit couldn't be more than six or seven years his senior. "I know the danger, but nothing will happen to me. Don't you trust God?"

The moment the words left his mouth, Johan regretted them. Cornelia's hot breath slapped his face. "I trust Him, but I also believe that we need to be wise and use the brains He gave us to make good decisions. Please, Johan, don't go."

"Will you?"

"I can't. I wish I could. There has to be another way."

Johan had the answer to his question.

CHAPTER 8

Gerrit watched Cornelia flee the room and heard her slam the front door. Just as Mies had flown from him—all because of his work.

Would Cornelia betray him too?

He had upset Cornelia, but he had no remorse. They both had secrets. He saw her raw, gaping wounds, much like his. She didn't share with him what caused her injury, but he recognized grief.

She chose to cope with it all by hiding in this house, in her safe and comfortable little world. Like so many others. They refused to help. He wanted to pound his pillow.

Mies had been the same way. Thinking only of herself, she had pleaded with Gerrit to keep out of it. And when he refused her, she betrayed him.

He couldn't contain a small groan as he shifted under the fresh-scented covers.

No matter what, the task needed to be done. Many had capitulated along with the nation in May 1940. The queen had fled. He tugged hard on the sheet.

The more who labored at freeing the Netherlands, the sooner it would happen. Johan could help. Cornelia shouldn't be withholding him from the country that needed him.

The incredible pain in his shoulder prevented him from adjusting his pillows. He would have to wait until Cornelia came back for that.

He had to admit, he enjoyed watching the fire in her hazel eyes. Underneath her retiring ways lived a tiger.

CORNELIA'S HEART—ALREADY beating at a breakneck speed—picked up its pace as she strode across the bridge, past the soldier, and into town. The late afternoon sun cast long shadows across the tree-lined road, distorting the shapes of the houses.

Once she reached the heart of the small town, its centuries-old center lined with narrow brick buildings topped with red tile roofs, she slowed to catch her breath. Women bustled around her, picking up groceries before the Sabbath. Many of them held the hand of a child or two. The smell of roasting potatoes made her stomach growl.

She heard two voices speaking German and she spun around, wondering who uttered that language.

Without hesitation, she changed her course, away from the voices, finding herself wandering down a residential street. The din of a busy Saturday in town faded and quiet settled over her. Long and slow, she inhaled a lungful of cold, salty North Sea air, yet her thoughts turned like a spinning wheel.

Never would she have the courage to contact Gerrit's friends. So much could go wrong.

Did that mean the job had to fall to Johan? Of course not. Neither of them had an obligation to Gerrit. Soon enough he would be able to go to his friends on his own.

Deep inside, her conscience stirred. She tamped it down.

The cross-topped spire of the church rose high above her. Its stone walls had stood through wars and weather, prosperity and poverty. The peace that emanated through its stained-glass windows beckoned her to come and rest. Her tired mind and body obeyed.

With a good deal of effort, she opened the heavy oak door. A chill radiated from the winter-soaked stones. The wood pews had been rubbed with oil hundreds, even thousands, of times, and the scent permeated the spacious interior. She slid into one of the middle rows where her family had sat every Sunday from before the time she had been born.

She leaned forward and rested her arms on the back of the pew in front of her. "Dear Lord, what am I supposed to do?"

Realizing she had spoken out loud, she turned to the left, to the right, and behind her. She saw no one.

"Father, show me what is right. I need to know. Hans would have told me that I must help, but I don't know if that is what You want of me. Please, Lord, help me find a way out of this. A way that doesn't involve me or Johan. A way that keeps all of us safe."

The wind creaked in the rafters.

She looked forward and examined the many gold-covered pipes of the massive organ. In her memory, she heard its deep, rich tones sound out her favorite hymns. No answer came to her.

"Dear God, I need Your help."

For a long, long time she sat there, hoping for, waiting for an answer. God laid nothing on her heart. The rainbow of colors from the windows lit the stone floor at her feet and the bench beside her.

She could not be the one to get in touch with Gerrit's contacts. She doubted she would be able to take five steps in the direction of the place before she would be drenched in sweat. And she would raise suspicions when she couldn't remain calm.

And Johan—she was responsible for her brother. Ever since

their parents died, it had been her job to look after him. Sending him on this mission, no matter how eager he may be to do it, was not responsible. Her parents would never have approved, nor would she.

At least she had resolved part of her dilemma.

Now she had to find a way to be rid of the Resistance worker. As soon as possible.

AS CORNELIA RETURNED home, she recognized the tall, slight form standing on her front step as her sister, her dark red peacoat pulled around her hunched shoulders. Her gaze darted here and there, at the truck parked at the end of the quiet street.

"What is going on?"

"They arrested Jap Boersma."

"Because of . . ." Anki nodded toward the house.

"Ja."

"Where are you coming from?"

"I couldn't stay in the house any longer. He asked me to help him. To contact someone for him. I went to the church to pray." Cornelia had to be careful what she said. Being outside, anyone could overhear their conversation.

"You won't do it."

"Of course not. I admire people like him, but I won't do it myself or allow Johan to join the battle. He is a naive twenty-year-old, so to him, danger and adventure look appealing. I know differently."

"That man is involving our brother?"

"Johan offered of his own free will. I put an immediate end to it. He won't go. But I suppose someone has to."

Anki gathered her sister in a hug, and Cornelia rested her head on her sister's shoulder. "You can't do this. Resistance workers are involved in dangerous things."

"I know."

"Wim may have blown up rail lines or brought stolen ration cards to Juden. He might have even helped plot the escape of an English pilot."

"I refuse to get involved with the Resistance—I just want Gerrit to heal and leave my house, you know. The sooner, the better. He insists the way I have to do that is by contacting his friends."

"You can't do it yourself. What about the *dominee*? Reverend Sikma has said things that make me wonder if he might be involved."

"If he is, he could relay the message. But if he isn't . . ." Cornelia shuddered. She moved to the back garden and fingered the few clothes on the line.

Anki followed her. "You know what happened to Hear Kampinga. One day he disappeared and no one ever heard from him again."

"I know all about places like Scheveningen and Amersfoort and Vught."

"Then why are you even thinking about this?"

Ja, despite her insistence that she couldn't do it, Cornelia was thinking about it. Because she had to get rid of Gerrit. And Johan couldn't be involved. If anything happened to him . .

She liked Gerrit's comparison of his work to David and Goliath. God used small people to accomplish big goals. That was a battle, a day Israel fought against her enemies. "How do I know what is right and what is wrong? What would God have me do? My head is being pulled in opposite directions by the ears." She studied Anki.

"It is always wrong to break God's laws."

Cornelia began ripping the clothes from the line, even though most were still damp. "The trouble is, if I don't lie, I all but kill a man."

"Doesn't he have any family? A wife? Parents?"

A light ignited in her mind. "Anki, that's it." Her neighbor on one side, a middle-aged woman she didn't know very well, opened her window and scowled at the pair.

Cornelia clamped her hand over her mouth. How much more of the conversation had the woman heard? Whose side did she sympathize with? She led her sister to the front of the house again and pulled her inside. The thump of the sentry's boots reverberated in her ears as he marched back and forth in front of the bridge.

"We can contact his relatives. Because of the censors we can't send a letter, but if we find his family, Gerrit will leave and no one will have to risk their life." Cornelia smiled.

From down the street, gunshots reverberated in the cool, dusky air.

GERRIT HEARD THE door open and click shut. From his isolation in this cupboard, he couldn't see Cornelia but trusted she would return. Quiet footsteps moved down the hall and into the kitchen. He smiled, excited at the thought that she soon would appear in the doorway.

He thought that kind of pleasure had left him along with Mies, but now it came back, in a smaller, seedling kind of way.

He shook his head. Until all the Nederlanders breathed free air, romance must wait. And Cornelia would be like Mies—not wanting him to work in the Resistance. She would never have him.

He lifted his head from the pillow to search for her and the thought struck him. Romance? Could he, in less than a day, be attracted to her? Nee, she cared for him with a tender touch and he appreciated her nursing. These feelings were nothing more than gratitude for her lifesaving treatment.

Then she came into view and his pulse climbed. Her flawless complexion, flushed from being outside in the cold, reminded him of his sisters' china dolls.

She entered and sat in the ladder-back chair next to him,

smoothing her auburn hair. Her hazel eyes shimmered, filled with a peace she didn't have before.

"Do you have a wife? Parents? Some family? They must be worried about you."

"Nee."

Cornelia scooted her chair back a few centimeters at his harsh word.

"You can't contact them."

Her eyes widened. "Why not? If I would go missing, my entire family would be frantic. They would want word about my condition and where I was. They would come and get me."

"You can't tell them where I am."

"I don't understand. If they know about it, you have to tell them you are alive. You can't allow them to believe otherwise. Your poor wife." She shook her head.

"I don't have a wife. Never have. The first time the Nazis became aware of the work I did, it was under my given name. The Gestapo found my parents' address and went to their home to question them. They continued to come, day or night, and interrogate them. I narrowly escaped their house once before. I haven't spoken to them in almost a year. The risk is too great."

Cornelia stood and fiddled with the hem of the sleeve of her worn blue housedress. "Then what do we do? I think Dominee Sikma is part of the Resistance. I could go to him."

"You think? Or do you know?"

"I suspect. But if we were wrong and he wasn't involved, he wouldn't turn us in." She sat and crossed and uncrossed her thin ankles.

"How can you be sure?"

She waved at the air. "Because he's the dominee, that's how I can be sure."

"Nee, not him. A friend of mine from Leeuwarden, where I

grew up, a school pal, is working with the Resistance here now. He told me to come to him if I ever found myself in trouble. Contact him."

"I won't do it."

"Why not?" For the right cause, you had to do what was required of you. "He would get me out of here faster."

She shook her head. "I won't go to the Resistance. Too many things could go wrong. I could be followed. There has to be another way. And do not consider recruiting my brother either." She stomped across the room, making as much noise as she could with stocking feet, stepping on the cat's tail. The animal screeched and bounded out of her way.

He scrubbed his face with his left hand, a few days of stubble scratching his palm. If she possessed half that spunk with the Nazis, she would have no trouble talking her way out of any situation.

The problem remained that the Resistance needed to know he was alive.

JOHAN WATCHED HIS sister pick up her laundry basket and then heard the latch click. Good. He could speak to Gerrit without her interference.

The man lay in the bedstee, staring at the ceiling. Even from across the room, Johan saw the distinctive Dutch bump just below the bridge of his nose. Johan cleared his throat.

Gerrit turned, smiled, and scooted up on the pillows. "I am glad to see you."

"Corrie went to get the laundry from the line, so we don't have long to talk, but I had to speak to you."

The man's forehead furrowed. "About what?"

Johan shifted from one foot to the other. "I want to help with the Resistance. I'll contact them for you. It must be important if you're so insistent."

"Ja, it is. What about your sister, though? She forbade you from going, and she made it clear to me that I was not to involve you. If she finds out, she won't be happy."

"I mean, you said it yourself—I'm a grown man now and I can make my own decisions. The Netherlands has no army anymore for me to fight in, so this is my chance to speed the release of our people. The queen needs to come home."

"There are risks."

"I may be in hiding, but I have ears. I know the dangers and what might happen to me."

"If you saw the carnage at the bridge, Johan, I suppose you do."

"You can trust me."

Gerrit nodded and a smile lit his eyes as blue as the canal water. "If you're here in hiding, I believe I can trust you. Are you sure you want to do this?"

"I sure am." He would show his bravery and his strength.

"Then this is what you have to do."

CHAPTER 9

Cornelia cinched the belt of her green Sunday dress the way she wanted to cinch it around Gerrit's neck. That stubborn man, not accepting any of her compromises and siding with her brother against her. At least she had talked Johan out of going.

She touched the white crocheted lace collar, now yellowed even though she scrubbed and scrubbed it. Nothing she could do about that. She rolled the top of her hair, securing the curls with pins, and caught the rest at the base of her head in the simple silver clip Hans had given her as a wedding gift.

She wouldn't think about Hans today. She pulled her brush through her tresses once more, then laid it on her dresser. Time to get Johan moving if they were to make it to services on time.

She knocked on his bedroom door, but he didn't answer. When no reply came from her second and third knocks, she dared to turn the knob and enter his tiny room under the sloped roof. The sheets lay mussed in a pile at the end of the low bed and clothes all but concealed the floor, but Johan wasn't there. Good, he must be downstairs waiting for his breakfast.

When she got to the kitchen, however, she found it empty and cold. Perhaps Gerrit had called for him. She stirred the fire in the stove and hurried to the front room. Gerrit sat in bed, stroking Pepper, who purred, curled in a ball on his lap. The chair beside him remained empty.

Her stomach twisted. "Where is Johan?"

Gerrit motioned toward the chair. "Sit down for a minute."

She stared at the wounded man, a small scar marring his square chin. The look in his eyes caused goose bumps to pop up all over her arms. "What do you have to tell me?"

"Don't be angry."

"That means you do not have good news for me."

"Johan is an adult and made this decision on his own."

Her stomach turned inside out. "He went, didn't he?"

"Ja. He left about ten minutes ago."

She shook her head, unable to believe the depth of her brother's foolhardiness. "You encouraged him."

Gerrit played with the edge of the blanket, his hands displaying the long fingers, leathery skin, and prominent knuckles of someone who worked hard. "I didn't recruit him, if that's what you're asking. He volunteered and I gave him the information."

Inside her, an icy-hot spring welled. "I begged you not to do that."

"He was determined. You refused, so he went."

"Don't make this my fault."

"No one's blaming you, Cornelia. He went to do a job that needed to be done, that's all."

She balled her fists and resisted striking him. "What if something happens to him?" Awful images slashed across her mind, pictures of something she wanted to forget but couldn't.

"I won't lie to you—what he is doing is dangerous."

She strangled her words to avoid from shouting and causing suspicion among the neighbors. "Then why did you let him do it?"

"We have been over this already." His voice contained a sharp edge of impatience.

"Have I worked to protect him for nothing?"

"He wants to fight for his country and his queen."

She struggled to keep from being overwhelmed by memories. "I knew another young man like that. Things didn't turn out well for him."

"That doesn't mean Johan will have the same outcome."

"If anything happens to him, I will hold you responsible." She pointed the tip of her finger at his chest. "I am not sure I can ever forgive you for what you have done, allowing my brother to risk his life to find your friend."

She spun on her heel and marched from the room, fanning the heat away from her face with her hand. That man had some gall, demanding they take him in and care for him, then sending her brother out on a mission that could cost him his life. Gerrit would go this afternoon, even if it meant she had to drag him to the street herself and leave him there.

ANKI DYKSTRA WANDERED through the small village, rows of narrow houses crowding the roads. Even though the Nazis had confiscated the church bell, women and children bustled toward the tsjerke at the appointed time on their way to Sunday service, heads bent against the light rain. This would be a good time to check on her siblings and their surreptitious visitor.

She worried about the peril that had ensnarled Corrie. Her sister hadn't always been this timid and frightened, but after Hans . . .

The other night when the Gestapo came to the door, Corrie surprised her with how well she'd handled herself.

Still, the sooner that man left her sister's house, the better for all of them. Corrie was softening, thinking of working with him. No matter what, Anki had to convince her brother not to get involved. Corrie couldn't survive another loss.

Anki couldn't keep lying to her husband either. She would not do it. He would figure out the truth in time and then . . .

She bumped into a German soldier on the edge of town. Her spine stiffened and she sucked in her breath. Her baby sister hid what they sought.

She crossed the bridge and came to Corrie's small, two-story house. She did nothing out of the ordinary, including ignoring the soldiers she passed. She rapped on the cheerful green front door.

Corrie pulled her inside. "What are you doing here?" she said, her words low and quiet.

"I came to see Gerrit. I didn't check on him yesterday."

Corrie nodded. "You can't let him know you were here the other night. He can't see you."

"Have the Gestapo been back? They are still watching all of these houses."

"Nee, not yet, anyway. I'm expecting them here any moment."

"This is much too dangerous."

"It gets worse." Cornelia's hands quivered.

"What's wrong?"

"Johan slipped out earlier this morning to notify a friend of Gerrit's who works in the Resistance. What are we going to do?"

Anki rubbed the back of her neck. "He didn't like the idea of contacting his family? Or didn't you present that possibility?"

Corrie chewed on a fingernail. "I did, but he said that his parents' house has been under surveillance for years. It would be too risky to try to contact them through any means. Even if we could get ahold of them, there is no way they could help him."

"What are we going to do?"

"Johan is gone, so there is nothing we can do about it except to pray. If he survives this escapade, he is going to want to get involved further in the Underground. He will get a taste of this adventure and want more. We have to find a way to stop him."

Anki's own hands trembled as she grasped her sister's. "You're talking about the boy who climbed trees when Mem told him not to and who jumped off the Tuinstras' barn roof into the pile of hay. He broke his arm that time, but two weeks later we caught him doing it again."

Corrie shook her head. "I am terrified that Johan is going to run into trouble."

"Me too." She prayed she was wrong.

JOHAN THANKED THE Lord for the cold drizzle that allowed him to pull Mem's old blue scarf farther over his head and keep his focus on the ground. Only a crazy person would dress in Mem's clothes, but Gerrit insisted he needed a disguise. He supposed he couldn't gallivant down the street, announcing himself to the world. He wished they would have had the time and resources to come up with a better cover, though.

After he crossed the bridge into town, he blended in with a group headed to the tsjerke for Sunday services. They lived in a small town where everyone was acquainted with everyone else, so he prayed none of the faithful would question this strange woman in their midst. Or recognize Mem's clothes on his back.

He knew the exact house Gerrit instructed him to find. It was brown brick, the middle one in a long row on quiet Prince William Street. Without any problems, he peeled away from the group and made his way to the house. He glanced to his right and left before ascending the single step to the door.

His hand trembled worse than an old lady's, and he didn't think he would be able to use it to lift the brass knocker. He raised his chin and braced himself. He sure had wanted this adventure. He couldn't turn and run now. For his people and his queen, he had to prove himself to be brave and trustworthy.

Lord, help me.

He summoned the strength to tap the code Gerrit had taught him. Three knocks, pause, two knocks, pause, three knocks.

He dropped the knocker against the door and held his breath.

Steps sounded from inside and stopped. "Who is it?" a masculine voice asked.

At first, his words squeaked and cracked. He cleared his throat and tried again. "I have come with a delivery for you."

"Bread or milk?"

"I have some vegetables."

He didn't know what it all meant—Gerrit hadn't explained—but the man on the other side of the door must have understood the code. "Good. Carrots, potatoes, or beets?"

"Green beans."

"Green beans? Are you sure?"

Johan thumped his head with his fist. Had he made a blunder? In his mind, he retraced every word of the conversation Gerrit taught him. Nee, he had said to tell the man green beans, Johan was positive. Could he have misunderstood him? Gotten it confused?

"Green beans."

He waited while his heart threatened to jump ship, then spun around, sure someone watched him from across the street. The road remained empty.

After a very long minute, the door creaked open and a hand pulled him inside. Anytime now he expected the Gestapo to shove him to the floor and arrest him. The small living area where he stood was dim and it took a few seconds for his eyes to adjust. A huge man, both in height and width, shut the door. Only then did he release Johan's wrist.

"You have a message for me?" he growled at Johan, eyes narrowed.

Johan stood firm, then asked a ridiculous question. "Are you Bear?"

The extra-large man nodded his bald head. "What is your message?"

He wiped his sweaty palms on his mem's plain dark skirt. "Gerrit Laninga is alive."

With those words, the hardness in Bear's face melted. "Are you sure? We got word they executed him three days ago, but we heard his body was missing."

Johan nodded and Bear lumbered away. "Rooster, you have to come hear this."

A tall, lanky young fellow with dark hair stepped out of the shadows after Bear. "What is it?"

Bear nodded at Johan. "Tell him what you said to me."

Rooster must be the code name for Gerrit's friend Maarten. He fit Gerrit's description. "Gerrit Laninga is alive."

Rooster's eyes widened. "You have to be kidding me."

"I sure am not. After the Germans left, I set off to cover one of the bodies in orange. I found him near the bridge, breathing but wounded, and brought him to my house. My sisters and I have been caring for him since. Gerrit sent me here saying he had an important message for his friend."

Rooster ran his hand through his hair. "Are you sure you have the right man?"

It must be unbelievable to them that someone survived their own execution. "He told me if you doubted me to remind you about the time you broke your mem's window playing ball."

Bear motioned for Johan to stop. "You could be a collaborator, setting a trap for us."

Rooster shook his head. "He isn't lying. Everyone thinks Gerrit threw that ball, but I did. He took the blame for me. Only he would know the truth."

Bear stared at Johan, his dark green eyes boring into him, testing him. The piercing scrutiny made him want to drop his look to the floor, but if he did so, Bear would think he lied.

"Tell me where you live."

"The small brick house with a green door on the other side of the canal bridge."

"I know it."

The hulking man went to the window, parted the curtains, and peered at the street. When he returned, he opened the door. For their safety, no niceties or small talk passed between them. He never asked Johan's name, just said, "Someone will be there soon."

Knowing he had made sure the street was clear, Johan stepped outside without another word.

A sense of triumph filled him. He had accomplished his mission. Now they would have to let him work for them. No more sitting prisoner in that house, waiting to be either arrested or liberated. He wanted to skip all the way home.

Excited about the adventures that lay ahead of him, he turned the corner without much care and ran smack into someone. He thought it might be a latecomer to church, hurrying not to miss the service. When he looked up, though, his stomach plunged like it did when he had jumped off the Tuinstras' roof.

He stared into the hard, grimacing face of a German soldier.

CHAPTER 10

You had better pray that Johan returns by the time I get back from the tsjerke." With those words, Cornelia slammed the front door, leaving Gerrit and the house in absolute silence.

She didn't give him a chance to tell her he had been doing just that.

Once he finished praying, he had time to assess his surroundings. The front room's peeling red paper transported him to another era. Across from the bedstee, a faded blue sofa dominated the wall. Cornelia's rocker sat next to it in the far corner beside the small but elaborate iron stove. Then he saw it—the photograph on the wall where she could see it from her chair, next to a schoolhouse clock and a picture of the queen.

A young man, full of joy and life, dressed in a dark suit coat and a loosely knotted tie, looked at him, his back straight and proud. Who was he? Not Johan. And much too recent to be her father. He recalled her once or twice mentioning Hans. Was this him? And who was he? When she came back, he would ask her.

How long before he could be up and around? He had been a little boy very sick with scarlet fever the last time he had to stay in bed this long.

For the past year or eighteen months, he had been so busy with Resistance work, he had little chance to rest and catch his breath, constantly moving from place to place, always carrying either stolen or forged ration cards and fake identity cards. While getting shot wasn't the way to go about it, he tried to welcome the rest. Maarten would come soon and Gerrit could get back to work.

He dozed. Through his dreams of home, he heard a persistent knocking on the door. He came fully awake.

"Open up. Schnell."

The pounding continued for a moment before he heard the door being kicked in and soldiers entering the house. "Search everything. Don't miss a thing. He is here. I can smell him." The voice reverberated through the small dwelling.

Though the movement caused heat to spread from his wound throughout his entire torso, Gerrit reached up and shut the cupboard doors. He prayed Johan wouldn't return just now and meet up with the soldiers.

The near total darkness enveloped Gerrit. He struggled to remain calm. He would never make it into the hiding place in time. Instead, he curled into a ball in the corner.

The thud of jackboots marched nearer to him.

He pulled the soft blue blanket over himself. When they discovered him here, he would have to hide the wound that would scream his identity.

Please, Lord, protect me.

He breathed in and out silently, but forced himself to maintain a slow, steady rhythm. He bit his tongue to halt the building scream.

Moments later light flared into his cubbyhole. He lay with his back to the soldier. With the butt of his gun, the Nazi turned him over. The Gestapo officer jabbed Gerrit's side with the barrel of the gun. Gerrit moaned and observed the man.

His heart catapulted to his throat.

He would never forget the cobalt-blue eyes that stared at him.

Looking back at him was the face of the officer who had attempted to execute him.

Silence covered Gerrit. His awareness of the other Nazis in the house faded.

His breathing ceased.

His heart arrested.

Lord, save me.

White-blond eyelashes blinked at him. Disbelief widened those unforgettable blue eyes. The soldier squeezed his gun's barrel.

Indecision worked his face. His jaw muscle twitched and his lips scrunched. He lifted the blanket. Gerrit wore Johan's clothes that hid his wounds. The soldier didn't probe.

He dropped the blanket and gave Gerrit a few good jabs to the ribs with the butt of his gun. "What a drunkard. A useless excuse for a human being." He shut the bedstee doors.

The commander called from the front room's doorway, "What did you find, Neumann?"

"A lazy old drunkard sleeping off his Saturday night binge."

"Strange, we didn't find any liquor bottles."

"Who knows where he got the spirits. But he is as drunk as any I have ever seen."

"Are you sure it's not Aartsma? If the man can escape death by firing squad, he can pretend to be drunk." The domineering officer's words caused Gerrit to flinch.

"*Nein.* He reeked of alcohol. I checked for wounds but I found none. It's not him. He is that woman's brother-in-law."

"Maybe I should check." Heavy footfalls stepped toward Gerrit.

Lord, turn him away.

"Sir, that's not necessary. I conducted a thorough investigation. This isn't Jan Aartsma. It is Piet Dykstra. And he has an ausweis."

The steps ceased. Gerrit's vital signs stilled.

"Fine."

Cornelia's knitting needles clanked to the floor and one rolled close to Gerrit. From the kitchen, pots and pans clanged and dishes clinked against each other as the men searched the kitchen cupboards. They stomped upstairs and thumps came as items were tossed to the floor. The men shouted things to each other in the guttural language he couldn't make out behind the bedstee doors. After a few more minutes, the boots marched to the front door. Cold air seeped in as the Gestapo left.

Gerrit wilted.

CORNELIA STROLLED OVER the bridge, almost home from morning services. The light rain had stopped and now she could put away the calm facade she had adopted while at the tsjerke. A burning sensation gnawed at her stomach. A strong foreboding had accompanied her all morning. She prayed she would walk through that door and see both Johan and Gerrit, safe and sound.

Her apprehension magnified. Her front door hung open, swinging to and fro on the wind.

The Gestapo had been back.

Gerrit lay helpless in there. And what about Johan? Had he returned? He could have walked straight into their open arms, hungry for a Dutch workforce.

She commanded her legs to hold her and keep the same pace up the path and over the canal to her house.

She glanced in all directions. No soldiers watched the bridge. She willed herself to breathe. They waited inside, not wanting to tip her off, not giving her a chance to flee.

Should she run? That's what she wanted to do. Run as fast and as far as she could. But she had to know about Gerrit and Johan.

Or maybe Johan had come to get Gerrit and take him to the Resistance safe house. They had left and forgot to shut the door. She always imagined the worst. Mem had told her she had a vivid imagination. Very likely things weren't as ominous as she envisioned.

Should she take the chance and walk straight into the house? She would look silly if she slunk around only to find Johan sitting at the table sipping his ersatz coffee. Then again, she would be downright foolish to strut inside to meet a German battalion waiting for her.

She would rather appear crazy than stupid. She and Johan would have a good laugh about it. Gerrit wouldn't be there. A wave of something—regret or maybe sorrow—washed over her.

Shaking off the emotions, she crept around to the kitchen window in back and peered through the parted curtains.

She covered her mouth to seal off a gasp. Cupboard doors hung open and pots and pans and silverware littered the floor. Her small table had been overturned, and the papers with the notes she had taken during devotions were scattered.

Her heart threatened to defect from her body.

The Gestapo had been here. And she saw no sign of Gerrit or Johan.

Not a single soldier roamed the place. But they would return. For her.

With her blood pounding in her ears, she decided to grab a few things and escape.

She sprinted inside and slammed the door, bolting it. First thing, she had to know about Gerrit and Johan. As she scurried to the front room, she wondered if they would be here or if they had eluded the Gestapo.

Maybe the soldiers shot them on the spot.

She steeled herself, then grasped the bedstee's hand-smoothed knobs and pulled the doors open.

Gerrit lay against the pillows, his yellow curls mussed, pale but alive. "I'm glad you are home." A dimple creased his right cheek.

"They were here."

"Ja."

"How did you . . . ? They believed your story?"

"You will never guess what happened."

"What about Johan? Is it safe for him to come out now?"

"He is not here."

She swayed. "Shouldn't he be back? It shouldn't take that long to deliver a message."

Gerrit's face remained calm. "He may have decided to wait to come until nightfall, under the cover of darkness."

His words made sense and she steadied.

"If you fix me a little lunch, I'll tell you everything."

With a great deal of speed, she straightened the house. She cut the last of her bread into thin slices, glad she didn't have any milk or cheese in the house from her employer's farm. They could have been in a great deal of trouble for withholding the milk from the Nazis.

In the days before the war, her family would gather for a big dinner each Sunday, with a roast and mashed potatoes. The smell would make her mouth water. If a person could travel backward, she would return to those times and cherish them.

She assisted Gerrit in sitting against the pillows. Beneath his soft cotton shirt, his muscles rippled. Emotions swept over her, recollections of another man and his sculpted arms and chest beneath her fingers. Her heart betrayed her.

She dropped him back and he winced. Feelings were dangerous things. "I'm sorry."

He shook his head. "I'm fine." He nibbled at the puny slice of unbuttered bread and filled her in on what had transpired.

"You're saying the man who shot you was here?"

Gerrit nodded. "In this very room, looking straight at me."

"Perhaps he didn't recognize you."

"He recognized me."

"Why would he protect you?"

"I don't know. If any of the other soldiers had discovered me, I would have been arrested or, more likely, shot without delay. But God led that particular soldier to me. Not another one, but the one whose sympathy I earned."

Cornelia fingered the edge of the blanket. "Amazing."

Gerrit's mouth, usually hooked a little downward, curved upward like a horseshoe. "God's fingerprints are over everything that is happening." He reached out and brushed the back of her hand.

His touch, his words, stirred feelings in her. Beautiful, awful feelings. What he awoke in her had died more than four years ago. She fought the emotions, not wanting to experience them, ever. Never again would she give her heart so freely it could splinter. It belonged to someone else. It always would.

She stood to adjust the blanket that had slipped from his shoulder. With his left hand, he stroked her cheek and his eyes drifted shut. She left his bedside, her gaze fixated on the opposite wall. The picture, as sharp and clear as her recollections, hung there, encased in a silver frame. A young man stared back at her, his straight, dark blond hair slicked back, his joy and love of life evident in his wide grin.

"Why, Hans, why? Why you?"

WHEN GERRIT AWOKE from his nap, as the light slipped from the sky, Cornelia brought him another bowl of warm vegetable soup. She wished for a little meat to help him regain his strength. Perhaps tomorrow, when she went to work at Frou de Bruin's farm, she would be able to get a little pork.

She sat in the corner, in her rocker near the bedstee, absorbed in her thoughts about Hans and her prayers for Johan. The school-house clock, which hung on the wall between the pictures of Hans and Queen Wilhelmina, ticked away the moments.

"Do you like to sing?" Gerrit's question broke her reflections and caught her off guard.

"Ja. I used to sing with the church choir, but I don't sing much these days."

"Why not?"

"There isn't much to sing about."

"We can't allow those Nazis to steal our reason to sing. If we do, they have won the war. Don't you ever defy them? Ever?"

"Of course I do. I hide Johan here, among many other things." She slid forward in her chair. "I don't speak German and I take yogurt and cheese and milk from Frou de Bruin, you know. But in a way, they have won the war by taking irreplaceable things from me. And that is why I have lost the will to sing. Perhaps on our liberation day, I will break into song. Not now."

"Be a little daring. Sing a song for me. A hymn. Maybe 'We Gather Together'?"

"Nee, I won't. Those words are almost rebellious."

"My mother used to sing that song to me. I miss hearing her voice. I miss being able to worship each Sunday with God's people. Won't you please sing for me?"

"Throw your mother in there to gain my sympathy. Did you think it would work?" She shook her head and a small smile tugged at her lips.

He shrugged. "Did it?"

"It has been so long."

"Then there is no better time than now. I would like to hear your voice."

He wore away her resistance like rain wears away the snow. "I don't sing that well."

"You sang in the church choir, so you must have a decent enough voice. Please."

"Only if you will sing with me."

He nodded.

> *We gather together to ask the Lord's blessing;*
> *He chastens and hastens His will to make known;*
> *The wicked oppressing now cease from distressing,*
> *Sing praises to His name: He forgets not His own.*

His weak but rich baritone joined her soprano. She moved from the rocker to his bedside, sitting on the edge of the mattress as the long-buried song washed over her.

> *Beside us to guide us, our God with us joining,*
> *Ordaining, maintaining His kingdom divine;*
> *So from the beginning the fight we were winning;*
> *Thou, Lord, wast at our side, all glory be Thine!*

> *We all do extol Thee, Thou Leader triumphant,*
> *And pray that Thou still our Defender wilt be.*
> *Let thy congregation escape tribulation;*
> *Thy name be ever praised! O Lord, make us free!*

Something happened in that moment, something Cornelia couldn't express in words. These shared experiences bound her and Gerrit together.

Like she had been bound to Hans.

CORNELIA'S CLEAR, BEAUTIFUL soprano broke on the last line of the third verse.

He didn't want to hurt her. "What's wrong? Have I upset you in some way?"

"Nee, nee, not at all. Not really, anyway. It's not you."

All the women he knew said that. "I'm sorry. I didn't mean to."

She shook her head and covered her mouth. Then a flash of gold caught his attention. A plain, thin band encircled the third finger of her right hand.

A wedding ring. He hadn't paid attention to it before. Maybe she didn't wear it all the time or maybe he had been in too much pain to see it.

Cornelia was married.

But where was her husband?

Did he work for the Resistance, or had he escaped to England in the early days of the war to fight with the British? Perhaps he had been detained by the Germans.

In the end, it didn't matter where the man might be. What did matter was that Cornelia was married. Likely the war separated them and they would be reunited once the Allies liberated them.

He had no right to be attracted to her. From now on, he would have to watch himself. And not watch her. He would have to restrain himself and not let his budding feelings bloom.

Men in the Resistance were taught to control their emotions. If they showed any signs of weakness—any fear, any love, any sadness—it made their jobs much more difficult. And dangerous.

Cornelia sniffled. "You're quiet."

"Am I?" He stared into her hazel eyes, the color of the fields in late summer.

"Ja," she whispered, looking right back at him.

The tender moment stole all rational thought from his brain.

The day's last ray of sunshine caught her hair, setting the muted auburn on fire.

"Cornelia."

She clutched her middle and stood, her rocker banging against the wall. "I'm going for a walk. You should rest awhile."

After she halted the motion of the chair, she left the house without even grabbing a sweater.

CHAPTER 11

A light mist fell, leaving Cornelia damp and chilled as she wandered the streets of town. She peeked in a few of the shop windows. Nothing but empty shelves.

Each building, though packed right against another, had a special uniqueness. Some were covered in light red bricks, so pale as to be almost pink. Others boasted brown or gray bricks. Many offered sloping roofs that pointed to the sky. Several were rectangular. Here and there, one had a green-striped awning, another a red-striped awning. All of them butted against the sidewalk that ran adjacent to the road.

She didn't think much, just meandered here and there. After thirty minutes or so, she discovered herself shivering on Anki's doorstep, hoping neither she nor Piet were napping.

Her sister invited her in, a much-loved book in her bony hand. "What brings you by?"

"I was out wandering. Would you like to take a walk with me?"

"In the rain? And you with no coat?"

"It's stopped. Please?"

Anki gave a reluctant nod and fetched her red wool coat, which she held out to Cornelia. "Wear mine. I have Piet's."

"Always watching out for your little sister, aren't you?"

"That's my job."

"You will make a great mother someday."

She and Anki linked arms and stepped outside. "Someday."

Anki's smile overpowered her face. She had a look like . . .

"Someday soon, Anki?"

"Sooner rather than later."

"Really?"

"That is all you are going to get out of me."

Could it be? Oh, Cornelia prayed it was so. Piet and Anki had longed for a child since the first day of their marriage. Four years later, perhaps God had answered those prayers.

They walked in silence for a while before Anki broke the quiet. "Did you see Frou de Bruin this morning at the tsjerke?"

Cornelia shook her head. "Nee. I should go and see her after service this afternoon. Her gout must be giving her trouble. I am sure she will give me all the details."

Anki chuckled. "I'm sure she will. And you will listen and nod in the appropriate places and make her feel better."

"Of course. That's how I keep my job, by agreeing to all she says." Cornelia stopped in front of the tailor-shop window. The dark blue door had been locked for many months now because of a shortage of cloth.

Anki leaned next to her, the sides of their heads touching. "Will we ever be free? Will the Allies ever get here?"

Cornelia lowered her voice. "The Boonstras have a secret radio. They told me this morning the queen is making plans for a new government once liberation comes. If the queen is that optimistic, perhaps she knows something we don't. But I agree—it's a distant dream."

They stood silent under the tailor's green-striped awning as the cold drizzle began again.

"So what did you want to talk to me about? I am sure it wasn't Frou de Bruin's gout."

Cornelia watched the rain drip from the gray sky. "They came back today while I was at church."

"The Gestapo?"

Cornelia nodded.

"Not surprising."

"Our little drunk ruse worked again. The same soldier who shot Gerrit was there and saw him. By God's grace alone, he didn't turn in Gerrit. I could have been arrested. We both should have been."

"Corrie, you have to get that man out of your house, especially with Johan home. Both of you will end up in prison. Or worse. And now Johan is involved in this clandestine work."

Cornelia massaged her hands together. "And he is still not home. I don't know. Gerrit said he is waiting until dark to brave the streets." Icy cold hands gripped her stomach.

Out of the corner of her eye, she glimpsed three NSBers patrolling the street, huddled in their black coats. She and Anki stood in silence as they approached. Cornelia shrank back and averted her gaze, her hands shaking as they passed and turned the corner at the next block.

Anki rubbed her arms. "You both are too involved. As soon as he can be moved, you have to get rid of Gerrit. You are both in too much danger. And Johan. What will you do if the Gestapo comes again?"

Cornelia stared at the spot where the NSBers disappeared. She shrugged. "I did well enough when they came to the house the other night."

Her sister blew on her hands. "I have to admit you did."

"I wished I could melt into a puddle on the floor." She giggled.

Anki laughed. "Me too."

Cornelia gazed at the little house across the street, squeezed in between two others. "If I turn Gerrit out, I would be signing his death warrant. Maybe his contacts will have a place for him to go. If not, I suppose he will have to stay."

"You are going to risk your life for a stranger." Anki shook her head in disapproval.

"He doesn't feel so much like a stranger. We get along well."

Her sister's mouth rounded into a circle, her brows raised. "You have a crush on him."

"I don't." Cornelia cut her sister off but then thought of her encounter with Gerrit earlier.

Nee, she didn't. She refused to open herself up to the crushing pain of loss again.

"Corrie, you don't know the man at all. Don't confuse your sympathy for him with anything more."

"Don't worry. There is nothing going on."

"Such a dangerous man. And he is putting you in danger."

"What else am I supposed to do?"

CORNELIA WOKE WITH a start, drenched in sweat, her heart thumping at an alarming rate. Bits and pieces of the nightmare came to her—the sound of shattering windowpanes and screaming women, the vision of shadowy figures and blood.

Her breath came in short gasps and she hugged herself to stop her quivering.

Several minutes passed before the dream faded and the adrenaline drained from her body.

She stretched, an ache in her back and a crick in her neck. Light framed the blackout shades.

This wasn't her tiny bedroom under the eaves. She found herself lying on the blue sofa in the front room with its red brocade wallpaper, Gerrit snoring in the bedstee. Why had she slept here? Her foggy brain searched for the answer, and as she roused, the realization hit her.

Johan never came home last night.

Gerrit told her he had waited for darkness, but she had sat up until the small hours of the morning in vain. Perhaps he had snuck in after she dozed and crept upstairs without waking her. Clinging to that glimmer of hope, she rose from her davenport, hoping the springs wouldn't creak and wake up Gerrit.

For the second morning in a row, she climbed the steps to Johan's door. For the second morning in a row, she discovered an empty room.

Her chest rose and fell quickly and her airway constricted. If Gerrit hadn't come into their home and disrupted their lives, none of this would have happened. Johan would be sleeping in his bed where he belonged.

How dare Gerrit send an impressionable young man into such insanity as strutting about the streets dressed as a woman, dodging Nazi officers on a Sunday morning? The gall of the man, telling a stranger how to live his life. Yesterday she had been willing to let him stay. Today she changed her mind.

She didn't tread lightly down the stairs but stomped, wishing she had on her klompen. Marching into the front room, she stood next to the bedstee, her hands on her hips as Gerrit left sleep behind. He smiled at her. Imagine that.

"Good morning, Cornelia."

"Where is my brother?"

His face paled. "He didn't come home?"

"Nee. You put him up to this crazy scheme, risking a young boy's life to let your friends know you were alive. Was it worth my brother's existence?"

"Don't think the worst. We don't know what might be going on. He could be well and safe somewhere."

"Don't think the worst? How can I help it? You sent my brother on a dangerous mission and now he has disappeared. People who vanish like that do not come home again. I used to know where my brother was and that he was safe. You have stolen him from me."

He reached out his work-worn hand to touch her, but she shrank away. "Listen, Johan volunteered to go. I didn't want to send him, but you were unwilling. What was I supposed to do? I needed to make contact with the Resistance here. You want to get rid of me as fast as possible—well, this is the way it needs to be done. In fact, you may have to go to the Underground cell yourself and find out what happened."

"Why did you come here?"

"If you remember, your brother brought me here. I didn't have much choice in the matter."

"You didn't have to shoot a missile through our happy life."

"Were you really happy?" His bright blue eyes bored into her, as if he could see into her head like a gypsy's crystal ball.

He had no right to ask her that question. Safe and secure— that's what she wanted. Happiness had died with Hans. Happiness carried too great a price.

She clutched her stomach and turned away from the man who made her think too much. "I have to go and check on Frou de Bruin, do a few chores for her, and get her noon meal prepared. I have a job. When I get back, you need to have a plan to find Johan."

She turned and strode out of the room, not wanting to give Gerrit a chance to say anything more. Especially not anything that would make her delve further into long-locked-away memories.

CORNELIA WALKED BRISKLY down the road lined with farm fields, away from Gerrit and the intense gaze of the German soldiers. She lifted her shoulders and inhaled a deep breath of cold air and tasted the ocean on her tongue. She had known Gerrit Laninga for less than sixty hours and he had toppled her world.

Because of him, Johan had disappeared. Would she ever see her brother again? Danger hung about Gerrit like a cloak. He brought only heartache and trouble with him.

Since that first night of the war, since her soul had been torn from her chest, she had structured her life so she might live in peace. Having Johan home had disrupted that some, and Gerrit disturbed her calm further. Just because she followed the rules didn't mean she liked them or thought them right.

A windmill rose above the flat, windswept landscape, its sails turning and whispering in the breeze. Her breathing slowed. The wind gusted and then calmed. The iconic structure kept spinning.

For a moment or two, she forgot the war, forgot Gerrit, forgot everything.

Then the drone of an Allied plane on its way to Germany split the quiet air. Though the sight of the aircraft had become familiar, especially in the last year and a half or so, it still caused a shiver to run through her. She tugged her sweater around her shoulders and picked up her pace. She needed to finish and hurry home to see what Gerrit had done toward finding her brother.

Cornelia discovered her regal old employer, no taller than a twelve-year-old boy, ensconced on a straight-backed kitchen chair in her sunny front room, rejecting the comfort of the light brown davenport and the dark brown wing chair. An ancient wood-burning stove chased away the chill.

Several rings adorned the woman's bony fingers, each of the many fake diamonds sparkling in the light. At least four strands of pearls weighed down her skinny neck. She rapped her nails on the wobbly end table. "You are rather late this morning, girl."

"I apologize. A matter came up that needed my immediate

attention." She should promise it would never happen again, but with a wanted man under her roof, she could offer no guarantees.

"What could be more important than getting an old woman her breakfast? It will be dinnertime before I have anything to eat."

Cornelia tipped her head to one side. Though Frou de Bruin was slight, she doubted the elderly woman would blow away in the wind. "Do you want an egg?"

"Ja, and some bread. It would be nice to have some of that new-fangled *hagelslag* on it."

Cornelia's mouth watered at the thought of the delicious choco-late sprinkles on a piece of light toast. "No hagelslag today." That was Johan's favorite breakfast. Would he be around to have it after the war?

Her shoulders sagged in defeat.

"Stand up straight, girl, and no pouting. We all have privations in war. You can't let a little thing like chocolate sprinkles get the best of you."

Frou de Bruin didn't understand. She hadn't lost anyone in the war. Cornelia shook her head.

Her employer shifted in her chair and scooted to the edge of the seat so her feet touched the pitted wood floor. "What's the matter with you? The only thing that should be blue is the sky."

"I, well, so much happened this weekend. It's, well, complicated." Cornelia stared at the other woman.

"I am not a dunce. I understand hard things."

The younger stared at the older. True, Frou de Bruin had been kind to her when she had come to work here two years after Hans's death, the pain still raw. But how far could she trust another person? Children turned in parents and brothers betrayed sisters. Benevolence at one time did not translate into trustworthiness in the present moment.

"I am not sure I can explain it." Her stomach writhed.

"I will let you know what you didn't explain well. Just spit it out."

Frou de Bruin stayed alone in her house, only going to church on the rare occasion when none of her many ailments were bothering her. She didn't have anyone to tell if Cornelia shared her secret. Secrets.

Cornelia studied the petite, majestic woman from her tightly pulled-back gray hair to her claw-like fingernails to her tiny yet ladylike crossed ankles. Today she wore a dark purple evening gown, the scooped neckline encrusted with darker purple beads, the entire ensemble more appropriate to the nineteenth century than the twentieth.

She appeared so harmless.

"My brother is missing."

Frou de Bruin leaned forward, like a child anxious to hear the ending of a suspenseful story. "Did those Nazis get him?"

Cornelia shrugged. "I don't know for sure, but I think so."

"How can you not know for sure?"

"He is missing, that's how I know. He was out and never came back." Why had she blurted even this part of the tale?

"And you have been hiding him? Good for you, girl. You have some fortitude after all. So now what?"

"That's the question. Perhaps he will be home when I get there. Maybe Johan spent the night at a friend's house." Cornelia needed to stop talking.

"Set me up with some nourishment so I don't wither away before tomorrow morning, and you can go and find out what happened to Johan."

"Are you sure? You will be okay here?"

"I don't think I will die before tomorrow, although at my age, you never know."

Cornelia wanted to jump up and down. *"Heel hartelijk bedankt, Frou de Bruin, heel hartelijk bedankt."*

GERRIT ROSE FROM bed once Cornelia left and sat in her rocker for a while, the quiet of the house broken only by the ticking of the schoolhouse clock, its hands inching their way around the dial. Clouds filled the sky throughout the morning and the wind blew hard. He pulled the blue blanket from the bedstee and wrapped it around himself.

Forgive me, Lord, for hurting Cornelia. Forgive me for any role I played in Johan's disappearance. May she forgive me too.

He couldn't bear it if she remained angry with him. He enjoyed her closeness, her tender care, her gentle touch.

She had ordered him to figure out a way to find Johan and bring him home. How would he go about that? His shoulder wound and the fact that he was a wanted man complicated things. He racked his brain for an hour or more but found himself no closer to a solution.

Gerrit didn't know how long it would be before one of the Resistance workers would arrive. The possibility presented itself that Johan had been rounded up in a *razzia*, along with the others. No one may come.

A knock at the door broke into his thoughts. No banging, no demanding to be let in, just a knock.

Did he dare answer? If the neighbor had come to visit as she had the other day, he would give himself away. But the neighbor should know Cornelia worked.

In the end, he didn't have to say anything. A voice he recognized as his friend Maarten called, "I have a delivery for Frou de Vries." Gerrit sighed. Maarten must be bringing Johan home.

Gerrit shuffled to the door and Maarten greeted him with a grin, his dark hair parted and slicked back, not a strand out of place, as usual. "The man you sent told Bear about your wound, so I won't give you the slap on the back I would like to."

Gerrit swallowed hard and he bit back the pain as he grabbed his chum in a hug. "So good to see you. A little bit of Leeuwarden in this place."

His friend's smile widened. "You manage to get yourself out of more scrapes than anyone I have ever met. Only you can fall into a manure pile and come out smelling like a rose. We thought you were dead."

Gerrit led him into the kitchen. "Pull up a chair and listen to my tale. No ersatz coffee. I have never been in this kitchen and feel strange about helping myself."

Maarten waved as he folded his tall, bony frame into a ladder-back chair. "Don't worry about it. I'm fine."

Gerrit launched into his story, still amazed at God's providence in his life.

Maarten leaned back and stretched his legs when Gerrit finished. "Incredible."

"I know."

"What about this man you sent to us? He said you were staying with him and his sister."

"She has been nursing me and fussing over me. Like my mother, only better because she is beautiful and compassionate and very sweet."

"Watch it. A wartime romance complicates things."

"Don't worry about that. No romance of any kind between us." After what happened with Mies, he wasn't sure he ever wanted another romance—wartime or not. "I have a message for you, some information to share. But first, I have to tell you that Johan, the man I sent you, has gone missing."

Maarten tented his long fingers. "He never arrived here? We sent him straight home yesterday morning."

Gerrit sucked in his breath. "Nee, he never showed up here."

Something had indeed gone wrong.

CHAPTER 12

Cornelia pumped her legs home from Frou de Bruin's farm at a rapid pace, her steps keeping tempo with the thoughts flying around her mind. Maybe Johan had come home while she had been away.

Please, Lord, let that be the case. Don't let anything bad happen to my brother.

This morning she had been so angry with Gerrit, blaming him for Johan's disappearance. He had argued that her brother volunteered all on his own. She hated to admit it, but he was right. Johan had always been adventuresome, and being cooped up in her small house, not able to go outside, had to be driving him crazy.

With everything inside her, she wanted to stay mad at Gerrit but found it impossible. He could have done more to discourage her brother from this mission, but Johan had been determined to go. Her brother usually got his way. His disappearance wasn't Gerrit's fault. Not entirely.

Johan had probably browbeaten him until he gave her brother the address of the Resistance contact.

If anyone held responsibility for Johan's actions, she did. Gerrit asked her first to go to his friend and deliver the message. Because she declined, Johan stepped in to do the job. Had she laid aside her fear and gone as Gerrit wanted, none of this would have happened. In truth, the fault lay with her.

If Johan went to Germany and never returned, she would be guilty of her brother's death. He would be the second person she had loved dearly but allowed to go into harm's way.

Please, Lord, please let Johan be home.

Her legs burned from her quick-paced walk and her fingers stung with the cold. She couldn't contain a smile when she saw her house. It welcomed her. She entered through the back door and kicked off her klompen. "Johan, I'm home!"

Her brother didn't answer. Gerrit did. "In the kitchen."

Her stomach plummeted like a shot-down plane tumbling to earth as she entered the room. "Where is my brother? Isn't he here?"

Gerrit shook his head. "Sit down."

She refused his invitation, gripping the back of the kitchen chair so hard her knuckles turned white. "Where is he? What happened to him?"

"I received word from Maarten a little while ago. Johan was arrested and is being held at the jail. First thing tomorrow morning they are transporting him to work on the fortifications in the south."

Dizziness swept over her and she tilted like a twirling top. Gerrit hurried to her side and steadied her with his left hand before pulling out a chair. "Please sit."

This time she took his advice. She had done it. She had sent Johan to the front lines. A young man from their tsjerke escaped and told of deprivation, disease, and death. And she could have prevented it all. "What can we do?"

Gerrit sat across from her and grinned. She wanted to slap away those dimples. "Maarten and I have devised a plot to help him escape." He sounded like a little boy excited about his scheme to pilfer cookies from the kitchen when his mem turned her back.

"What might that plan be?"

"It's best you not know."

"That's not a good enough answer."

"Never ask an Underground operative questions unless you want the same answer every time. The less you know, the less you can tell."

"This involves my brother."

"All the more reason for me to keep quiet."

She clenched her fists. "Nee, all the more reason to tell me."

"Not going to happen. I will tell you that we will steal Johan right out from under the Nazis' noses."

She rubbed her temples, conceding defeat. "Will it work? Will it bring Johan home?"

He sobered. "Hard to say. But I'm responsible for getting your brother into this trouble. I'll do all I can to get him out of it."

"This trouble is my fault. If I had gone, he would be here now. They would never have stopped me, you know."

"Johan wanted to go. Even if you had volunteered, he would have slipped out of the house. Right now we need to work on securing his release. First thing tomorrow morning I leave to bring him home."

"But how? You have just been shot in the shoulder." Wait a minute—he sat in a chair, not in bed. "Why are you up? Are you that much better?"

"The pain is less, and other than preventing you from falling to the floor, I have stayed in this chair."

"If you open that wound again and get an infection, I don't know what I will do with you. Let me help you back to bed so you can rest." Why one minute did she want to slug him and the next minute she cared about his welfare?

He acquiesced without complaint. "I can make it on my own."

MORNING CAME ALL too soon for Gerrit—not really morning, but the end of his night. Maarten would arrive in a few minutes. This operation needed to succeed for many reasons, the least of which was his redemption in Cornelia's eyes.

A vision of his sister Dorathee appeared before him, her sweet, innocent face. Another human being had hurt her. Today they wouldn't hurt another.

He groaned as he swung his legs over the side of the bedstee. His shoulder complained at the movement, but he ignored it. The Underground leaders had taught him that any discomfort could be willed away. Good advice if you were being tortured . . . good advice if you survived your own execution.

Cornelia greeted him in the kitchen with a bowl of yogurt and a steaming cup of ersatz coffee. He turned up his nose. After the war, he vowed never to touch the bitter brew again for as long as he lived.

"Good morning." Red rimmed her eyes and dark crescents appeared below them.

He went to her and stroked her cheek. "Didn't you sleep well?"

She turned and pretended to wipe crumbs from the counter. "Sleep doesn't come easily when your brother is under arrest, scheduled for shipment to the front lines in the morning."

"If I could change anything, you know I would."

"That is the worst part. I believe you would." She shrugged.

She paced the room several times, worrying the hem of her sweater as she walked. Then she plopped into a kitchen chair. "I am scared, Gerrit."

Her vulnerability broke his heart. He went to her and, hiding a grimace of pain, gathered her into his arms. "Don't be frightened. God is on His throne."

"I know, but what I believe in my head is different from what I feel in my heart. I don't want anything dreadful to happen to my brother."

"Everything will be fine."

"This war has cost me everything. I have nothing more to give."

"And I'm going to try to make sure you don't have to give any more. We won't let them take any more from you. Not this time."

She gazed at him with such hope in her eyes. He had to bring Johan home with him. And he would.

He ate the breakfast she had prepared. The yogurt tasted good and revived him. Cornelia sat across from him after a few minutes, turning her coffee cup round and round. They didn't speak until he finished.

"Shall I pray?"

She nodded.

"Dear Father, be with this mission today. Bless it, and if it be Thy will, grant us success. Return Johan to his family and his home."

Cornelia sniffled and he couldn't continue. After pausing a few moments, he said, "Amen."

They both stood. She came around the table to him, gave him a hug, and climbed the stairs. A moment later Maarten knocked on the door.

DARKNESS PRESSED IN on Johan. The old brick walls of the jail cell seeped with moisture and a chill enveloped him. Odors of filthy bodies and unsanitary conditions permeated the air. No one shared the tiny room with him, a gift.

He paced the perimeter—six steps forward, turn, six more steps, turn, and so on. Not knowing what would happen to him today, he couldn't sit on the filthy straw or the damp floor.

Where might he be headed? He hoped to the fortifications in the south. If he was surrounded by somewhat familiar territory, he had a greater chance of escape. He would blend in better with his own people, and the likelihood increased that he would find a sympathetic countryman to help him get home.

And he would be able to breathe the fresh air. Home sure was as much a prison as this cell.

Six steps forward, turn, six more steps, turn.

He had a plan he would put into motion when the guard came for him. At some point in his journey, he would be alone with one or two soldiers. When the opportunity presented itself, he would kick one of them in the groin, then spin and disable the other in the same manner.

And then he would run. In the schoolyard, all of his classmates commented on what a fast sprinter Johan Kooistra was. He could outpace any of them on any given day.

He would be a hero. He would repay those Germans for what they had done to Corrie, how they had broken her spirit. And for how they had stolen Mem and Heit from him. If it weren't for the war, he would have been able to get medicine for them and they would be alive and well today.

The Nazis would get a small taste of the misery they had caused his family.

GERRIT GAZED AT the town hall, an old, square, three-story brick building with rows of gleaming windows and twin chimneys jutting into the sky. He smoothed down the green-gray wool German officer's uniform, cinched the belt at his waist, and adjusted the black bill of the hat, complete with a laurel wreath and an eagle. As he left Cornelia's, he had caught a glimpse of himself in the mirror. He looked every inch the German officer.

The stolen German transport truck Maarten drove idled behind him. When Gerrit had pressed his friend to tell him where he had gotten the uniform and the truck, Maarten gave the standard reply, "It is better that you not know." That suited Gerrit just fine.

He slipped his left hand in his pocket and fingered the forged papers granting him custody of Johan. If they had made even a small error on the documents, they would all suffer a fate worse than building reinforcements along the southern front or working in a German factory ripe for Allied bombing. He withdrew his sweaty hand, fearful of smudging the ink.

He shivered in the early morning chill, then climbed the stone steps. Taking a deep breath, he pushed open the heavy wood door, which creaked in protest. Each step he took in his boots echoed down the corridor. He reached the main reception area and crossed to the big desk.

"Heil, Hitler." He bit down hard to keep from crying out as he raised his right hand in salute, all the while hoping his Dutch-tinged German didn't tip off the man. Then he handed the documents to the scrawny clerk with wire-rimmed glasses and held his breath.

The clerk took his time, reading every word once, twice, three times. Gerrit didn't dare try to guess if all this perusal was good or bad. The big clock on the wall ticked away the seconds and minutes.

At last the clerk peered up at Gerrit over his glasses. "I'll get the prisoner."

Gerrit nodded and clicked his heels, hoping he didn't over-act. He concentrated on releasing his breath bit by bit. If he let it whoosh out, he might arouse suspicions.

Many more ticks of the clock passed before the clerk returned with a guard.

And Johan.

The young man's soft blue eyes widened when he saw Gerrit standing there, ready to take custody of him. He gave Johan a slight nod and straightened his back. Johan cleared the emotions from his face. He might make a good Resistance worker yet.

Gerrit stepped forward and grasped Johan's elbow, then led him out the big door, to the steps and toward the canvas-covered transport truck.

Cornelia's brother paused. "What . . . ?"

Gerrit squeezed his elbow hard, wincing at the pain in his shoulder. "Hush. Don't say a word. Things could still go wrong."

They took one step down, the truck idling across the street, Maarten waiting for them. Before they descended farther, two German soldiers sauntered to the driver's side of the truck. Both had close-cropped blond hair. One had wider shoulders and a broader body than the other. They poked their heads into the window and gestured at Gerrit's friend.

Gerrit pulled Johan back. "Don't move, in case the cover is blown."

No sooner had he said the words then Maarten gestured for them to come.

Gerrit led a trembling Johan down the stone steps. "We have to see what they want. Don't say a word. Follow my lead." He straightened his own spine.

Maarten spoke to him in German, though his Dutch accent was apparent. "They would like to see the papers."

Gerrit fished them out of his jacket pocket and handed them to the soldiers.

"Where are you taking this prisoner?"

Gerrit nodded to his fellow Resistance worker. "We have orders to deliver him to Amersfoort."

"What for?"

"Working with the Resistance."

The older, smaller of the two pulled a pair of reading glasses from his jacket pocket. Much as before, the officers examined the forged papers with an exacting thoroughness. That much could be said for the Germans.

"Have a nice drive." The soldier with the glasses handed the papers back to Gerrit before taking the time to sneer at Johan and spit in his face.

Gerrit's temperature rose by ten degrees.

Johan strained forward.

Even though the idea of kicking the officer sounded appealing, Gerrit hissed at Johan, "Don't. Do you want to truly be on your way to Amersfoort?"

Cornelia's brother relaxed and Gerrit shoved him into the back of the truck with what he hoped was convincing roughness. His shoulder burned.

Maarten grinned at him as he climbed into the cab. "That was easy."

"Don't speak too soon. We have to get him home."

CHAPTER 13

The sound of a truck rumbling down the street interrupted Cornelia as she spread fresh sheets on Gerrit's bedstee. Only the Nazis had petrol. She parted the curtains and peered out, her heart racing when the truck screeched to a stop in front of her house. At the end of her walkway sat the same kind of transport that took away people who never came back. The same kind that took Jap Boersma away the other day. The same kind that might take her away today.

Something must have gone wrong with Gerrit's plan. Terribly, horribly wrong. They had tortured Gerrit and Johan for information, and now they had come after her. Her entire body quivered and her breath came in short spurts. She sat on the bed, helpless, smoothing her maroon A-line skirt.

The sharp clack of jackboots approached the house. Without a knock, the front door opened. "Cornelia, we're home."

Her breathing ceased altogether. She couldn't trust her ears. "Johan, is that you?"

He bounded into the room. "You will never believe it. I sat in my cell this morning, waiting for them to take me away at any moment. I mean, I had this escape plan all ready to go. Then the guard arrived and led me upstairs. I was prepared to say good-bye to this place forever. And there in the lobby stood Gerrit. They actually handed me over to him. It sure was amazing. Though I didn't get a chance to put my plan in motion."

"What plan would that be?" Another one of his crazy schemes.

"How I would get away from them and be a hero myself. Everyone would cheer me. Gerrit would help me join the Resistance."

Cornelia peered behind her brother but didn't see Gerrit. "Where is he?"

Johan's brows furrowed. "He was right behind me."

Gerrit stumbled into the room. "Not a hero. Just doing my duty."

She flew to his side, embracing him loosely so as not to cause his shoulder more pain. "Bedankt. You brought my brother back to me. Heel hartelijk bedankt."

He winced and beads of sweat dotted his forehead.

"I am sorry. I didn't mean to hurt you. Is it your shoulder?"

He nodded.

"Johan, help me get him to bed."

Her brother slipped under Gerrit's good shoulder and eased him to the bedstee. They laid him down, careful not to jostle him. Her hand brushed his shoulder as she pulled up the blanket, and it came away sticky with blood.

Cornelia's stomach did an about-face. "Look at the wound. It opened again."

Johan did as she requested, unbuttoning Gerrit's shirt and peeling away the dressing. "Get a towel. Fast. He is losing blood."

She ran to the kitchen and grabbed two or three old dish towels, scurrying back to the front room. Her brother yanked them from her hand. "Go get Anki."

Gerrit shook his head. "Nee. I told you nee."

Panic wove itself through Johan's words. "She already knows

about you. In fact, she took out the bullet. If she had wanted to turn you in, she would have by now."

Johan wadded the towels and pressed them into Gerrit's wound. "Let's not argue. Go get her."

ANKI SAT IN the sagging brown sofa next to the long window, sipping her warm water. The weak late winter sun matched the pale yellow of the front room's walls. She rested her head on her husband's shoulder. "What I wouldn't give for a cup of real Indonesian tea."

He stretched his head, first to the left, then to the right. "Let's be thankful for all we do have."

"Can't you play along with me just once? What do you miss the most?"

"I miss you when I go to work."

She sat straight and studied his long profile, his almost pointy chin. "Not that. What do you look forward to the most when the war ends?"

"Okay." He smiled. "Enough raisins to make *olliebollen* and enough sugar to roll them in."

Anki could almost smell the sweet donut holes frying. "And you shall have as many of them as you can eat the first day I find raisins and sugar in the market."

He kissed her cheek and stood. "Now that I have played your game, I have to get ready for work."

Quiet descended and her thoughts scattered. What might have happened to Johan? Had he come home yesterday? Her hands shook and she set her mug on the floor so she didn't slosh the water.

She shouldn't deceive her husband. Spouses should tell each other everything. Piet didn't favor either the Germans or the Allies but favored telling the truth no matter the outcome.

He said God would protect them and His will would be done.

Anki rubbed the back of her neck, a headache niggling the edges of her brain.

Corrie could deny it, but she had a crush on that Resistance worker. On a man who had involved her and her brother in illegal activity. Never in her life would Anki have imagined Corrie would become a criminal, aiding an Underground agent.

Protect my family, Lord.

She rubbed the spot below her navel, her special secret. Would this child, newly conceived, ever know his aunt or uncle? That was her prayer. She hadn't told Piet her news yet. She had been waiting to choose the perfect moment but couldn't wait much longer. The baby would start making his or her presence known soon.

If the Lord answered their prayers and they had good news about Johan, maybe she would tell Piet tonight. She would fix a special dinner, as much as she could with the rations, and they would celebrate. Perhaps confiding in Piet with one bit of news would ease her conscience when she hid more from him.

A gentle rap on the door drew her from her daydream. She was surprised to find Corrie.

"Aren't you supposed to be on your way to Frou de Bruin's?"

"Can I come in for a minute?"

Anki opened the door all the way and stepped aside for her sister. "What is it?"

"Is Piet around?"

"He went upstairs to get dressed."

Corrie spoke so softly Anki had to lean close to hear her. "Gerrit's shoulder wound has opened. Johan tended to him and told me to get you. You have to hurry and look at it."

Anki attempted to process one piece of information at a time. "Johan's home? Praise the Lord."

Her sister nodded.

"Where has he been?"

Corrie went to the hook by the front door and grabbed Anki's old red wool coat. "There's time for that later. Gerrit needs you now. Every second he loses more blood."

Anki slipped her arms into the jacket her sister held open. "I don't like this. What am I going to tell my husband now?"

The words had just passed her lips when Piet came down the stairs, buttoning the top button on his white collared shirt, now yellowed because of the lack of good soap. He surveyed the situation—Cornelia in the front hall, Anki with her coat on. "Where are you going? Don't you have to be at work, Corrie?"

She nodded. "That's why I'm here. Frou de Bruin isn't feeling well but won't send for the doktor. With her age, it would be good for Anki to lend her opinion, you know."

"And it looks like you are going, my dear, without a word to me."

Anki snuggled into her husband's arms. She missed the sweet aroma of his pipe. "Don't be silly. I was going to say good-bye, but I hadn't had the chance yet."

"This couldn't wait?" Piet kissed her cheek, then nuzzled her ear and neck.

Corrie coughed behind them. "Nee, I am worried about her. She didn't eat well yesterday."

"Maybe she wasn't hungry."

Anki sensed her husband's suspicions and needed to deflect them. "I have a surprise for you tonight."

"What?"

"I am going to make you wait until after work. Now you will have to let me go."

He released her. "You seem in an awful hurry to get rid of me. What's going on? Corrie's had a lot of sick friends in the past few days."

With each word she spoke, Anki's list of lies grew. Keeping

secrets from Piet wasn't something she could do much longer. "There is a bug or something going around. Now you need to get over to the milk plant and I need to see to Frou de Bruin."

"If I didn't know any better, I would say you two sisters were up to something."

CORNELIA STOOD IN the hallway, peeking into the front room where Anki examined Gerrit. She didn't want to see everything that took place in there, but she did want to hear.

"Anki," Johan said, "thank goodness. The blood has soaked through three towels."

"Let me take a look."

The two remained silent for a time, and Cornelia assumed her sister was checking Gerrit. Then Anki sighed. "He ripped open the stitches. The wound is jagged and beyond my ability to do a really good repair job that's going to hold once he starts moving. A doktor needs to see him."

Cornelia stepped into the room. "That's out of the question."

"If we don't send for a doktor, he may well die."

"Nee, we can't let that happen."

"Then we have to get Doktor Boukma."

Gerrit stirred and winced in pain. "Go to Maarten."

Johan's broad face lit up like a sunrise over the Frisian plains. "What disguise should I use this time?"

She couldn't allow Johan to venture out again. Anki couldn't go either. She didn't like lying to her husband, and maybe one day she would tell Piet everything, including the location of the area Underground cell.

That left her.

If she wanted Gerrit to live, she had to be the one to go to the

SNOW ON THE TULIPS

Resistance and find out what they should do, and if there was a doktor in the area who could be trusted.

She had been helpless to prevent Hans's death. She had gotten Johan arrested and almost sent to dig trenches at the southern front.

But they asked her to do the impossible.

Her stomach swung back and forth like a pendulum. So did her mind. She needed to go and save Gerrit's life, but could she do that while risking her own?

Places like Scheveningen and Vught, which had been vague imaginations, shadowy places where other people went, became real to her. She could smell the death these places implied. And what would happen if the doktor they thought could be trusted turned out to be working for the Nazis instead?

There went her stomach again, slamming against her midsection, sending foul-tasting bile into her throat.

"Inasmuch as ye have done it unto one of the least of these . . ."

She covered her ears, trying to drown out the Lord's admonition.

Johan rubbed her back. "Corrie's not going to be able to do it. I will have to go."

"Nee!" The word burst from her clenched mouth before she could stop it. "I will be the one to go this time. I will do it."

CHAPTER 14

Cornelia walked the route to the Underground's headquarters, acting as if she did this every day. She waved to Frou Huizenga when she spotted the woman across the street and stopped for a moment to coo at Mot Portinga's new daughter. Inside, however, she quivered like a poplar tree in the breeze.

She should be on her way to Frou de Bruin's house now, but getting help for Gerrit took precedence. From the time he had walked into her house this morning until the time she left to fetch a doktor—not much more than thirty minutes—Gerrit had weakened and faded. The feisty old lady would peck at her to no end when she did arrive, but she would have to make her employer understand that some things were more important than peeling potatoes and washing floors.

A man's life—Gerrit's existence—rested in her hands.

She passed the old, familiar shops. At Hear Smeet's bakery, a few women milled around, waiting for their little loaf of bread, their daily ration. Their thin coats were drawn around their shoulders, their bare legs exposed to the elements.

The same scene played out at the greengrocer's. Though the

man did not have his usual prewar bounty of fruits and vegetables, the town's women who weren't at the bakery stood in line here, waiting with open hands for their few potatoes.

Again, she passed the shop without stopping. She rehearsed Johan's directions to the house and the code knock and words she would need to gain entrance.

Though the walk to the center of the small town didn't take long, by the time she arrived at the nondescript house stationed in the midst of a row of dwellings sagging under the weight of the occupation, her legs shook and her knees banged together. She didn't know how much longer she would be able to stand.

She raised her hand, which trembled more than Frou de Bruin's. Clasping her own wrist to still it, she closed her eyes and inhaled and exhaled a few times.

She tapped the cold metal knocker in the rhythm Johan taught her, praying she had remembered it correctly. With Gerrit losing blood at an alarming rate, she had not been entirely focused.

A deep voice rumbled from the other side of the door. "What do you want?"

"I have a vegetable delivery."

"Carrots, beets, or potatoes?"

"Green beans."

Johan told her he had to wait awhile for Bear to open the door, but it flew open wide a few seconds later. Thankful she remembered the code, she crossed the threshold into the dim interior. The man slammed the door shut behind her and bolted it.

He towered over her and, despite the food shortage, appeared well fed. She shrank back until she leaned against the door.

"What do you want?"

"Are you Bear?" Her voice squeaked.

"Ja."

She swallowed hard around the lump in her throat. "Gerrit's

wound has opened and he's losing blood. He needs a doktor. If he doesn't get care soon, he will die."

"Doktor Boukma can be trusted. Get him and he will take care of Gerrit. He won't say anything."

"But I have to get to work."

"I thought you said Gerrit is about to die."

"Ja, but I have a job." Frou de Bruin would be furious with her for being so late. "Can't one of you go?"

"It's too dangerous for men to be on the streets. Maarten has a forged ausweis, but that means right now he is supposed to be somewhere working. I couldn't send him until later. If Gerrit's condition is as grave as you say, you need to be the one to go."

Once, when she was small, maybe five or six, she had played along the edge of the canal. Rain had fallen earlier in the day, making the bank slippery. As she played, she lost her footing and slid into the water. Though she struggled, she hadn't been able to keep her head above water.

That same drowning sensation washed over her now.

"I'll go."

Doktor Boukma had delivered her and her siblings, had removed her tonsils, and had stitched up Johan's head more than once.

"Then you had better hurry."

She restrained herself from curtsying when she fled Bear's house.

She didn't need directions to the doktor's office and she picked up her pace. Time was slipping away for Gerrit.

Doktor Boukma welcomed her with a wide smile, his blue eyes warm. "Cornelia de Vries. To what do I owe this pleasure?"

"I need you to come with me."

He didn't hesitate and didn't ask questions.

Together they bustled down the streets, past women going about their daily business. That had been her a mere four days ago.

SNOW ON THE TULIPS

Many of them greeted her and the doktor, and he returned their greeting, relaxed and confident.

She tried to disappear behind his slender frame.

"Won't people wonder why you are coming with me when I live alone?"

He shook his head. "They are busy with their everyday lives. And if they wonder, let them wonder."

How many of these women also harbored secrets?

Doktor Boukma went straight in to see Gerrit as soon as they arrived home.

She stood in the entry to the front room. "Do you need me to do anything? Otherwise, I should start a pot of water for coffee."

He waved her toward the kitchen. Part of her sagged in relief that she didn't have to see the blood spurting from Gerrit's wound or the signs of death in his face. The other part wished she could be in there with him, holding his hand, willing him to live.

She placed the kettle on the fire and sat on the kitchen chair. Then she jumped up, checking to see if the water boiled yet. She opened and closed cabinet doors without putting anything in or taking anything out. A moment later she arranged four coffee cups on the counter, then rearranged them.

Johan came through the door and leaned against the jamb, his entire face wilting with exhaustion. "Sit down, Corrie. He will tell us about Gerrit when he is through. I think once Doktor Boukma stitches him up, he will be fine."

Cornelia thumped into her chair and played with the handle on her blue coffee cup. "I hope we got here soon enough. What if he dies?"

"Then it is in God's hands. He will take care of everything."

"I couldn't stand it if he died."

Johan stood straight. "Are you falling in love with him?"

Cornelia sat back, almost tipping over her chair. "Nee. Absolutely not. Never."

"A lot of denial for a straightforward question."

She spread her hands on the table. "I have loved Hans since I was a little girl. He gave me piggyback rides, and even then I enjoyed being near him. We had so little time. We had no time, really."

"I want to see you happy."

"I don't love Gerrit or anyone else. And I never will."

But as Cornelia spoke the words, she wondered if they were true.

Doktor Boukma stepped into the room and over to the sink to wash his hands. "All finished." The tall, strong man Cornelia used to know had changed. He stooped a little when he walked and his hair had turned white. Anki followed him.

Cornelia rose. "Let me get you some coffee."

He waved her off. "Nee, bedankt. I can't stay. You did a great job, Anki. You should think about becoming a surgeon."

She laughed, her green eyes shining. "I have other things that will occupy my time. My nursing days are over."

Now Cornelia knew for sure. It would be a matter of waiting for Anki to announce her news.

Doktor Boukma turned to Cornelia. "The wound looked clean, so all I had to do was stitch the hole closed. The most important thing is to keep him still. He got up too soon and moved about too much, causing your sister's beautiful sutures to come apart. Even while I worked on him, he started asking me when he could get out of bed. Good luck keeping him quiet. In a few days, I will check back."

Cornelia steadied herself on the edge of the table. "Heel hartelijk bedankt for everything you have done."

The doktor touched Cornelia's shoulder. "You are doing the right thing. Don't doubt it. God will bless your efforts."

He served as an elder in their village tsjerke. As a church leader, shouldn't he know these things? "Do you truly believe it?"

He mussed the little hair he had. "Yes, I do."

Anki wiped her hands on her apron. "What about the lies? Isn't that wrong? Surely God will protect us if we tell the truth."

"Is it right to sacrifice another life? Think about Rahab in the Bible. She hid the spies under the flax on her roof. Then she misled the soldiers, but God blessed her actions by saving her family when the walls of Jericho fell and by including her among the ancestors of Jesus. God credited all this to her as righteousness. Keep doing what you are doing and God will reward your faithfulness."

Cornelia didn't want any part of this. Why had God brought Gerrit here? Was He testing her? Or using her?

Anki circled the table. "I understand what you are saying, but the commandment not to bear false witness is pretty clear to me. God doesn't put in any provisions for extenuating circumstances."

The older man nodded. "The commandment not to kill is just as plain. I don't have to put a bullet through someone's head to break that commandment."

A fierce headache throbbed behind Cornelia's eyes. "But what if you have to break one commandment in order to keep another?"

CHAPTER 15

Gerrit's shoulder burned like someone had lit it on fire. Every time he moved, the incredible heat increased, so he stayed still, despite how much he wanted to be up and about business.

He and Johan both napped the afternoon away, exhausted from their ordeal of the past few days. He woke as soon as he heard the front latch click open. Cornelia entered the room and announced herself to Gerrit with a smile much warmer than the pale, cold winter sun.

"Has Johan taken good care of you?"

He nodded.

"How about some soup?"

He nodded again. Johan hadn't brought him anything to eat, not that he had been hungry until now.

When she walked away, he missed her. Then he recalled her marital status. He must turn off the switch to these feelings. Out there, somewhere, she had a husband.

From the kitchen, he heard Cornelia and Johan speaking but couldn't understand their words. He tried to move to a more comfortable position, one that would ease the pain, but that only increased his discomfort. After a while, she came back and helped him, her touch gentle.

"Here you go."

He raised his right hand to take hold of the spoon and winced.

"Let me help you." Her soft, cool palm brushed his hand as she went to take the spoon. The fire moved from his shoulder to his fingertips.

She fed him the salty golden broth, and the carrots and potatoes floating in the steaming liquid. He obeyed her commands but didn't say anything, watching her every gentle, graceful move. Her presence calmed and soothed him. If only she didn't wear that band of gold around her finger.

He finished the soup and she stood. He had to stop her from leaving. "Bedankt for getting the doktor. Again you saved my life."

She turned her gaze to the floor and the smile faded.

She didn't answer.

"Did I say something wrong?" Maybe she missed her husband. Perhaps today was a special day for them, like their anniversary or his birthday.

She gathered the dirty dishes on a tray, then turned to take them to the kitchen.

"Where is your husband?"

He heard her sharp intake of breath. The glass wobbled on the tray. The bowl clattered to the wood floor, shattering.

CORNELIA STOOD STATUE still, her back to Gerrit, staring at the smashed glass.

She didn't want to talk to anyone about Hans, least of all to this man who generated in her the emotions reserved for her husband.

"Why do you want to know?" she whispered.

"You wear a wedding band but never talk about him. I have never seen him. Is he in hiding? Or did he get transported to Germany?"

She shook her head. If she spoke about Hans, she would open the sea, all those horrible memories and amazing feelings flooding her, overwhelming her. In the end, she would drown.

"You can trust me. I won't betray him. You should know that by now. Perhaps I can help."

"You can't help." The room spun in front of her. "No one can. He is dead."

"I am so sorry."

She pinched the bridge of her nose. "I don't want to talk about him."

"I don't want to push you, but I have been told I am a good listener."

"There is nothing to say." Nothing that wouldn't squeeze her heart until it hurt.

"Is he the man in the picture?"

She nodded. "I need to get a broom."

She returned and began to sweep the shards of glass into the dustpan.

"Was he in the Resistance? Is that why you don't like us?"

"Nee. And I never said I didn't like you. You Resistance people, I mean."

"But you are afraid of us."

"Ja. I suppose I am. Death follows you."

"Death follows all of us, and more so during war."

She straightened and rubbed the small of her back. "Do you always talk about such morbid subjects?"

"Nee, I can be fun. I am a champion domino player."

She knew so little about this man. "You don't play cards, do you?" Did he drink or dance?

He laughed. "Don't worry, I don't. With my bad shoulder, I

can't even play dominoes. But I would like it if you would sit and talk with me."

Johan had said he planned to read for a while before turning in early, so she wouldn't have his company. And Gerrit had quit prying about Hans. If he didn't broach that subject again, she wouldn't mind talking to him.

She held up the dustpan. "Let me empty this first."

A few minutes later she returned and drew the rocker close to the bedstee. Gerrit reached out and touched her hand. "I apologize again for upsetting you. I shouldn't have pushed you to tell me something personal."

She settled in the rocker. "I appreciate that. Now, can we talk about something else?"

He smiled, a dimple creasing his right cheek. "Anything you want."

"Well, you know I have a brother and a sister."

"About that . . ." His smile faded.

"I wouldn't put your life in jeopardy. If she turned you in, she would turn in her own brother, and me too."

"Good point."

"The other night she did a fine piece of acting when the Nazis came searching for you. She had them believing you both were passed out from too much drink."

"If you trust her, so do I."

There came that incredible dimpled smile again, the one that reminded her of spring and sunshine.

"Anyway, tell me about your family." She picked up her knitting, fashioning a new sock from yarn she had used several times over. Before the invasion, she had never thought of a new skein of yarn as a luxury.

He stared at the stark white ceiling and she watched as his memory traveled the miles to his home. "I feel for Johan because I have three sisters and no brothers. Two older sisters, just like him, and a younger sister. Both my older sisters, Beatrix—like the princess— and Elisabeth, are married. Last I heard, Beatrix was expecting her second child and Elisabeth her first. Those children would be born by now, but I haven't had contact with home for a long time."

She dropped a stitch and ripped out the row. "Did you get along well? Sometimes Anki and Johan and I were best friends and other times we were worst enemies."

"My older sisters thought I was a nuisance. They complained to Mem all the time that I pestered them."

She smiled a little. "I went to my mem more than once about Johan. But what about your younger sister?"

"Dorathee." His voice took on a faraway, dreamy quality. He smiled. "She lives at home in Leeuwarden with my parents. When she was a baby, she had a very high fever and never fully recovered. She has a hard time learning things and remembering them. The other kids in the neighborhood laughed at her and teased her, but they didn't get away with it."

"Why not?"

"I got in trouble for fighting more times than I can remember, but all of my brawls were in her defense." He shrugged. "Most of them, anyway."

"So you fought for her?"

"Ja, because she couldn't fight for herself." His smile faded. "When the occupation first started, Dorathee went outside to play. Even though she was sixteen, she still played with dolls. I was coming up the street from working with Heit when three soldiers approached her. One of them ripped her doll from her hands and smashed it on the pavement."

He tugged on the edge of the sheet. "When she began to cry, they sneered at her and yanked her braids."

Cornelia sat forward. "The Nazis don't have hearts at all."

"Before I could think, I sprinted toward the house, charged those soldiers, and shoved one of them to the ground. The others went after me. One landed a good punch to my face and the other kicked me in the stomach. Before I could catch my breath, they ran off."

"She is the reason you work with the Resistance."

All softness left his voice. "I want this land rid of those Nazis before more people are hurt or killed. Before they do worse to Dorathee. I heard rumors about them killing off the mentally and physically disabled in Poland and Germany. I have to protect her. Perhaps I can't bring those exact three soldiers to account, but I can hold their like responsible for what they have done."

"Revenge will eat you away."

"This isn't revenge. This is justice."

"Is there a difference?"

"Vengeance is getting even. Justice is giving what is deserved. Justice seeks fairness."

Cornelia sat back. "If you let this desire to retaliate consume you, then you will have done Dorathee no good."

"I do her no good sitting here."

"You do. You are healing, so when the war ends, you will be able to go home to her. God will take care of the rest."

"Are you always this serious?"

"Are you always this intense?"

Gerrit smiled. "Touché."

"Tell me something about yourself that isn't serious."

"I'm only serious when it comes to children, redheads, and olliebollen."

Her mouth watered. "Olliebollen is serious business. As far as redheads, you're only trying to get into my good graces with that remark."

"Maybe so. Did it work?" He yawned.

"That remains to be seen. Right now, you need to get some sleep."

As she leaned over him to pull the blanket across his shoulders, he kissed her on the cheek, a little peck, but it started her heart throbbing. "Good night, Cornelia."

She swallowed. "Sleep well, Gerrit."

Even with the Allied planes droning overhead on their way to Germany with their fatal cargo, contentment flooded her.

ANKI PREPARED FOR bed, taking more time than usual washing her face in her little bathroom sink. By the time she had returned from Corrie's house, she was tired and didn't feel well enough to make a special dinner for Piet. He hounded her all evening to reveal her surprise.

She wanted to tell him. They never kept anything from each other. Secrets ate away at the trust needed to sustain a marriage. Everything in her screamed to tell her husband the truth. All of it. A tiny but powerful little niggle restrained her.

She hated what she was doing.

With little room to squeeze in, her husband came behind her and wrapped his arms around her. Still with her back to him, she reached up and stroked his stubbly cheek.

"You look worn out, Anki."

She playfully jabbed him with her elbow. "That is a nice thing to say to your wife."

"I mean that I am concerned about you." He kissed her neck.

"No need to be." She couldn't quite bring herself to tell him about the baby. The time didn't feel right.

"Then what is going on?"

"Nothing. You are worried for no reason."

He released her from his embrace, pulling her into the bedroom, holding her at arm's length, examining her from head to toe. He didn't believe her. "What is that? You have a stain on your dress."

SNOW ON THE TULIPS

She looked down at the top of her light brown skirt. A streak of red crossed just under her waistband. Gerrit's blood. She must have wiped her hand on her dress without realizing.

"Just a little dirt that will wash off. Let's go to bed."

"That's not dirt. It looks like blood."

"Blood?" Anki stared at her skirt for a moment, trying to think of a story he would accept. "Ja, how silly of me. This afternoon the neighbor's littlest boy cut his finger and they asked me to help bandage it. I must have gotten some blood on me then. I will wash it in a little cold water and it will be as good as new."

Piet raised a single eyebrow. "I was thinking. Since Frou de Bruin has been sick so much, why don't we go see her tomorrow first thing in the morning. You can bring her a pot of meatball soup."

CHAPTER 16

Morning came much too soon for Anki. Her nightgown had tangled around her legs and she had thrown off the blanket. All night she had tried to devise a way to talk Piet out of going to see Frou de Bruin.

You reap what you sow. A harvest of hurt awaited her.

If Piet knew about the coming baby, she could plead morning sickness. But that was another lie that haunted her. Not so much of a lie as an omission.

Nee. There was no difference between the two.

She poured the meatball soup left over from last night into a pot, some of it splashing onto the counter. When she picked up the dish towel to wipe the mess, she dropped the cloth onto the floor. She had to quiet her trembling hands before Piet came downstairs when he finished shaving.

Perhaps she needed to tell him the truth before they went on their visit. That would be best. No public scene. Piet would never turn in Gerrit or Johan. Especially not Johan, her only brother. He wouldn't hurt her that way.

A moment later her husband towered over her, leaning in to

place a peck on her cheek. "Are you just about ready? I do need to get to work soon."

"Can't we go once you get home from the milk plant? It is too early to be making calls."

Piet stood to his full height, hands on his narrow hips. "Nonsense. Corrie gets there much earlier than this. If we bring the soup, she will not have to make Frou de Bruin any dinner. It saves her that much trouble."

"I have so many chores to finish today."

"We will only visit for a few minutes."

If she didn't know any better, she would say that Piet was bent on uncovering what she had been hiding from him. Yet she could not get the truth past her padlocked lips. She could not tell him. Instead, she papered a smile onto her face.

Once she had curled her shoulder-length hair under and caught it in a clip, she pinned her little brown hat to her head. She pulled on white cotton gloves to just past her wrist and was ready to go. To whatever lay in front of her.

Hand in hand, she and Piet walked through the small town, past the windmill churning in the breeze, toward the de Bruin farm.

Piet squeezed her hand. "What is the matter? You are shaking like a frightened puppy."

"Even four years after marriage, your touch still makes me tremble."

He gave her a cross-eyed look.

All too soon, they drew near to what had been the finest farm in the area. The de Bruins had been renowned for the quality of their milk and cheese.

They approached the property. The thatched barn roof sagged like an old woman's face. Dark red paint peeled from the front door of the attached house.

Corrie answered their knock within seconds. Her eyes grew as large as a harvest moon when she saw them, and panic raced across her face. "What are you doing here?"

Piet kissed his sister-in-law's cheek and stepped inside. "That is a fine welcome. Since Frou de Bruin has been under the weather, we thought a bowl of soup might speed her recovery."

Anki held the pot forward. "If she isn't up to receiving visitors, we understand. You can wish her all the best and tell her we are praying she recovers soon." Corrie wouldn't want Piet to see Frou de Bruin either. She would do all she could to protect their secret.

"Who is that at the door?" Frou de Bruin banged her cane on the floor. "Bring them in here."

Corrie shot Anki a what-in-the-world-are-we-going-to-do-now look. She had no answers for her sister.

Piet grabbed the pot from Anki's hands as they entered the kitchen where Frou de Bruin sat, her chin high in the air, her hand wrapped around a gold-tipped cane, her arm festooned with gold and silver bangle bracelets. She wore a white lawn dress she must have bought before Anki's mem and heit had been born.

Piet held the pot high. "Anki tells me you haven't been feeling well, so we brought you some soup." He set it on the coal-burning stove and took a place at the table next to the old woman. A red-and-white luncheon plate with an Oriental garden design held a slice of toast, and a matching bowl contained a few spoonfuls of yogurt.

Anki stood in the doorway. "See, Piet, we are interrupting breakfast. Let's go so she can finish eating."

He leveled a steady gaze in her direction. "I would think you would want to make sure she is feeling better."

"No need. I can see she is fine. You need to get to work, so let's leave her in peace. I will see you later, Frou de Bruin. Sorry to be in your way."

Corrie all but lifted Piet from his chair. "That was such a nice thought but not necessary. All is well here and so you should go ahead to work. Besides, it won't do for Anki to examine Frou de Bruin while you are here."

Anki dared to breathe. She would get out of here without Piet learning the truth.

Then a big voice boomed from Frou de Bruin's little body. "Why would Anki examine me? I'm not sick."

Piet smiled, almost triumphant. Anki grabbed him by the elbow and steered him into the hall. She hushed her words to a whisper. "We don't want to say anything that would upset Frou de Bruin, but she has been quite forgetful recently. Dementia is setting in. If she has a bad day, she doesn't even recognize Corrie. She can't remember being sick or me being here. So sad, but not surprising given her age."

Piet acquiesced, poking his head into the kitchen. "Sorry to have bothered you. Have a good day and enjoy the soup. No need to see us out, Cornelia."

Anki drooped like a flower in the heat.

As she shut the door behind them, she heard Frou de Bruin say, "Why would Piet Dykstra bring me soup?"

Anki broke into a near run to keep up with her husband's long strides. "I told you we shouldn't have bothered them."

Piet came to a sudden stop and made the quarter turn to face his wife. Red blotches covered his cheeks. "You lied to me." The words sounded as if he squeezed them through his throat.

Her stomach flip-flopped and she fought the bile gurgling from her stomach. "What are you talking about?"

"Frou de Bruin is not sick. Never was she sick. She is not senile. Why would you lie? Where were you if not here?" He raised his hand.

Anki took a step back. "Please, Piet, calm down. Don't hit me."

He dropped his arm to his side. "I would never hurt you. But I want you to tell me the truth."

"I can't. I promised."

"This involves Cornelia somehow." He balled one hand into a fist and rubbed it with the other.

"Piet . . ."

"Quit your lying." The cows in the field raised their lash-framed eyes in their direction.

She stared at her husband, her heart flailing in her chest, fluttering like a sail in a gale.

"Tell me the truth."

She had no choice. "I have been helping the Resistance. That is all I am going to tell you."

"How have you helped?"

"I have been nursing a man back to health."

"A man." He stepped toward her. "What else?"

"Nothing. Cornelia was there the entire time. Nothing inappropriate happened. I promise you that. Anyway, they have found a doktor now to take care of him."

"You will not help this man anymore. Do you hear me?"

She nodded.

"The blood on your skirt had nothing to do with the neighbor boy, did it?"

This time she shook her head.

"No more, Anki, no more. I forbid it. You are lying to me. You are breaking the law. Breaking God's law. Do you understand me?"

She wanted to shout yes and no at the same time. Not knowing what to do—help an injured man and her own brother or obey her husband—she said nothing.

"Do you understand?" Piet thundered and her heart sped away like a race car.

She gave one simple nod of her head.

CHAPTER 17

March 1945

ood morning." Piet, ever the dutiful husband, gave Anki her customary wake-up kiss as she stood over the coal stove and fried a little ham Corrie had brought for them.

"Good morning." She slid the meat onto a white china plate and set it on the kitchen table. Without saying another word, she poured a cup of ersatz coffee and placed it in front of her spouse.

Her stomach rebelled at the sight of the food, but she choked back the wave of queasiness and sat across the blue-cloth-covered table from Piet.

He folded his hands and bowed his blond head. "Dear Father, thank You for the provision of this food and for the hands that prepared it. Bless it to our bodies and strengthen us for this day. In Your Son's name, amen."

Though it was located in the front room, separated from the kitchen by a wall, Anki heard the mantel clock keep time while Piet's fork and knife clanked against the plate. She heard him swallow as he kept his attention focused on the food. She nibbled at a bit of dry toast and moved the meat around her dish without taking a bite. Piet didn't comment on her lack of appetite.

When at last he pushed back his breakfast and downed his coffee, she went to the light and bright front room and brought him the Bible from its spot on the end table beside her brown chair. He read a psalm—Anki had no idea which one—closed in prayer, scraped his chair back, and left the room.

Both of the dishes and the pan were washed and put away before he descended the stairs. With another peck on her cheek, he slipped into his klompen and disappeared out the back door.

A typical day in her life now.

She ran her finger over the bookcase and end table in the front room. Dusty. She did not have the umph to clean it. She walked a circuit of the room and into the kitchen. An oppressive weight bore down on her.

How long would it be until Piet forgave her? It would have to be before she told him about the baby so he didn't pay attention to her for the baby's sake. Then again, telling him about their child might lessen the strain between them.

She had to get out of this house. She grabbed her ration book and set a course for Hear Smeet's bakery.

The cool air refreshed her.

The line in front of the little shop stretched out the door and onto the street. When the war first started and standing in line for bread was a novelty, it was almost fun to go shopping. Women chatted and preschool children played. It could be a pleasant way to spend a morning.

That didn't last long. For the most part, the women greeted each other, then drew their coats around themselves to ward off the North Sea chill, stamping their feet until they reached the counter inside.

Anki queued up and said a hello to the women, all of whom she recognized. Other than that, she didn't engage in idle chitchat.

Someone tapped her shoulder, jostling her in the crowd. She tapped again. Frowning, she turned to see Nell, her childhood friend. She jostled one infant on her hip while three other little ones, their button noses all running, clung to her legs. A brown strand of hair had escaped from its pins and she struggled to get it under control.

"Anki." Nell hugged her. The baby, crushed between them, whimpered. "Is everything good with you? I have been thinking about you so much. I never get a chance to talk to you anymore. Ach, that is how it goes. Never does the house stay clean for more than a minute. Rikhart, please keep your hands off your sister. And the kids require my attention, so I don't have a spare minute to breathe, but I am glad I ran into you today."

Anki found herself smiling. "I am fine. How about you?"

"Fine, fine. The kids don't go to school at all because the schools are closed. They stay at home and drive me crazy. Margrit, please get off the ground. You have dirt all over. Luuk works in the garden a little here and a little there when he can, but I have had to take in washing and mending for the Germans just to feed us. Another thing to do."

For that one thing Anki could be happy. Piet had a job.

"And now baby number five is on its way. Can you believe it? This is not the time to bring a child into the world, but God had different ideas. What can we do? Falco is only nine months old. Hillie, don't put that in your mouth."

Anki peeked at her friend's stomach, a slight bulge announcing the blessed event. "Congratulations." She leaned in. "We have some news of our own."

Nell clapped her chapped hands. "That's wonderful. When is the baby due? What did Piet have to say when you told him? I wish I could have been there to see his face. He must have been so surprised. You waited so long for this and will make a great mother."

"He doesn't know."

"He doesn't know? How far along are you? You have to tell him. He won't be upset. Rikhart, I told you not to pinch your sister."

"Far enough that I am going to have to tell him soon."

They moved forward with the line. Anki's stomach tossed when she caught a whiff of the yeasty bread.

Nell scrunched her round face. "Why aren't you telling him? He will be so excited. He will want to know right away."

"You know." Anki waved her hand. "This comes up and that comes up and the subject of babies never comes up."

Nell shook her head, another strand of hair escaping from its pins. "Nothing should come up. Hush, Falco. I know how many years you have wanted this. You should be making an announcement in front of the tsjerke. You can't hide it forever. What is happening that you don't want to share this news with your husband? Is the pregnancy not going well?"

"The baby is fine." She paused for a moment and gathered her thoughts. "Has Luuk ever been so angry with you that he stopped speaking to you?"

"Is that what is happening? Nee, Luuk has never stopped talking to me. Not for long, anyway. He often tells me not to talk so much. Listen, I have known you both since we were children. Whatever squabble you are having will pass. Especially once you tell him about the baby." She squeezed Anki's arm.

They now entered the small bakery, the once-laden shelves bare save for a few small loaves of bread. In times past they had held *banket* and olliebollen and other pastries, as well as raisin bread and brown bread. All of that had disappeared. Now their ration coupons would get them nothing but a small loaf of bread, more like a roll than anything.

"Ja, you are right. I have to tell him. Soon."

"Now, Anki, now. In this time, with the war, you can't waste a moment with each other. As soon as he comes home from work, you have to tell him. He will be so happy, all the anger will be forgotten. I know these things. You need to listen to me."

Anki laughed. "You always were the smartest of the two of us, including when it came to boys." She presented her coupons and the baker wrapped up two loaves for her. "Here, let me take the baby so you have one hand free."

Anki cuddled with the little boy, dark hair peeping from under a blue knitted cap. The infant alternated between studying her and screwing up his face. She jiggled him. To think, soon she would have a little one like this at home.

Nell made her purchase and took back the infant. "I will come to your house tomorrow and we can talk babies. How fun. Margrit, please hold your brother's hand. Our children will be the same age. Imagine it. They can play together and if I have a girl and you have a boy, perhaps they could even get married."

Hoping not to step on a child, Anki leaned in and kissed her friend's rosy cheek. Piet did need to know. Right away.

THE MONOTONOUS WEEKS passed slower than the snow melts. All of Gerrit's nerve endings pulsed. He walked about the house, played checkers and dominoes with Johan, and stroked Pepper.

Maarten had become a regular visitor to the de Vries's house, but today his banging at the door held an air of urgency. Gerrit shooed Pepper from his lap, left his spot on the blue davenport in the front room, and went to admit his friend.

Without a word, Maarten pushed past him and shut the door behind himself. He swiped the sweat from his forehead. "I came as soon as I could." His forged ausweis allowed him some measure of freedom of movement.

"What is going on?"

Maarten shook his head. "I am having a hard time believing this."

Gerrit waited. His friend took a minute to catch his breath.

"First thing this morning the Gestapo raided Doktor Boukma's home. They ransacked the place and found the false bookcase. When they opened it, they discovered five Juden hiding."

Gerrit's stomach dropped to his toes. "Nee. Nee."

Maarten tousled his dark hair. "The Juden went without a fuss, but Doktor Boukma resisted. Who knows why he did that. Things might have gone better if he hadn't. He struggled with one of the soldiers, shouting, screaming. The soldiers shot the doktor dead on the spot."

A surge of heat raced through Gerrit's body. He pounded his fist into his hand. "Those brutes. Those beasts. He was an old man. How many more will die before all of this is over?" He paced from one end of the hall to the other. "These men need to be brought to justice. We have to find a way to give them what they deserve."

Maarten blocked his way, halting Gerrit's pacing. "We will. Don't doubt that. The sweetest revenge will come when the Allies march into town."

"Nee. We can't wait that long. We have to take action. Now. Otherwise, too many more innocent people will be hurt or killed. Too many have already been hurt and killed." He closed his eyes to block out the image of Dorathee crying. "Put me to work, Maarten."

"Don't rush it. Remember what happened the last time you moved around too soon. Get stronger and then we will talk. For the time being, we will make do."

"There is no reason for me to sit in this house any longer. You need me and I need to get back to work. I can step right in. When all the Juden and onderduikers appear after the war, we will show those Nazi pigs who was triumphant."

Gerrit returned to the davenport in the front room and Maarten followed, taking a seat on Cornelia's rocker. "Nee, we aren't going to rush you. That is my final word."

"I can't sit here all day long while I could be out there giving assistance to all who need it and kicking the Germans back to their Fatherland. Don't turn me away. You need me."

Johan picked that moment to thunder down the stairs and into the room. He stopped short and studied Gerrit.

"Sit down." Gerrit motioned to the empty place next to him on the davenport.

Johan obeyed. "This doesn't sound good."

Maarten opened his mouth, but Gerrit shook his head. He needed to be the one to deliver this news to Cornelia's brother. "Doktor Boukma's house was raided this morning and the Juden hiding there were taken away. The doktor was shot and killed."

Johan's mouth swung open and his eyes widened. "This is a joke, right?"

"Nee. It's the truth."

The young man paused for a second, staring at Gerrit, then Maarten, then Gerrit again. A second later he bounded from his chair. "Corrie needs to know."

"We will tell her when she gets home."

"That is too long to wait. I have to go now. I mean, she'll want to know."

Cornelia would not be happy about Johan leaving the house. Gerrit had to keep her brother from putting himself in peril. "Fish won't keep, but bad news will. She will find out soon enough."

"And when she finds out we have known all day and haven't told her, she will scold each one of us. I, for one, have had enough reprimands from her."

Gerrit stood and grabbed Johan by his upper arm. "Stay put, please. Maarten has an ausweis and can bring her word."

"Information like this needs to come from a family member. I will stick to the fields and stay alert."

A second later the door slammed.

CHAPTER 18

Johan wanted to skip and jump and twirl as he crossed the road and cut through the fields to Frou de Bruin's. The expansive sky welcomed him to the daylight.

Then he thought of Doktor Boukma. Because of Gerrit, Johan had known he was affiliated with the Resistance, but none of them suspected him of hiding Juden.

If an old man like him could serve his country, then Johan would do so as well. He refused to sit idle in the house any longer. His capture taught him that he had to be extra cautious. He had learned his lesson and would not get caught again.

Off in the distance, two dark spots appeared where the land met the sky. They grew closer and closer, heading toward him. The speed at which the spots grew left no doubt in Johan's mind that they were German trucks. No Dutchman had petrol.

See, he had been paying attention. Now he needed to find a place to hide from the Nazis. In the fields, he stood exposed. He hadn't managed to get far enough away from the road yet. He scanned the area. The flat, open landscape offered him little protection. A few white sheep grazed on the tender grass and water sparkled in the ditches between the fields. There by the windmill, a little stand of trees.

He hurried in that direction and flattened himself against the back of the largest of the dozen or so trees. The rough bark scratched the back of his neck. He dug his fingernails into the soft wood.

Now he heard the humming of the motor, the pitch growing higher as the vehicle approached. He held his breath. The tires whispered across the pavement.

The jeep whizzed past and the drone of the engine grew deeper. He exhaled but dared not move.

When Maarten heard about how watchful Johan had been, he would rush to give him an assignment.

Heit would have been so proud.

"WELL, CORNELIA, LATE to work again this morning." Frou de Bruin sat as tall as she could and as erect as Queen Wilhelmina on her throne, rapping her bony, gnarled fingers on her large, well-worn kitchen table. Today she had put on black mourning garb so outdated she must have worn it to her mem's funeral forty years ago.

"I will get right to the chores." She slipped on her full-length apron that crossed and tied in the back. "Did you have your breakfast already?"

"Of course I did. It's well after eight. Did that brother of yours get into more trouble?"

She laughed. "Nee. Now, let's plan dinner. What would you like?"

"A thick beefsteak and an entire stick of banket is what I would like."

Cornelia tipped her head to the side and gave a fake, toothy grin. "What will you have?"

"I will have sauerkraut and a little pork."

"And the cow has been cared for?"

The elderly lady tsk-tsked and shook her gray head. "Bram has been here. He's dependable and always on time. He took care of the cow. If not, the poor dear would have burst." Bram was the neighbor boy who saw to the farm chores.

"I apologize for being tardy."

"There is nothing that can be done about that now. Today you should air out the front room and dust in there."

Cornelia didn't like to go into this particular front room alone, because she remembered Hear de Bruin laid out in his coffin, his beady eyes staring at her, following her. She shivered every time she entered the room.

Picking up her dust rag and a broom, she headed to her task. If she made quick work of it and got Frou de Bruin's dinner, maybe she could head home early. Gerrit had promised her a game of checkers tonight.

Her employer's voice at her back startled her and Cornelia jumped, the broom in her hand clattering to the floor. Her hand over her heart, she turned toward Frou de Bruin.

"I have never met anyone as jumpy as you. And I have met a fair number of people in my long life."

Cornelia's heart slowed to a normal rhythm. "What can I get for you?"

"I saw Johan coming up the lane."

"Nee, he has changed so much in the past few years, grown up. I am sure you don't recognize him, you know. Besides, what would he be doing outside?"

Even as she spoke, from the corner of her eye, she spied her brother walking up the lane.

She would strangle him later. She let him in and wasted no time in slamming the door behind him. "Whatever are you doing here? You are out of your mind."

Johan stood with his hands on his knees, gasping for breath, his face pale.

An icy shudder shot through Cornelia as she hurried to get her brother a chair. "Sit down, breathe, and then tell me what is going on."

Johan studied the pine floors. "Maarten came to the house."

She turned even colder. "Tell me."

"Early this morning the Gestapo raided Doktor Boukma's house. He was hiding Juden."

"Nee."

Frou de Bruin sank into a chair of her own. "Tell us all."

"I don't know many details. Someone must have turned him in for aiding the Resistance." He looked at his sister. "You sure need to brace yourself, Corrie. There is more."

She steadied herself on the table.

"He refused to be taken into custody without a fight. They shot and killed him right in front of his house."

The world faded and Cornelia slumped to the floor, unable to catch herself.

Johan rushed to her side, though it seemed like hours before he reached her.

"Why? Why? He didn't hurt anyone. He was only trying to help people."

"Get your sister a glass of water. Don't stand there now."

He grabbed a glass from the cupboard and pumped the water, handing the cool cup to Cornelia as the old woman continued, "Underground work is dangerous. Whoever gets involved with it knows this. He followed his convictions."

"Who would have believed he had been hiding Juden?" Johan's

eyes gleamed in that now-familiar way. The way that made Cornelia as skittish as a rabbit in a garden. "If only I had known before, I could have helped him. Next time I see Maarten, I will ask to be put to work. They must need more assistance with Doktor Boukma gone."

Cornelia reached to set her water on the table and clutched her heart. She remembered how Doktor Boukma had encouraged her to keep doing what she was doing, hiding Gerrit, because it was the right thing to do. But Doktor Boukma paid the ultimate price for doing right.

She stared at her brother, who oozed eagerness the way a child did when waiting for *Sinterklaas*.

"THAT'S IT. I beat you again. I believe that has me in the lead a hundred games to none." Gerrit pushed his chair back from the kitchen table, his shoulder much better than it had been even a week ago when Doktor Boukma died. "That is enough victory for me for today."

Johan picked up the checkers. "Just wait until tomorrow. Then it will be different."

Cornelia, home early from work today, came around with her broom. "Don't get too cocky there. Pride goeth before destruction. Now please lift your feet."

Instead of complying, Gerrit stood and took the broom from her hands, brushing her fingers with his. "Let me help you."

A blush rose in her cheeks. "You don't need to."

"I want to."

Johan groaned. "Oh no. You have fallen for her charms."

Now heat crept up Gerrit's neck into his face. "I believe I have." He focused his gaze on her hazel eyes. She returned the look. He would be happy to spend the rest of his life right here.

The sound of Johan smacking his forehead brought Gerrit back to reality.

"We should help your sister because we do make most of the mess around here."

Cornelia laughed, the sound pure heaven. "This I have to see."

Gerrit grabbed another broom from the closet and chased her around the kitchen. "Are you saying I'm not capable of cleaning a house? Let me strap on my apron and you watch how it's done." He pulled a clean apron from the drawer and hung it around his neck, not bothering to tie it.

She assumed a fencing stance. "With a mem and three sisters, I doubt you know a dust rag from laundry soap. *En guarde*."

Gerrit swung his broom and connected with Cornelia's. She danced back and forth and lunged, missing as he dodged her attack. Her face glowed. *Thwack, thwack, thwack*. The broom handles clacked several times. He leaped onto a chair, noticing that a few tendrils of hair had escaped from her side rolls. "Do you concede defeat?"

She grinned. "Never. Do you?"

He struck her broom handle again. "Not if you don't." With that, he jumped to the floor for another exchange. She fought back with spirit, around the table, past the old stove and the sink until he had her pinned against the wall.

"Do you surrender now?"

She dropped the broom and raised her hands, giggling all the while. "I give up, oh gallant knight."

He laughed with her. "You will never best me."

"Is that a challenge?"

He had never seen her more beautiful. "It is." But he didn't want to fight her. He wanted to kiss her, long and hard.

Johan cheered. "Bravo, you beat your girlfriend."

Gerrit's blood pumped even harder. "At least I have a girlfriend.

But look, we have raised Pepper's kitty hair and made more work for ourselves, not only having to sweep, but having to dust too."

Johan grabbed the broom from Gerrit, set the bristles on the floor, and got to work, moving to the hall. "Have fun dusting, old man." He disappeared around the corner.

Once they were alone, Cornelia came to him, hooked her left arm around his waist, and kissed him on his right cheek. "Bedankt."

He lifted the apron over his head and set it on the counter. "For what?"

"Helping. Laughing. Everything."

"You're welcome. And bedankt."

"Why?"

He didn't know how to answer her question. "Because."

"That's not a real answer."

"Of course it is."

"It doesn't tell me anything."

"What would you like to know?"

"Did you ever have a girlfriend? Do you have one now?" She searched his face, as if she looked for answers there.

The knife that sliced his heart didn't dig as deeply as it had before. "Yes, I courted a woman some years ago, but not anymore."

"What was her name?"

"Mies." The word tasted bitter on his tongue.

Her voice softened. "What happened?"

"It's a long story. One I'm not sure you would care to hear." Not one he cared to tell.

"I would."

CHAPTER 19

Cornelia wanted to hear Gerrit's story. She took Gerrit by the hands and led him to the table and they sat. "Please tell me."

He traced a water stain with his finger. "I don't like talking about her."

"Where did you meet her?"

"One day she came into Heit's furniture shop. This was right before the war. Her boss at the bank wanted a new desk and sent her to price them. I helped her and we talked and that is how it started. A few days later the war came."

Cornelia's heart stuttered. "Did she . . . ?"

"Nee. Worse."

"What could be worse?"

"Pepper has nothing on you in the curiosity department."

"Will you tell me?"

He gulped. "After the incident with Dorathee, I got involved with the Resistance movement. I couldn't let those Nazis get away with what they did to my sister. They hurt her so much. She became fearful and distrusting. A different person altogether."

He clenched his fist. "Mies and I were engaged to be married and looking forward to spending the rest of our lives together. Things changed when I became involved with the Resistance. Mies became clingy, afraid I would never return to her. She didn't want me to have anything to do with the Underground. She wanted me to stop my work for her sake. The last words she said to me before I left were angry and hurtful, accusing me of using her, of deserting her, of not putting her first. She couldn't love a Resistance worker."

"I understand."

"Could you ever love a man in the Underground?"

Could she?

SILENCE THREATENED TO drown out Anki's thoughts. Perhaps that was a good thing. She ran her dust cloth over the night table in the bedroom she shared with Piet. She had to use caution not to hit her head on the sloping ceiling when she stood straight.

He punished her for lying to him with his silence. If he said three words in a row to her, that was a day to have a celebration. She had been faithful to the promise she had made, but he told her only time would prove if she would remain true to her word.

She returned her brown leather Bible and her round, white alarm clock to their places, then straightened the red blanket on the bed before pulling up the blue-and-white quilt decorated with Delft scenes.

Perhaps she would go to see Corrie. She studied the black numbers on the timepiece. Her sister would soon be on her way home from work. If Anki met her along the way, they could spend a little time together and she wouldn't see Gerrit. Her promise to her husband would remain intact.

She swept down the stairs, returned the dust cloth to its place, and pulled her sweater from the hook by the door. The rest of the chores could wait.

Only a few steps out of the front door, she noticed a small woman, a fringed blue scarf tied over her head. The young stranger nodded to Anki and stopped in front of her. "Are you Anki Dykstra?"

"Ja. Can I help you with something?"

"A woman at our farm needs you."

"I'm not sure I understand."

"She is in labor. I was told that you had worked with Doktor Boukma."

"She needs a midwife then, not me. It's been a few years since I worked with him."

The woman touched Anki's arm. "I was told I could trust you."

"What do you mean, trust me?" Although she knew the answer.

"This is a sensitive situation, Frou Dykstra."

Of course it was. More lies. More deceit. A shattered vow. And if Piet found out she had delivered a Jewish baby in hiding, he would never forgive her. "You can trust me."

"Will you come? This is the girl's first child and she is frightened and having a hard time of it. Doktor Boukma is gone and the situation is beyond what I can handle."

Anki looked at the sky, as if God would drop an answer to her from heaven.

She put herself in the girl's place. When it came time for her own child to be born, she would be afraid. If there were complications, she would want a qualified professional to help her.

Nee, God didn't need to send her a reply from heaven. He had placed it on her heart.

Piet, please forgive me. "Let me go inside and get a few things. I will hurry."

While the woman waited outside, Anki pulled a set of clean sheets from her wardrobe along with a few old towels. Digging in her drawer, she located her stethoscope and added it to her bag, in addition to a bar of strong lye soap, heavy string, and a pair of sharp scissors.

Her mother's words to her on her wedding day rang in her ears. *"Be a good and submissive wife, Anki. If you do that, you will have a happy and successful marriage."* She had stood there in her cream-colored wedding dress, about to walk down the aisle to be married to Piet, and told her mother she would obey him. With all the lies that slid out of her mouth with alarming ease, she hadn't kept her word.

Her fingers trembled as she wrote a note to Piet.

> *I have been called to help with a birth. I don't know how long it will take or when I will be home. All my love, Anki.*

CORNELIA HAD GROWN quiet after Gerrit asked his question about loving a man in the Underground. She soon retired to her room with a headache. Johan, too, had gone upstairs to read.

He had been too hasty in asking the question, knowing the answer. Gerrit wanted to make amends with her. Perhaps a cup of hot coffee would ease her headache.

He had watched her in the kitchen a little but had not paid attention to where she kept everything. Sitting around doing nothing for almost a month had rusted his observation skills. Not a good thing for a Resistance worker. Cornelia kept the place neat and tidy, much like his mother's kitchen. Mem had always said, "A place for everything and everything in its place."

He searched the cabinet next to the sink, where his mother kept their coffee. This one contained a set of pretty blue glasses and some Delft china, rimmed with scrolls and curlicues. Had these things been a wedding gift?

In the next cabinet, he discovered several pots and pans but no coffee, so he moved to the next one. This cabinet was stocked with tins. Most of them contained nothing. The spice jars sat forlorn. He picked up another container, a wooden box with a tulip etched onto the lid, that perhaps once held tea. Though he suspected Cornelia had emptied it long ago, just maybe he could gather a few leaves. A cup of tea, a commodity that disappeared years ago, would be a real treat. A sure way to win her heart.

Upon opening it, he found not tea leaves but letters. He set down the container and pulled out the first.

He turned over the note. Straight, masculine words strode across the paper. *To Cornelia Kooistra. From Hans de Vries.*

He sifted through the papers in the box. There must be a dozen or more crammed in here. Why didn't she keep them in the bedroom, hidden in a drawer? He had been born a snoop, and when he got older, it didn't take him long to unearth his sisters' hidden treasures. Always in the bottom drawer of the wardrobe, with the unmentionables. They had gotten so angry with him when they came upon him one day with their love notes spread over their bedroom floor.

Should he?

He remembered his sisters' wrath and the paddling he received from Heit. While curiosity drove his desire to find out more about the very attractive woman who stirred his heart, his recollections of the ire he had incurred at the time of his youthful indiscretion made him return the letters to their place. In time, perhaps Cornelia would open her heart to him and tell him everything. He replaced the lid and opened the cupboard door to put it back in its spot.

At that precise moment, the floor behind him creaked. He turned to see Cornelia in the doorway, her mouth open like a gasping fish. Horror twisted her lovely features.

Gerrit looked down. In his hands he held the box with the tulip carved on the cover.

CORNELIA STARED AT Gerrit, the white cupboard door open behind him, the precious wooden box Hans carved for her clutched in his leathery hands.

A bubble built in her chest, ready to burst. She dropped the mail she had retrieved, rushed forward, and snatched the box, hugging it close. "How dare you?"

They both stood stock still, Cornelia breathing hard. The clock suspended its timekeeping for a minute as they gawked at each other, a muscle jumping in his square jaw.

Then Johan bounded down the stairs, paused, and touched her shoulder. She brushed him away, keeping her focus on Gerrit. "How could you?"

Gerrit licked his lips, clearly uncomfortable. And he should be. Those letters were between Hans and her. No one else had a right to touch them.

"I let you into my house. I nursed you back to health and risked my life for you. I have lied for you and protected and trusted you. You betrayed me. Is that who you really are? A liar and a traitor?"

His face turned ashen and he opened his mouth to speak, but she couldn't stop the stream of words. "You have violated my privacy. You intruded on my life with my husband. I should have known better than to give you refuge here. What else have you uncovered?"

Johan squeezed her elbow, probably trying to restrain her from clobbering Gerrit. "Give him a chance to say something."

"What can he say? There is no defending what he did."

"Just give him a chance."

Gerrit stared at the floor, tracing circles on the scarred wood planks with his stocking toe. He said nothing for a full minute. Cornelia clenched her teeth until her jaw ached.

Then he directed his focus on her, his scrutiny enough to make her squirm. He squared his shoulders, looking ready to defend himself to the death. Because of what he did, he might have to.

He gazed hard at her. "I will tell you the truth because I want you to be able to trust me. I decided to make some coffee because I know my question startled you. I didn't know where you kept the canister, so I did search your cabinets. I saw that box and thought maybe you might have a few tea leaves left in there. Never did I expect to find letters."

Cornelia crossed her arms, the box still clasped in her hand.

"I didn't read any of them. I didn't even pull any of them from their envelopes."

"Because I surprised you."

"Nee. I was about to put the box away when you came in. Please believe me."

She turned to her brother.

"I think he's telling us the truth, Corrie."

She looked at Gerrit, who continued to stare straight at her, his blue eyes fixed and unmoving. Her shoulders slumped.

Without saying a word, she returned the box to the cupboard. After the men went to bed tonight, she would move it to a more secure spot. She withdrew another tin, the one with the ersatz coffee made from chicory. "I haven't had real tea for a long time, and I won't be able to make any substitute until spring."

Gerrit touched her hand. "I am sorry."

His touch caused her skin to tingle. She yanked back her hand. "If you would like coffee, I will make you some."

"Cornelia, please tell me you forgive me. I stumbled on the box by accident and I was about to put it away. I am sorry for upsetting you."

She wished he didn't sound so sincere. Squatting, she gathered the mail scattered on the floor. An official-looking letter addressed to Johan caught her eye. Her heart pounded and moisture dampened her hands. "Wait."

The paper shook as she stood. "We have a bigger problem." She handed the letter to Johan, who opened and read it while she held her breath.

CHAPTER 20

Johan's face turned as white as the winter snow. "A razzia. At eight o'clock tomorrow morning we are to be on the front stoop with our cases packed, ready to go to work for the Germans."

Gerrit watched as Johan handed the piece of paper to Cornelia. She read it, her fair face paling. Then it fluttered feather-like toward the floor. Gerrit swooped it up before it touched the ground. He scanned the page, then his hands crushed the paper.

All of the men of the town between seventeen and forty-five were to be on their front steps to report for work for the Fatherland.

All of this, most likely, because of him. The Nazis took their revenge on the entire town because he had escaped execution and they couldn't find him. Because he had survived, many of this village's men would be taken away. Probably never to return.

And Cornelia, was she now angry enough to turn him in like Mies had done?

Would it be better if he turned himself in? Would that stop this nightmare?

Nee. The authorities had given the order and their underlings would carry it to completion. No matter what. If he went to the

Gestapo or to the NSB, he would sacrifice his life for nothing. That was the greatest waste of all.

Cornelia came to his side, smelling like the fresh outdoors. "Look at the bottom." She pointed one trembling slender finger at the type. "Even men with an ausweis, like my brother-in-law, Piet. But what are we going to do? The hiding place isn't big enough for both of you."

"You could throw me out on the street."

She stared at him in disbelief, her hazel eyes wide. "Nee, I could never do that."

"Even though not five minutes ago you were ready to do such a thing?"

She straightened. "I wouldn't have put you out."

He searched her face, studying the light in her eyes, the arch of her brows, the tilt of her mouth. What he saw surprised him. She didn't hate him. Quite the opposite.

"I know you wouldn't. And as to where I will hide—in the attic, between the wall and the rafters. Johan will keep his usual place."

"Can you get in there with your shoulder?" A crease marred her brow.

He nodded. "Ja, I can do it." For her, he would do anything.

She grabbed the corner of her apron and crushed it in her hands. "Will this work?"

More than anything, he wanted to reach out and touch her, but he held his hands at his sides. "It will have to. Otherwise, we will all be on our way to build defenses against the very people who are on their way to save us."

ANKI WATCHED PIET move about their home, carrying that hated letter with him. He climbed to the attic and found her small, pale blue overnight case.

She followed him like his shadow. "What are you doing?"

"I'm packing the things on this list." He flashed the notice that all men had to report for duty.

She blocked his path to the stairs, unable to believe what her husband was doing. Piet was about to leave her alone and pregnant. She stood there, numb.

"Please move. I want to finish this and get a good night's sleep."

"You are not seriously going to stand on the step, are you?"

He pushed past her and marched down the attic stairs. She followed close on his heels, her stomach threatening to spill its contents.

He entered their bedroom and packed a few pairs of the warmest clothes he could find. Some she had just put away this morning.

"Piet, you can't do this."

His green eyes met hers. "Why not?"

"You are punishing me for going to deliver that baby, aren't you?" The baby boy had entered the world an hour ago, healthy and hearty. She had arrived home as Piet opened the letter requiring him to report for duty to the Fatherland.

"That wasn't just a baby, was it? It was a Jewish baby."

Enough of the lies. "Ja, it was. A boy who is alive because I went. A life precious to God."

"And your marriage vows and His law aren't precious to you?"

"Is your child precious to you?"

"My child?"

"I am carrying your child, Piet. If there were complications to the delivery, you would want a doktor or a nurse to be there, wouldn't you?"

"You aren't a Jew. The doktor wouldn't be breaking the law by coming to you."

She flopped on the bed, unable to believe his mule-headed stubborness. "Haven't you heard what happens to these men who go to Germany or to the defense works? And to the women who are left behind? They don't receive what is promised them.

"Remember Putten? After all the men were gone, they burned the town to the ground. None of those men sent a single guilder to their wives. Or their children. Never are they coming home. The Allies bomb the factories where they work and kill them, or they die because of poor conditions on the front. I don't know why I am telling you this. You know the facts."

Piet nodded once. "I know. I don't want to leave you, but I must obey the authorities no matter what the consequences."

"Aren't you even happy about the baby?" She hadn't been able to bring herself to share her news with her husband as Nell had told her to do.

Piet shut the wardrobe door. He turned to his wife and for the first time in weeks, his expression softened. "You really are pregnant?"

"Of course."

"You weren't lying about that?"

So many lies, each one eroding the trust between them.

"Nee, I wasn't. I am expecting. We are expecting."

A smile turned his mouth upward. He sat on the bed next to her and held her hand. "Ja, I am happy. Imagine me, a father."

She kissed him on the cheek. "You're going to make a wonderful father."

"I will take him out on the canals when they freeze over and teach him to skate. He will be so fast he will skate the *Elfstedentocht* and make it all two hundred kilometers. Or he will skate in the Olympics, maybe even win a gold medal."

"What if she is a girl?"

"She can learn to skate too. She will have her mem's green eyes and pouty mouth."

She relaxed against him. "I don't have a pouty mouth."

Now he kissed her. "A puckered mouth, then. Perfect for

kissing." His lips met hers once more. She returned his ardor, wanting him always.

He broke their connection. "When is the baby due?"

"In the fall."

"Good. I will be back from my work detail then. Everyone says the war will be over by summer."

"Piet, we are going to have a baby. You have to stay with us. You can hide. I have heard talk about men hiding in the attic walls, those without an ausweis who have been through this before."

"That would be lying. Please, stop worrying. Nothing bad is going to happen." He touched her cheek.

She must be going deaf. The short-lived joy vanished. "Nothing bad? Where have you been these past five years? Look at what happened to Hans. And to all the Jewish people. What about the men who were executed by the canal? And Doktor Boukma."

This was what happened when you went behind your husband's back and lied to him. If only she hadn't helped Gerrit, none of this would have happened. She should have gone to the authorities. Then her husband wouldn't be talking so crazy about going to work in Germany.

"You will be fine, Anki."

"You don't think I will be distraught when you leave?" Her voice raised in pitch at a steady rate until she screeched. "You will never return. I can't live without you."

He closed the small valise and latched it shut. "My heavy work boots, where are they?"

Again she stood in his path, this time grabbing his upper arms and shaking him. "Listen to yourself. You can't do this. You can't do this to me, to us, to our child. Please." A lone tear fell across her cheek.

He brushed it away. "If I had my choice, I wouldn't go. But they have given the order and I must obey."

"Obey at the cost of your own life? Risk having your child never know you?"

He sighed, like she was a little child who didn't understand complicated grown-up things. "The Bible tells us we are to submit to the authorities. Like a wife is to submit to her husband. That is what I am doing. I am following the Lord's command by following the occupiers' command."

"You are punishing me. For the sake of our child, reconsider. Please."

"Not punishing, Anki, obeying. Even if you had done what I asked, I would still go. One thing has nothing to do with the other."

"What will happen to me? And to our baby? Have you thought about that?"

"You and your sister will look out for each other and you will be fine. The money I send home will be enough to support you."

"Haven't you heard anything I have said? You won't send back any money. You won't send back anything because you will be dead."

"I cannot lie. I must obey." He moved past her and she followed as he located his mud-caked work boots by the back door.

"Piet, please. I'm begging you, don't do this."

"All I need in the morning is my coat and I will be ready to go."

"Think about our child."

"I am."

She collapsed onto a kitchen chair.

The one thing she thought would keep him home wouldn't.

CORNELIA SAT AT the kitchen table, the notice spread in front of her, though without electric lights or lamps, she couldn't see it in the shadows of the night. She had tried to sleep but couldn't stop the horrific images chasing through her mind, the past mingling with the present. Sitting in the dark hadn't erased them.

A stair creaked and a moment later Johan entered the room. "I couldn't sleep."

"Neither could I. I am thinking about tomorrow."

"We sure are good at hiding. Another adventure come morning." She didn't miss the near-excitement in his voice.

"Aren't you tired of all of this?"

She heard his shirt crinkle as he shrugged. "It's exciting. I will have something to tell my children and grandchildren. Sitting around all day is making me crazy. Tomorrow will be a break from the routine."

"You don't know what life is all about yet."

"I have seen enough of it to know." He pulled out the chair across the table from her and sat. "You didn't have to be so rough on Gerrit. He told us the truth. He didn't read any of Hans's letters."

"But he found them and touched them. He stumbled onto something very private and personal, you know."

Johan leaned across the table. "Hans has been dead for over four years."

Cornelia clutched the edge of her chair. "It feels like only yesterday."

"You need to let him go."

Could she? "I can't."

"Do you still love him?"

"Of course I do. Never will I love another."

Johan moved to the chair beside her, his voice deep and quiet. "You think I don't understand, but I do. I have watched you over the years. In your eyes, I see your sadness. I sure want you to be happy."

"You remind me of Heit before he died and of Anki every time I see her."

"Mem and Heit should never have died. I should have gone out and gotten the medicine for them."

"There was no medicine to be had."

"You don't know what I would have found."

"Doktor Boukma would have had the medicine if there had been any. It's not your fault and it's not mine. Risking your life won't bring them back."

"And mourning will never bring Hans back." Her brother sounded far older than his years and not at all like the kid who came home a couple of months ago. Had he grown up so much in the past few weeks?

"You don't understand. You are young and have never been married, or in love, for that matter. God robbed us of a life together."

Johan scraped back his chair and patted her hand, his skin cool against hers. "Maybe God is giving you a different love, one just as amazing as the love you shared with Hans."

Cornelia thought of Gerrit and the way her soul danced when he touched her. Closing her eyes, she also closed her mind to the suggestion.

GERRIT WOKE EARLY the next morning from his fitful sleep. Cornelia was already in the kitchen, so he washed in the sink in her room, which provided a measure of privacy. As he splashed cold water on his cheeks, he thought about the emotions that played on Cornelia's face last night.

Did she have the beginning of feelings for him? Did it matter? She believed she still belonged to Hans. Maybe she always would.

He scrubbed his face. If only he could wash away his feelings with as much ease as he washed away the dirt. Thinking about Cornelia all the time, wondering how to get her to leave Hans behind, jeopardized his work. He needed to remain focused to be effective and to avoid another arrest.

He descended the stairs and found her preparing breakfast. He watched her struggle to open a jar. "Let me help you."

She turned and smiled, holding out the container. As he took it from her, their fingers brushed and his heart zinged. He released the lid in one motion.

"Bedankt. Frou de Bruin sent this. If they find you, at least you won't be hungry for a while."

"About last night and the letters, I am sorry."

He expected her to turn away, but she continued to peer at him. "I believe you. But I did move the box."

"I am sure you did." Was that a sparkle in her eye?

She wiped her hands on her apron before taking back the jar. "I had better get breakfast on the table. Soon enough eight o'clock will come."

A few minutes later Johan joined them and she carried the yogurt to the table, along with a little cheese and some bread. "Will you pray for us this morning, Gerrit?"

He nodded. "Dear Father in heaven, we thank You for the bounty You have bestowed upon us. You have lavished more on us than we deserve. Lord, Your blessings to us are innumerable.

"And now, today, we ask that You would be with Johan, Piet, Cornelia, Anki, and me in a special way. We pray that You would keep the soldiers from entering this house. If it is Your will, we petition You to blind their eyes and lead them away from here, as You did to the soldiers from Aram coming against Elisha.

"Father, we acknowledge that You are sovereign over everything. You reign and exercise absolute control. We bow to Your plan, Lord, whatever that plan may be. For we know You always work for the good of those who love You, who have been called according to Your purpose."

Gerrit prayed that he may truly believe the words he uttered.
Together they chorused, "Amen."

After each had finished the meal, they headed to prepare for
the arrival of the German soldiers.

CHAPTER 21

Gerrit stood in the attic with Cornelia, cardboard boxes and old leather trunks scattered around the finished room. They had stashed Johan in his hiding place and now Gerrit's turn had come. He flexed his shoulder. This wouldn't be painless, but at least he didn't have to be underground like her brother.

She wrung her apron. Her gaze darted around the perimeter of the room. She looked like a child lost on the street.

Gerrit's heart broke for her. Not able to help himself, not sure if he would ever get another chance, he swept her into his arms, pulling her close until her heart beat against his ribs. He inhaled her scent. How could she smell like roses when there wasn't perfumed soap with which to wash?

She quivered under his touch as he played with the small tendrils of hair not caught in her pins.

"Shh," he whispered against her neck.

She clung to him and he etched this memory into his brain, forever seared in his recollections as one of the loveliest moments of his life. He didn't want to leave her.

"Cornelia." The name swirled on his tongue, sweet as the sugar on olliebollen.

She touched his lips with the tip of her finger. "Don't say it."

Fire surged through him. "What if this is our only chance?"

"Then it won't hurt so much."

He let go. "God be with you."

"And with you."

He wanted to hold her forever. Outside, a truck with a loud-speaker traveled the road beside the canal. "Men seventeen to forty-five, report or face arrest. All others must remain indoors."

Cornelia's eyes widened. "Hurry, please hurry."

Gerrit scrambled for his secret place in the attic, a niche he had fashioned between the wall and the rafters. Cornelia's breakfast settled in his stomach like a rock at the bottom of a canal.

He attempted to inhale as much fresh air as possible before he crawled in. He wouldn't be able to breathe down in that dark, cramped space. They heard the squeal of brakes as a truck stopped near the bridge. The sound of German boots reverberated on the street.

"Cornelia, I—"

"Get in there," she hissed.

He liked this rush of spunk. He wiggled in, then huddled in a ball. It was dusty and smelled musty, and he hoped that since it was only mid-March, there wouldn't be many spiders sharing this spot with him.

Closing his eyes, he fought for breath and willed his wheezing to stop.

Her footsteps faded and she banged the attic door shut.

CORNELIA PEERED OUT of the lacy white curtains at the same window where she had seen the men marching toward their executions. Another green truck with a canvas top screeched to a stop at the foot of the bridge, opposite the house. Soldiers stood at attention, their machine guns pointed down the street.

She dropped the curtain and tried to sit and knit, as if this were any other day. But she couldn't concentrate and kept dropping stitches. It didn't matter. With the yarn shortage, this was the third or fourth time she'd knitted the same scarf. Anything to keep busy.

She set the work aside, her entire body pulsing with fear and . . .

And what? She shivered when she thought about the passion rushing through her. For the first time since her terrible loss, she awakened, like her endless night of sleep had ended. She had wanted that moment in the attic to continue forever.

Nee. Love could be exquisite.

And exquisitely painful.

Love could be taken away at any second. She thought she would have Hans forever. She only had him for one night.

The soldiers' footsteps grew louder. When she had looked out the window, she saw two men at the neighbors' front doors, their rucksacks slung over their shoulders, but most stoops stood empty.

They pounded on the neighbor's door across the canal where Maria and her husband lived. Cornelia's heart pounded along with them. She prayed he had hidden well.

Curiosity overcame her and she dared to spy out the window.

"Open up, open up," the soldiers yelled.

Maria stepped over the threshold, playing with the tassel on her cream-colored shawl, not looking the Germans in the eye as they questioned her. Unsatisfied with whatever answers she gave, they barged past her, knocking her to the ground. Cornelia pressed her nose against the windowpane.

A few minutes passed. Maria screamed as they dragged her husband out the door. She tried to hold on to him, but they pushed her inside. Cornelia dropped the curtain and stood still, feet frozen to the floor. Her breath came in short gasps.

In the recesses of her mind, she recalled the bliss of being held in Hans's arms, loving him all through the night in the hotel in the town of Nijmegen, near the German border. As morning neared, off in the distance something had boomed and the ground had shaken.

Hans sat up in bed. She pulled him down on his side, facing her. "Darling, it's only thunder."

The muscles in his bare back tightened as she ran her hands over them. More explosions sounded. Cornelia willed them away. She couldn't believe war had come. She didn't want to believe it had come.

He switched on the light and reached for his pants. "I need to go. We are under attack."

She laughed. "Didn't the bellboy tell us about Hitler's speech last night? He promised to respect our neutrality. It must be something else."

"Hitler has proven in the past that his word means nothing."

He spoke the truth, but she continued in her denial. The predawn sky flashed red and orange and yellow.

She tugged on his arm. "Please don't go."

"It is my duty as a Dutch soldier to protect our country and our queen."

"It is our wedding night. Surely they don't expect you to report when you have been married for mere hours."

He stroked her hair from her face. "I have to do what is required of me."

"What is required of you is to stay with your wife."

He sat beside her and held her hand. "What is required of me is to fight for our liberty, so you and I and our children can live in freedom."

The hotel shook with another, much louder reverberation.

The Germans had come.

They were at war.

She cried, "Please, Hans, please." She could barely force the words around the swelling in her throat. "I am begging you."

He drew her to her feet and pressed her into him. Through her lacy nightie, she was aware of his every muscle and sinew. He crushed her, trembling, in his embrace as she soaked his chest with her tears.

He drew away far too soon. "I love you. I will always love you."

"I love you too." She kissed him, hard and long, hoping the passion behind it would convince him to stay.

It hadn't.

GERRIT SAT CRAMPED in the dark, cold recess of the wall, trying to make himself as small as possible. The soldiers had been known to poke bayonets through the plaster, searching for anyone hidden within. *Please, Lord, make them miss.*

Darkness closed in on him like a cloak. Shivering, he told himself over and over that the walls weren't caving in, that he had plenty of air, that he wouldn't be crushed to death.

He would rather be out there, taking his chances with the Gestapo, concocting some wild yarn about why they shouldn't haul him away to Germany. But he stayed put, unwilling to leave Cornelia.

Instead of plaster and studs surrounding him, he imagined her arms around him. She had felt so good, so right inside his embrace. But the walls were cold in the unheated attic, not like the warmth of her trembling body. He shivered.

His favorite Bible passage, Psalm 56, came to mind. His dominee preached on that passage at the beginning of the war, and the Lord's words touched him so much he had memorized the entire chapter.

Be merciful unto me, O God: for man would swallow me up; he fighting daily oppresseth me.

Mine enemies would daily swallow me up: for they be many that fight against me, O thou most High.

What time I am afraid, I will trust in thee.

Almost imperceptible at first, warmth seeped through him, but his release from this prison couldn't come soon enough.

He heard a scream. Cornelia? *Nee,* it didn't sound like her and it came from too far away.

A while passed. He forced himself to breathe in and out with a regular, steady rhythm.

The soldiers yelled for Cornelia to let them inside. *Please, Lord, help her remain calm. End this search soon.*

He heard furniture scraping against the floor, pots and pans crashing. After a time, they climbed the stairs to the attic. The door banged open and boots marched across the wooden floor. He held his breath, convinced the men could hear him exhale. He heard them poke bayonets into the wall. One came within centimeters of his foot.

"Did you find anything?" One soldier spoke in a deep voice.

"Nein. No one here. We should move on."

The first one with a deep voice wasn't convinced and spoke in Dutch. "Where is your brother, Frou de Vries? We have records of a boy living here who has never reported for his labor detail."

"He died of influenza along with my parents during the second winter of the war."

"We have no record of that."

"Someone must have overlooked recording it, because he has been gone for over three years now." The tears in her voice made her sound convincing.

"Let's move on. There is no one here."

Gerrit wanted to cry with relief. They had survived this raid.

He let out the air he had been holding, then inhaled. Along with oxygen, he breathed in a good amount of dust that tickled his nose, throat, and lungs. He worked not to release the explosion building behind his clenched lips. Tears watered in his eyes.

Then he coughed.

CHAPTER 22

Cornelia heard the cough explode beside her, behind the wall. Everything inside her froze. *Dear Lord, nee.* The three German soldiers in the attic ceased their ransacking. She attempted to cover it up with a hacking cough of her own.

"Did you hear that?" The fierce-looking soldier with a turned-down mouth stopped moving boxes and tilted his head.

Father, protect him. She hugged herself.

The one with a big nose shrugged. "I don't know. Maybe."

Cornelia faked a coughing fit, continuing the charade until she became dizzy. Anything to make them believe the noise they heard came from her. "I am sorry. Allergies."

The two soldiers stared at her, bewildered. They must not speak Dutch, and she didn't translate. A third Nazi, rummaging through Mem's old trunk, too close to Gerrit for her comfort, stood. "That wasn't you coughing. It sounded like a man. Who do you have hidden here?" He spoke in the Netherlands' official tongue.

"No one." Her voice warbled and her body commenced trembling.

"You lie." He threw the words in her direction.

She shook her head, concentrating on his Hitler-like mustache.

He had been here before, when Gerrit first came. She couldn't look him in the eye.

Her heart thrummed in triple time. "I am not hiding anyone."

He slapped her across the face with the back of his hand. Tears stung her eyes. The world buzzed. "Liar. I won't tolerate any more of your fabrications." He directed his attention to the other two. "Turn this place upside down. We won't leave until we find whoever is here. Schneider, watch this woman. She is coming with us."

Cornelia's knees buckled and she slid to the floor. Gerrit and Johan would be located and all of them shipped off to someplace she couldn't allow herself to think about.

"Oh God, oh God, oh God." She whispered her prayer under her breath, hoping no one heard.

They flung boxes. Heit had plastered the walls in here, making it a pleasant place for his three children to play on rainy days. With bayonets affixed, the soldiers stabbed the walls more than they did before, puncturing holes. Each thrust pierced her heart. The Hitler-like one stomped on the floor. Any minute now they would drag the men away, like they had Maria's husband.

She bit her lip to halt its quivering and folded her hands, clutching them until her knuckles turned white. She didn't whimper. Gerrit had warned her not to show her emotions in as stern a voice as she had ever heard. If she cried or screamed, she would be signing their death sentences. Already she had slumped to the floor. She couldn't do anything else that might give him away.

Herr Hitler yanked her to her feet by one arm. "Take her away. If we can't find who she is hiding, we will burn the place to the ground."

Fear coiled around Cornelia and squeezed. The soldier with a permanent frown propelled her forward, down the stairs, out of the house, and into the yard, the barrel of his gun in her back. The buzzing in her ears grew louder.

God, have mercy on me.

Was this how Hans felt? How Gerrit felt?

She marched a few steps, the weapon's barrel digging into her spine. She wanted to crumple to the ground and beg them for her life. Instead, she concentrated on the still-brown grass under her feet. Well-shined black boots appeared. She dared to peer up. Piercing blue eyes met hers. Her heart skidded. The soldier who lied for Gerrit blocked her way.

"Where are you taking this woman?"

"She is being arrested for violating the order and hiding a man. We heard him coughing but can't find him. Meisner is going to burn down the house to flush him out."

The once-kind German interrogated her. "Is there a man in the house?"

Unable to trust her voice, she shook her head. Her stomach completed a few Ferris-wheel turns.

"Who coughed?"

"I did."

"They claim it was a man."

"It wasn't. I coughed."

"Where is your drunken brother-in-law? How about your sister?"

"I told them if they lived with me they couldn't drink. They left."

"Should we burn down your house?"

What should she say? If she said no, they would continue searching until they found one or both of the men inside. If she said yes, they might do it. *Oh Father, grant me Solomon's wisdom.*

She took a moment to compose her thoughts, daring to stare directly into the man's eyes. "Please don't. My *pake*, my father's father, built this house, and it is the only place I have ever lived. I have no family left but my sister, nothing but memories here. It would make me very, very sad if you burned down my house. If you don't believe me and think it is necessary to prove that I am alone here, go ahead." May God in His providence keep the soldiers from burning down her house.

She hugged herself so he wouldn't notice the way she shook. Would he call her bluff? She couldn't breathe, couldn't think, couldn't move.

The man turned to his comrades. "Meisner, here. Schnell."

A short, ruddy-faced soldier answered the call.

"Did you find anything?"

"Nein. But we will burn him out. I know he is in there."

"I have questioned this woman. Release her and leave the premises. There is no one here."

Meisner opened his mouth to protest to his superior.

"Move out. Schnell."

The Nazis marched across the yard and out to the street. On their way, they trampled her tender tulip shoots.

GERRIT HAD HEARD the slap of the Nazi's hand against Cornelia's fair cheek. He wanted to fly out of the wall and pummel the Gestapo soldier. Instead, he clenched his fists and bit his lip. One day he would return the favor.

"Take her away. We will burn the place down." Gerrit imagined them leading her out of the attic and down the stairs, a gun probably in her back as it had been in his. How could he have been so careless? They had taken her into custody. If she came to any harm, he would never forgive himself.

He would never forgive them.

He concentrated on getting out of here, formulating a plan to gain Cornelia's release. Fast.

The echo of heavy Hun boots moved down the street. He waited for the smoke to begin to rise, for the heat of flames to burn him. He cocooned as still as possible. If he got himself arrested, he could never free Cornelia. Only that thought kept him contained here.

How he would survive the fire, he still needed to figure out.

His mind whirled as time ticked away. He couldn't devise a plan. Any idea that surfaced, he discarded as too risky. She couldn't get hurt in the attempt. He didn't know which guards to bribe even if he had money to pass. Enlisting the services of Maarten and Bear seemed the only option.

So far, no smoke. No flames.

Soft footsteps tapped below him. Had Johan come to get him? But the footfalls indicated someone who weighed much less.

Whoever it was rapped on the wall. "You can come out now."

"Cornelia?"

"It is certainly not Sinterklaas." She laughed and no music ever sounded sweeter.

He sprang from that chasm, though the movement sent pain crashing down his arm and chest. He didn't care.

She grasped him. Cornelia, beautiful Cornelia, safe and here with him. He stumbled out of the hiding place, steadied himself, then lifted her from her feet, embracing her.

"Oh, *leafde, leafde*, I am so happy to see you." He fingered the crimson stain of that beast's hand on her cheek. "Are you all right? Did they hurt you? Those monsters. They deserve whatever they get." He strained in her embrace.

She held him. "Nee, nee. I'm fine. Just fine. Don't worry about me. Anger won't help." She collapsed against him. "Just never, ever cough again."

He rubbed her back. "I won't, I promise. The dust tickled my throat so much. I tried to contain it."

"I was so scared, so sure they were going to arrest me and send me to Germany. Or worse . . ."

"You were so brave."

"They threatened to burn down the house. They wanted to smoke out you and Johan. I told them to go ahead!"

"I would have loved to have heard that conversation." He kissed her forehead.

"They trampled the tulips when they left."

"The shoots will come back. They always do."

PIET STOOD IN the front room, his packed valise on the chair, several layers of clothes on his back, his work boots on his feet. His much-worn klompen sat beside the door.

Anki glared at him. He was nothing but a stubborn old Dutchman. He couldn't forgive her. He wouldn't listen to reason. How could he place the orders of the occupiers above her and their child? "There is still time. We can hide you in the attic walls and you will be safe here with the baby and me. Stay where you belong." She clenched her fists.

Piet straightened his back. "The baby doesn't change the order. I have to go."

Nee, God, nee. Her words rose in pitch. "You can't. I need you. Our child needs you. Don't punish our child because of me."

"Our child isn't born yet. I will be back before he is here."

She screamed at him, as if the louder she spoke, the more likely he would listen to her. "You cannot do this. Don't go." She pounded her fists on his chest. "Please, please, please, I am pleading with you, don't do it. Don't leave me."

He caught her wrists and held them. "Do not make this more difficult than it is. Remember, God is sovereign and in control of everything. His ways are perfect. We don't always understand them, but we must trust Him. In all of this, His plan will be fulfilled."

She believed God was sovereign. Without that conviction, how could she live her life? But she didn't think it meant that fighting back against evil was wrong. Doktor Boukma had said so himself, and he was an elder in the tsjerke. Maybe Corrie was rubbing off on her. She was confused and didn't know right from wrong anymore.

Deflated, she plopped onto the brown davenport, her arms crossed in front of her. Inside, a fire burned. Piet sat beside her and neither of them spoke. All the things they had to say to each other had been said. The persistent *tick-tock* of the mantel clock marked off their last moments together.

She studied his profile, drinking in the sight of this mule-headed man she loved, knowing she would never see him again. He tilted his proud jaw upward, his green eyes clear, while a muscle worked in his cheek.

Trucks mounted with loudspeakers traversed the streets, their order to report for duty for the Fatherland. The Netherlands and Friesland were their Fatherland, not Germany. Brakes squealed and soldiers marched. The little clock chimed the hour. Piet rose and so did she. He gathered her into an awkward embrace. "I will miss you, Anki. Take care of our baby. I love you."

She couldn't have cried even if she wanted to. He was leaving her. "I love you. I am sorry." What more could she say?

He opened the door, exited, and shut it behind him.

She watched at the window, her hand covering her unborn child. All emotion had left her—the anger, the grief. Later, the pain would come. Now there was nothing besides numbness.

Just two other men on their street waited on their clean-swept steps, their cases at their feet. The neighborhood held its breath. Many more men lived here. Most of them, Anki assumed, hid somewhere inside.

The troops swept down their road. They didn't lay a hand on Piet. He went willingly.

When he disappeared into the green truck, she turned from the window.

CHAPTER 23

The Nazis had turned over Cornelia's rocking chair and the kitchen chairs. They had torn pots and pans from the cupboard and pulled the mattress from the bedstee.

The one spot they missed, only by the grace of God, was the spot in the wall where Gerrit hid. Half an hour ago Cornelia wouldn't have thought it possible that the three of them—she, Gerrit, and Johan—would be at their home, safe and together.

Her shoulders wilted and her knees unlocked.

Best, though, to leave her churning emotions untouched. If she didn't acknowledge them, perhaps they would fade, as they should.

Gerrit leaned against the wall, the lines around his mouth smooth, as relaxed as a man on holiday as he related the story to Johan. "You should have seen your sister. She is a professional Nazi handler. Her coughing fit almost had me convinced."

Johan gripped the back of the rocking chair and laughed. "An actress extraordinaire in the making."

"And then she told them to go ahead and burn down the house. That took some nerve."

"I can't believe I said that." A tremor passed through her. "If they had done it, you both would have roasted."

Gerrit shrugged. "I had a plan."

"Don't you always?"

"Of course I do. Mem told me never to leave the house without a plan."

She allowed herself to smile. "And what would that plan have been?"

"I would have ridden my gallant steed out of the house, felled all the Gestapo with one swoop of my sword, galloped straight into the police station, swung you beside me in the saddle, and ridden far, far away where they would never find us." Light danced in his blue eyes.

Her cheeks warmed at his romantic, if far-fetched, tale. She needed a smart comeback, but she hadn't flirted with anyone in a long time. She copied the actions of her school friends who went to the motion pictures. Clasping her hands to her chest, she said, "My hero."

Gerrit touched her cheek and her knees weakened.

Johan cleared his throat. "There is one problem with your plan. You would have left me in my hiding place to fry."

The men roared until they cried and she joined them, the soul's medicine washing over her. Mirth had been in short supply.

Their merriment came to an abrupt halt when someone knocked at the door. They must have made too much racket and a neighbor must have tipped off the Gestapo, telling them they had missed two men here.

She glanced from Johan to Gerrit and back again.

Gerrit reassured her with a slight nod. "It is not the Gestapo."

"How do you know?"

"They announce themselves."

"At least go upstairs until I know who is here. It might be Maria. They took her husband."

"I will do anything to make you happy." He winked.

Gerrit's words and actions did nothing to steady her rattled nerves.

After giving the men a moment to climb the stairs, she cracked open the door. The pink of a woman's sweater—Anki's sweater— greeted her. Exhaling in relief, Cornelia swung the door wide.

Her sister's mouth looked like it had been drawn in a straight line with a pencil across her ashen face. "Are Johan and Gerrit here?"

"What is wrong?" She gripped her sister's hands.

"Please tell me they are safe." Distress marked Anki's features.

"They are. I insisted they go upstairs because I thought the Gestapo had come back. What is the matter? Sit down and I will get you a glass of water."

"I don't want a drink." Anki's words fell lifeless to the floor.

"Then what?" As soon as she asked the question, she knew what troubled her sister. "Piet?"

Anki nodded.

Cornelia propelled her sister into a kitchen chair before she fainted and got her a glass of water, whether she wanted it or not. Then she sat beside Anki. "Tell me."

"They took him. Or rather, he went with them. I am pregnant, and he went with them."

Her suspicions had been correct. Her sister would be a mother at long last. "Did you tell him about the baby?"

Her sister pursed her lips. "Ja, but it didn't matter because he thinks he will be back before it comes. He believes every lie they have forced us to swallow."

Cornelia wasn't surprised. Piet obeyed the authorities because he believed God commanded him to follow them.

She glanced up and found Johan and Gerrit standing in the doorway, both of their mouths round with shock. "Piet went of his own accord."

Sweet Gerrit stepped forward. "We might be able to mount a rescue of some kind. I had a plan half formulated when I thought Cornelia had been arrested."

Anki shook her head. "Even if you did, he wouldn't come with you. He wouldn't want that because it might be against God's will."

Cornelia leaned on the table. "Then what? What can we do to get him released?"

"Nothing. How can you release a man who doesn't want to be rescued?" Anki's voice cracked. She wiped her nose with her embroidered handkerchief. "What am I going to do?"

Cornelia gave her sister a sideways hug. "Have hope. He may return for you."

"Or not. Maybe I, too, will lose my husband and grow old alone."

Cornelia dared to glance at Gerrit.

She smoothed back Anki's dark auburn hair, rolled at the top and curled under at the bottom. "Let's wait and see what the Lord has in store for us. For now, you will stay here where we can take care of you."

"Nee. I need to be where Piet can find me if he comes home."

Cornelia remembered how she didn't want to leave that hotel room in Nijmegen. If Hans came back to her, she needed to be where he could find her. Such a long time she sat in that room waiting for him, passing the hours praying for him, planning their life together, how many children they would have, how they would love them and spoil them, how they would be devoted to each other to the very end.

"You are going to stay for supper, at least."

Anki nodded, staring at the canal shimmering in the early spring sun but not seeing it.

That old, too-familiar pain bore down on her once more. God may be sovereign and have a perfect plan. That didn't mean Cornelia had to like it.

ANKI WOKE WITH a start the following morning. Bright sunlight streamed through the lace curtains and hints of spring tinged the air. The hyacinths and daffodils and tulips would soon bloom, and this long, horrible winter would end.

Reenergized, she rolled over to wake Piet. She found only pillow and blanket and not his smooth, strong shoulder. He must have risen early. Being pregnant made her so tired, she must have overslept. She would need to hurry to prepare his breakfast before he left for work.

She sat and stretched, then swung around to stand. The instant her bare feet hit the icy floor, the cold reality of Piet's deportation hit her.

Panic cinched her stomach. Where had he spent the night? Had his coat been warm enough? Was he hungry? Had he left the Netherlands already?

She needed to know the answers to these questions. They might bring her a measure of comfort. If she knew where he laid his head at night, what he did, and what he ate, their connection could remain unbroken.

Without much thought to what she wore or what her hair might look like, she donned a simple blue cotton housedress and slid into her washed-out pink sweater. Morning sickness kept her from wanting a meal, so she left the house fifteen minutes later.

She made her way through the familiar streets with haste, not paying any attention to her surroundings until the town hall stood in front of her, three stories of white brick and windows.

She climbed the few stairs that led to the front entrance. The heavy wood door creaked as she pulled it open. She focused on what she needed to do.

Around fifty men or so milled about the large lobby, ringed by armed guards. Some acted careless and casual, talking and joking with the other inmates. Those were the ones who surrendered themselves, Anki figured. Others sat to the side, heads bowed under the weight of what lay in store. These must be the ones who were discovered hiding in their homes.

Though tall, she had to stand on her tiptoes to scan the sea of faces for her husband's. She found him without too much trouble—one of those who looked like this might be a pleasant church gathering.

Her body ached, needing to be in his arms. Leaning forward, she went to push through the crowd toward Piet.

"Halt." A German guard pushed the side of a rifle into her midsection. "Where are you going?"

"I need to see my husband. You have to let me go to him."

"Nein. Go home. Your husband will be well cared for and he will send you money soon."

Anki wasn't going to let some foreign kid barely old enough to shave stand between her and her mission. "Nein," she answered in fluent German. "You don't understand. I have to see my husband. It is urgent."

He pushed his rifle into her harder. Fearing for the baby, she stepped back. "Where is your superior?"

He pointed at the gray-haired man behind the counter across the room. "But he won't let you see your husband either."

"Don't be too sure of that." With her head held high, she strode to the desk.

"Excuse me, sir, do you know Piet Dykstra?" she asked in German.

He peered at her from behind wire-rimmed glasses. "What can I do to help you?" he answered in perfect Dutch. So he was a collaborator. Anki didn't know if this would make her job easier or harder.

"He is over there, with the group of men rounded up yesterday."

He stared at her, eyes enlarged behind his glasses, as if she asked him if he knew why the sky was blue.

"He shouldn't be transported with the others. He has an ausweis and works in the milk plant. You need him here to process the milk you take back to Germany." She hadn't come here to attempt to win his release, but now that she had seen him, she didn't intend to leave without him, even if she had to drag him out of here by his ear.

The man scratched his head, fingers mussing his dark, slicked-back hair. Good, she had made him think.

"Frou Dykstra, right now your husband is needed in the Fatherland. In order to beat back these Allies, we need men like him to help us build planes and make ammunition. We can find someone else to process milk. Maybe you."

Anki refused to take this as the final word. Not today. No matter how much Piet wanted to stay. She leaned across the counter, her face mere inches from the man's. Her words seeped between clenched teeth. "You must release my husband. I am pregnant."

The man had the gall to shrug. "About half of these men have pregnant wives at home. That argument will not sway me. I don't know why you are here."

"Because I need my husband." She tamped down the tears rising in her throat.

"You owe this to the Fatherland."

"I owe *nothing* to Germany."

The man rose, the top of his head coming to her shoulder. "It is time for you to leave, Frou Dykstra." He nodded and two armed guards materialized at her side.

"I will get my husband released."

"Do what you want. The transport leaves in thirty minutes. You can't save him."

"Please, please let him go."

"If I free all the men whose wives have been here to plead their causes, I wouldn't have a single man to deport. Good day, Frou Dykstra."

He turned on his heel and disappeared into a back room.

She nodded to the guard on her left, the one she had a word with earlier. "I will speak to my husband." Not waiting for an escort, she edged around the group of men until she came within audible range of Piet.

He glared at her. "What are you doing here?"

"If you won't come to your senses and fight for yourself, I will do it for you."

Bruise-like circles hung under his eyes. A little of her anger ebbed away.

"Go home, Anki."

"Not without you."

"I have made my choice, relying on the care of my heavenly Father. You need to do the same."

"Sometimes He cares for us by providing the means for us to take care of ourselves."

Disappointment shone in his green eyes. "Where is your faith?"

"Where is your common sense? This is not how you punish your wife."

He didn't reply. This conversation wasn't going the way she hoped. She didn't want to think the thought, but this might be the last time she would ever see her husband. She didn't want to argue, so she released more of her irritation and softened her tone. "Are you warm enough? Did they give you something to eat?"

His stance relaxed. "I am fine, so please don't worry about me. Take care of our baby."

Behind her tears, his long face looked like it had when they had toured a house of mirrors as teenagers. "You need to come home to us."

"If God wills."

Like an uncorked bathtub, her fight and resolve drained. "I love you, Piet. I will always love you." And she did, no matter what passed between them. She could no longer contain her tears.

He moved forward into the crowd until he stood as close to her as possible with the guards between them. He lowered his voice to a whisper. "I love you too."

"That is enough now." The child-soldier grabbed her arm and steered her toward the exit.

She wiped the moisture from her cheeks and looked over her shoulder.

The last she saw of Piet, tears streamed down his face.

CHAPTER 24

An Allied plane buzzed over Cornelia's house, low in the sky. Her insides turned to ice and she froze, holding her breath, her dust cloth clutched in her hands. The pilots sent to liberate them often shot at any moving target, regardless of what it might be. They killed an older woman on an outlying farm last week as she pinned her clothes on the line. Cornelia no longer hung her laundry out to dry but instead strung another line across the kitchen and dried her dresses with the men's garments.

She hated biking home from Frou de Bruin's farm and pedaled as fast as she could, praying the entire way that she wouldn't encounter any British or American planes.

Fear held her hand all day long and slept beside her at night.

The droning of the aircraft died away. Cornelia released her breath.

She tucked the dust rag into her apron pocket and straightened her back. Gerrit chafed more and more every day under his confinement, so it surprised her that he dozed, Pepper the cat cocooned against his chest. With the coming of the warmer weather, she had all she could do to keep him and Johan from stepping outside.

She went to the hall closet for the broom.

Pepper's soft cat hair floated on an air current as she swept.

She moved the coffee table in order to better clean under it and it scraped against the floor. Gerrit stirred, then sat up and stretched, Pepper doing the same. Weeks ago when he did this, he gasped in pain. Now, only a small grimace marred his smooth forehead.

"I didn't mean to disturb you. I can finish later." She moved to go to the kitchen, her broom in her hand.

His words stopped her forward progress. "Don't go."

She turned and caught his pleading look. Her breath hitched. With his wavy blond hair, square jaw, and blue eyes, he was handsome. Hans had been good-looking too, but with a different, more boy-like quality.

She stood her broom in the corner and sat next to him on the blue davenport, her leg brushing his. She shivered.

He snaked his left arm over the back of the couch, cupping her shoulder. She didn't protest.

She settled into the crook of his arm, her head on his shoulder. She had never been able to do that with Hans because he was so much taller than she. When they nestled, her head had rested on his chest. A few silent moments passed as she didn't know what to say, awkward like a girl on her first date. At last she blurted out, "How are you feeling?"

"For a man who was executed, pretty well."

She giggled at his dry wit, feeling like a schoolgirl. "You look well too." Heat tinged her ears. "Does it still hurt? Your arm, I mean."

"Not much. Only if I move a certain way." He rotated his shoulder, the muscles in his arm contracting and relaxing beneath his blue cotton shirt.

She forced herself to study the red painted floor instead of staring at him. "Good. Maybe you won't have any lingering effects."

"I'm ready to build furniture with Heit."

"Is that what you want to do afterward?"

"It's hard to think about the war being over."

She dared to look at him once again. "It will be strange. Strange not to have to watch every word you say. Strange not to have the soldiers on the streets."

He smiled, the dimple dancing in his cheek. "Strange to be able to go outside."

"Strange in a good way, though."

"Wonderful." He cracked his knuckles. "We will be rid of the Nazis at last. Get rid of them so they will never hurt another person."

"You have done all you can for your sister. She doesn't know how blessed she is to have you."

"She is the one who is a blessing to me. I need to do more for her."

"You're a good big brother."

He shifted in the chair and settled in again. "And what about your big sister?"

Cornelia shook her head. "That first night Anki seemed so lost, but now she has changed. She has become strong and hard. She is better at accepting God's will than I was."

"Is that good or bad?"

"Piet is still alive, so I suppose she has hope and that is what has kept her from falling apart. Perhaps in a few weeks, when all of this is behind us, he will come home. He has to come home. I don't want to see my sister suffer like I did."

He stroked her knee, sending tingles from her toes to her head. "What about you?"

"A dear older widow in our church told me soon after Hans died that the grief would lessen over time. I didn't believe her, not understanding how I could go on without him. But her words were true. The ache has lessened, slowly, over a long time." And Gerrit was the cause of it. A light had dawned in her life and pierced the darkness.

She touched his upper arm and heat suffused her entire body, replacing the cold of earlier. Johan was upstairs.

"Cornelia."

"Ja." Her thoughts scattered and she couldn't say more.

He held her chin and caught her full attention. "The time has come for me to resume my deliveries. I'm well enough to get around now"—he swallowed hard—"but your home is safe for me, if you don't mind me staying here. Otherwise, I can always find another base."

She shot out of her seat like an antiaircraft rocket. They had such a nice conversation, and now he ruined it with this talk. The war intruded every time. "You can't go outside. As soon as you step foot out of this house, they will nab you."

He pulled her back beside him. "I got to the police station without any problems, didn't I?"

"That was before they rounded up all the men. Now it's too dangerous for any man to move about, least of all you." Why did he insist on doing this? She worried the hem of her gray sweater.

He held her hand. "Just because it's dangerous doesn't mean I shouldn't do it. The war may be over in a few days or weeks, but there is still work to be done."

"They'll find you, and this time you won't survive the execution, you know."

She withdrew her fingers from his grasp and walked in circles around the room, her hand against her heart. Losing him might be worse than losing Hans. She had already lived with Gerrit longer than she had with her husband.

"These days we all live in terror."

She stopped and looked at the side of his blond head. "But you aren't afraid."

"I am. All the time." He turned to face her and she saw the sincerity in the sure set of his pink mouth.

"You?"

"When I'm out, I hear the footsteps of soldiers behind me, about to grab me. When I'm home, I see them outside of my window. They haunt me."

"Does Mies haunt you?"

He nodded, then he tipped his head, staring at her.

"There is more to the story."

"Ja."

She returned to her seat beside him, this time careful not to brush against him. "What about her? Did she hurt Dorathee?"

"Nee. I tried to explain to her why I had be involved in the Resistance, for Dorathee, but either she didn't listen or didn't understand. We broke off communication for a while.

"At last I managed to get home and I brought a fellow Resistance worker with me for a break. Already then, the Gestapo was watching my parents' house in Leeuwarden. Going there was dangerous, but we were careful and didn't arouse suspicion." He stopped and rubbed his temples.

"Please continue."

"Mies came to see me, but the meeting went much as it had the last time we had been together. She screamed and yelled and stormed out of the house. In the midst of her hurt and anger, she ran into a soldier just outside our door."

He paused, gasping for breath. Cornelia held his hand. "She turned you in, didn't she?"

He nodded. "I got out the back way and hid in the neighbor's bushes. My friend didn't make it. They arrested him. No one has seen or heard from him since."

"What about your parents?"

"They weren't home at the time. The Gestapo questioned them but released them a few hours later."

She lowered her voice. "And then you witnessed the deaths of nine more men."

"Ja, Mies haunts me in a way. That night I realized how dangerous this line of work is."

"You don't show it."

"Emotion will sign your death sentence."

"Is that what happened to you? Did you show emotion? Is that why they shot you?"

"Nee. In the Leeuwarden area, there was a failed attempt to blow up some rail lines. In retaliation, they rounded up some men at a house they suspected of being used for Underground purposes. They were right, and I was there with stolen ration cards and forged identification papers on my person."

"Even with all that, you are ready to go out and face possible execution again?"

"Ja."

"Why?"

He leaned forward, his breath on her cheek. "I see my sister's helpless face in all of those in hiding. There are so many to help who would starve to death without ration cards."

She slid away a little. "How can you make yourself do it if you are frightened?"

"'In God I will praise his word, in God I have put my trust; I will not fear what flesh can do unto me.' That's from Psalm 56. Throughout the entire psalm, David reassures himself that he doesn't need to be afraid because God will turn back his enemies. Our dominee preached on it early in the war. I repeat it to myself during the long hours on my bike and on foot, when I'm delivering my cargo."

"That helps?"

"Ja."

"Yet you hate the Germans."

"I don't hate them."

"You do."

"I want to see them defeated. I want them to leave our country forever. How can you not work toward that?" He stood, his face over hers, then turned to pace the room. "You should want to."

ANXIOUS AS HE was to get back to work, Gerrit waited until dark that night before making his way to Bear's house. The group leader must have work for him to do here. Going back to work near his home in Leeuwarden would be much, much more perilous.

The fresh air tasted of salt and earth and grass.

He stopped and did a few neck circles, loosening the kinks. If more Nederlanders had resisted, if they had worked to kick the Germans out of their country, this war would have been over years ago.

So much loss of life because people refused to stand up for what was right. He kicked a stone.

Clouds scuttling across the black sky hid the moon and cloaked everything in an eerie darkness. No light eked out from behind the blackout curtains. He could easily run into a patrol never having seen them.

"When I cry unto thee, then shall mine enemies turn back: this I know; for God is for me."

He heard the stomp of feet in front of him and to the right. His heart tripped over itself. He dashed ahead into a narrow space between two buildings.

Not breathing, he listened as the footsteps approached, two men speaking in what sounded like German, though he couldn't hear their words. They passed directly in front of him and he flattened himself against the brick wall, his shoulder aching.

He waited for a full five minutes after the footsteps died away before venturing out again. Taking a circuitous route through numerous side streets and back alleys, he reached the group's headquarters half an hour later—about twenty minutes longer than it should have taken. But as the door opened, his heart rate returned to normal.

Maarten admitted him, clapping him on the back with his large, work-roughened hand. "Hey, here you are."

Gerrit gave his friend a playful shove. "I can't sit back and let Cornelia wait on me for the rest of the war."

"Why not?" Maarten grinned and jabbed him back. "She is beautiful and I know you are smitten."

"This is not why I risked my life to come here. Is Bear around?"

Maarten led him to the kitchen where the hulking man sat at the table, a coffee cup dwarfed in his hands. Another man sat across from him.

Maarten motioned toward the man. "This is Junior. Sit and I'll get you some of our best coffee."

For half a second, he thought the cell had gotten their hands on some genuine coffee beans. One taste of the bitter brew Maarten handed him told him that was not the case.

His friend pulled back his chair and took his place at the table. "We were discussing some logistical matters. One of the group got caught in the razzia the other week."

"I may have the solution to your problems. I'm healed enough to take on deliveries again, but I cannot go back to Leeuwarden. The moment I step foot inside the town limits, I will be arrested. The entire area is too dangerous for me to work. I have decided to stay here for a while, so I can take on some of the load."

Bear played with his mug's handle, then looked at Maarten. "What do you think?"

The dark-haired man nodded. "I have known Gerrit since we were in knickers. He is religious and trustworthy. You won't find anyone so loyal. He will work hard and won't betray us."

"But he was arrested once. He is a wanted man here as much as in Leeuwarden." Bear pushed away his empty cup.

Gerrit leaned forward. "That is true. They are on the lookout for me here too, but I don't think the outlying areas are as dangerous. I'm not known around here, so there is no risk of being turned in by sympathizers. They don't realize I have a price on my head. If you make me some identity cards, I will be even safer."

Junior leaned his tall frame back in his creaky chair. "We need the help and Rooster has never given us bad information." Rooster was Maarten's code name. When they were kids, he did have this uncanny ability to imitate any farm animal.

Junior continued, "He wouldn't put us at jeopardy by recommending someone unreliable. For weeks this man has known about us, since Rooster went to see him right after the execution. If he wanted to turn us in, he has had ample opportunity."

Adrenaline pumped through Gerrit. More than fish needed water, he needed to be busy.

Bear growled. "Are we agreed, then?"

The two others gave their assent.

"I have your first assignment for you, Jan Aartsma."

He felt like a kid waiting for a school vacation.

"It won't be easy. In fact, it is very dangerous."

Gerrit couldn't wait to finish the job he had started.

And then Bear told Gerrit what he needed to do.

CHAPTER 25

You are asking me to do what?" Gerrit gripped the edge of the well-polished kitchen table in the Resistance house. "I can't do that."

Bear rubbed his bald head. "If you can't accept this assignment, we don't have any work for you."

He couldn't sit in confinement anymore, couldn't watch others working for the end of the war and the liberation of all of the Netherlands. But in his years of Resistance work, never had he been asked to do something like this. He had heard of others attempting such a brazen act. Most often it hadn't ended well.

He fidgeted in the hard chair. What Bear asked of him bordered on the area where he vowed never to go. He had done plenty of illegal things in the past years, always convinced he stood on the side of right. But this . . .

He wiped his damp hands on his brown pleated trousers. Then he stood and walked to the back of the chair. Wrapping one hand around his stomach, he cupped his jaw in the other, shifting his weight from one foot to the other.

He had been raised in one of the strictest tsjerkes in all of the

Netherlands and had been taught right from wrong at an early age. He knew the Ten Commandments. Theft was wrong. But if he didn't complete this task, many people would die. What would his dominee say? What would God say?

He looked into the angular face of his friend with the strange code name. "What do you think?"

"The decision is yours; I have already made mine. What does your conscience tell you?"

Gerrit shook his head. Any sailor would be proud of all the knots in his gut. He shifted his weight again.

Lord, help me to do what is right.

Conviction filled his heart. This was the job his heavenly Father had for him. He took a deep breath. "I will steal the ration cards."

Bear, Maarten, and Junior all nodded and smiled. Gerrit rejoined them at the table and together they worked out the details of the plan. Everything had to be precise and without flaw. Backup plans needed to be made in case of glitches. He concentrated on each word they said, committing it to memory. Writing it down posed too much risk to himself and the others if he got caught.

Hours later Gerrit's eyes itched. He prayed his exhausted mind would retain all of this information.

Bear scraped back his chair and stood. "You know the plan. If anything goes wrong, we can't help you. You will be on your own." He offered his paw-like hand. "Good luck."

Maarten also stood. "God will watch over him and he will be fine."

The man with a trunk like a tree showed Gerrit to the door. "In case of a raid, the fewer who are in this place at one time, the better, so I want you to go two houses down on the left. An elderly couple lives there. Tell them I sent you and the woman will give you a hot breakfast, a place to sleep, and the money to bribe the guard. You can leave from there tonight."

Bear turned to go, but Gerrit touched his arm to stop him. "I can't do that. I have to get back to Cornelia. She must be sick with worry by now. If I don't show up until after supper, she will be in a state."

"You can't do a lot of things, can you? Distractions aren't good. We can't afford them. If you are involved with a woman, perhaps it would be best to find someone else to do the job."

Gerrit needed to get back to work, but what about Cornelia? He couldn't lose this opportunity. Perhaps he could slip by and see her later today, before he began his assignment. "Nee, I won't be distracted."

"Good, then you will go to *Beppe* and *Pake's* house for a little rest."

Gerrit relaxed a little with the thought that Cornelia did have Johan with her. He would occupy her time and keep her calm.

He hoped.

He said a prayer for Cornelia's peace of mind before striding the short distance to the house of the people Bear referred to as Pake and Beppe. A shriveled little man cracked the door. These people weren't Bear's grandfather and grandmother. Even their identity must be protected.

He sent Bear's greetings and the man opened the door wide. Gerrit stepped inside the cozy house, the large front window almost hidden behind houseplants. Sunshine streamed in and fed all those green leaves.

Beppe, a hunched gray-haired lady, took him by the arm and led him to the tiny kitchen. He could stretch his arms and reach from one wall to the opposite. "Come in and let me get you some breakfast. A little fried ham, maybe, would be good."

His mouth watered as the delicious smells permeated the petite space. He watched the woman's hands tremble as she prepared the meal.

He prayed for Cornelia, asked a blessing on the food, wolfed it down, then settled into the soft bed Beppe prepared for him.

Despite the weight of the job looming in front of him tonight, sleep claimed him in a matter of minutes.

CORNELIA PACED THE length of the front room, down the hall, around the kitchen, and back again. She didn't care that she might wear a hole in her shoes and have to go barefoot the rest of the war. One thought possessed her.

Gerrit never came home last night.

She had waited for him. At first, she knitted a little, then tried to read the Bible, the passage he had recited to her earlier. The words grew hazy. She dozed on the big blue davenport, the one Gerrit occupied most often. Every little while she jerked awake, thinking she had heard the door open. The noise had only been the wind creaking in the rafters.

She paused her pacing and prayed for him, pleading with God to protect him.

Where could he be?

She remembered those long hours after Hans disappeared, how she paced their hotel room, waiting for him to march through the door and hold her again.

He never came.

Maybe the same fate awaited Gerrit.

Her body still tingled from where he touched her yesterday. She rubbed the spot on her shoulder where his fingers had rested. When she reached the window, she parted the curtains, hoping, wishing, praying for a glimpse of him.

Where could he be?

Johan came downstairs buttoning his red shirt, the thin material straining across his shoulders. "Where is breakfast?"

How could he be so calm when Gerrit was—where? She grasped her brother's wrist. "Gerrit never came home last night."

He glanced up at her, both eyebrows raised, blue eyes gleaming. "They must have put him to work right away. He is out on some grand mission, an adventure, working to save our country and our queen. Now that the southern part of the Netherlands is free, we have to do everything we can to help the Allies liberate the rest."

"Anything could have happened to him. He might have been arrested. Or worse." She shuddered.

Johan rubbed her arm. "What happened to Hans isn't going to happen to Gerrit."

"You don't know that. He is not here."

"He could have found another place to stay."

"Nee. Yesterday we talked about it, right before he left. If we would allow him, he wanted to stay here."

"Maybe it got late and he decided to wait until morning to come home."

"None of this makes sense. Last night he went out after dark. That wouldn't keep him away."

"Maybe his meeting went long, until daylight, and now he needs to wait until dark."

She released his wrist and made another circuit around the kitchen. "Be serious. How long does it take to tell them you want to help and for them to give you ration cards? So often he has done this, he could do it in his sleep. Where could he be?"

"You are borrowing trouble, Corrie. He's fine."

That's what she had thought about Hans.

Someone knocked at the door and she scampered to open it, sure she would find Gerrit on the other side. "There you are at last."

Anki stood on the other side of the threshold. "I didn't know I was late."

Disappointment weighed down Cornelia's shoulders. "I thought you were Gerrit." She gave her sister a quick hug.

"Why would I be him? Where is he?"

Cornelia ran her hand through her already mussed hair, the pins holding her curls loose. "If we only knew. Last night he went to tell the Resistance he was ready to go back to work, but he didn't come home."

Johan joined his siblings in the front hall. "Tell her she is making windmills out of pinwheels. He is doing something for the cause and will sure have a grand tale to tell when he returns."

Cornelia pulled Johan away from the door. "He would have stopped here to let us know. If he could, he would have gotten word to us."

Johan headed toward the kitchen and the women followed. He cut a thin slice of bread for each of them. "Members of the Underground don't keep regular hours. All times of the day and night they come and go."

Anki and Johan sat at the table, but Cornelia couldn't. Rubbing her hands together, she stood behind her sister.

Anki turned and placed her hand on top of Cornelia's. "Do you think something bad has happened to him?"

Cornelia pulled away and rearranged the empty salt and pepper shakers on the counter. "My heart doesn't feel the same cold absence it did when Hans died. Deep inside me, I knew it." She tapped her chest. "But my mind insists on conjuring up the worst scenarios."

Her sister brought her empty plate from the table. "So you care about him. As a man." Anki turned Cornelia to face her, her touch gentle.

She leaned on the counter. "He is warm and tender and awakens my senses. Some of these emotions are familiar. Some are new and different. I don't know what to think or what to feel."

"Corrie, you more than care for him. You love him."

Cornelia slammed the door in the face of that notion. She brushed past her sister to clear Johan's plate.

He got up and handed it to her. "Anki's right. For the past few weeks, I have seen the two of you together. I would have to be blind not to see how he looks at you. And how you look at him, following his every move. 'Oh, Gerrit, let me help you with that.' You are as taken with him as he is with you."

"You two are crazy. Especially you, Johan. You are more starry eyed over Gerrit than I am." She tipped her head. "'Oh, Gerrit, you are so brave. Let me help you.'"

Johan gave her a little shove. She shoved him back.

Anki switched into big-sister mode. "That is enough from both of you. I guess I am the only one not smitten by Gerrit's charms." She wrapped an auburn curl around her finger.

Now Johan gave Anki a playful push. "That is only because you are married."

Shadows crossed Anki's face. "I miss Piet terribly."

Recollections assailed Cornelia. She and Hans gliding down the frozen canal on their skates, later sipping hot chocolate to warm their icy insides. Their long walks through the fields, jumping *sloten*, ditches filled with water, laughing when she didn't quite make it over one and got soaked. Holding hands as they sat beside each other in tsjerke. Stolen kisses under the moonlight on the cobblestone street. One night of bliss as he made her his wife.

Though it ended in tragedy, their love had been amazing. She had been blessed to have him for the time she did. After all, it had been worth it. Even had she known the end, she wouldn't have missed out on that happiness.

That kind of joy came along once in a lifetime. Nothing could compare.

CHAPTER 26

Gerrit hurried through the dark, deserted streets toward Cornelia. The kind old couple, Pake and Beppe, had been most good to him, but he missed her. Twenty-four hours without her laugh or smile or touch and his world had ceased to spin.

Was this what true love was like?

And if it was love blossoming between them, did she have room in her heart for him? Or would it forever belong to Hans?

Not that it really mattered. Bear was right. Distractions could cost him and many others their lives. Already he put himself in additional, unnecessary danger so he could see her. But he had to spend some time with her. He wanted to breathe in her fresh scent, touch her soft hand, hear her lilting voice. Maybe he would get brave and kiss her when he left.

Or maybe not.

He shook his head. He didn't want to hurt her. She had lost someone dear already. He thought she loved him, but he wouldn't take a chance and play with her emotions. He would put on his mask, the one he used to hide what churned inside him, and try to keep his distance.

But he just had to see her.

Tonight the streets remained empty and he didn't encounter any soldiers. He made it across the canal in a short amount of time. Not wanting to stand exposed, he didn't knock but opened the door and stumbled inside.

"Hello?"

Cornelia came running from the kitchen, sliding to a halt in front of him.

And then she embraced him. He couldn't breathe and didn't know if it was because she squeezed him so hard or simply because she was in his arms. Whatever the reason, he relished her—being so close to her, her heart pounding, her breathing heavy.

"I thought something had happened to you. All this time, where have you been? Don't ever do this to me again."

He tilted her chin upward and studied her. She did care. At least enough to have worried about him. And he very well might break her heart tonight. Now his breathing became heavy.

Should he change his mind? He didn't have to do this.

Dorathee.

His fellow Resistance workers.

The men executed at the canal.

Ja, he needed to do this.

He kissed her forehead in a brotherly manner, though he wanted so much more. She clung to him. "They gave me an assignment for tonight and we had to go over all the details. All night we worked, until dawn arrived. By then, it was too dangerous for me to come home. I got some sleep and came as soon as I could. Pray for me, but trust God."

She stroked his cheek and a static charge rushed to his toes.

He moved toward the front room. "We need to talk."

"About what?"

"You know what they say about curiosity. The cat who sticks his nose in the mouse's hole will get bit."

"I have never heard that before."

"Because I just made it up."

She laughed then, a beautiful laugh, almost like a song. "You have a strange sense of humor."

"Bedankt." He bowed and she laughed harder, the sound full of joy.

How could he leave her?

HIS LAUGHTER WASHED over her and its warmth seeped through her. Cornelia hadn't meant to be so bold when Gerrit came home, but she couldn't help herself. He was safe. She wished he would stay here, protected under this roof with her.

But then his smile dropped like weights had been hung on each corner. He sat on the sagging, old blue davenport. "Come here and talk to me for a while." He leaned forward, hands on his knees.

She sat next to him, his blond brows drawn. He cracked his knuckles. "I need to tell you something."

If she kept the conversation neutral, maybe she could delay the bad news. "This morning I got a little yogurt from Frou de Bruin, you know. Johan and I had some for supper, but we saved you a bit for tomorrow."

Neutrality didn't work for the Netherlands when it came to Germany, and it didn't work for her.

"I need to leave in a couple of hours on an important mission."

A flock of birds fluttered in her stomach. She cocked her head but didn't answer.

"I don't want to worry you, but it is dangerous."

Telling her not to be concerned was like telling water leaking through a dike to go back behind the barrier. "How dangerous?"

"Many men don't return from it. For your own safety, it is best that I not tell you more."

Nee. She covered her ears, as if not hearing the words could make them go away. A minute ago they had been laughing. Now he told her he may not come back from his mission.

How much more would the Lord demand of her?

She turned her back on him and unplugged her ears. "Please don't go. Please. I, we . . ." Just a little crack in her heart and this happened.

Unable to face him anymore, she fled to the sanctuary of her bedroom and slammed the door behind her. She hated this—all of it. The war, the destruction, the loss.

Oh God, why have You forsaken me?

She lay on her bed, overwhelmed and spent. As the night progressed, she drifted in and out of sleep, memories intertwining with dreams. Sweet kisses and gunshots. A caress and the whistle of bombs. Love and loss.

A light knock at her bedroom door woke her. "Cornelia? Are you all right?"

Gerrit. She didn't want to face him now. She answered without opening her door. "I'm fine."

"I'm leaving."

How could he? "Please be careful."

"I will."

NO BREEZE STIRRED the night air. Darkness cloaked the town, only a sliver of the moon shining in the sky. Gerrit patted the pocket of the old, long, black wool coat that once belonged to Cornelia's father. Inside the pocket lay the bribe money.

As he did last night, he scuttled through the dark, deserted town, keeping close to the buildings, hiding in their shadows. He met no patrols. To him it seemed as if there were fewer soldiers around. Perhaps troops were being called to the front to fight the advancing Allies. The Canadians knocked on Friesland's door. The people could almost feel their liberators' breath on their necks. Yet so much remained to be accomplished.

In a little while, the town hall loomed before him, its old brick facade weathered and discolored over the years. Peeling paint marred the small cross-topped dome. Yet it stood prominent in the town, only a little shorter than the tsjerke steeple. He had rescued Johan from here, but tonight things were different. The building loomed in front of him. He locked his knees to keep them from clunking together. He needed to be as quiet as a breeze but as swift as a gale.

He slid around the corner. With his back against the wall, he moved to the rear of the building and found the door the employees used to gain entrance. One guard stood sentry, the one he needed to pay off. He steadied his breathing, then strode forward as if out for a Sunday stroll.

He nodded to the soldier, a Dutchman from what he had been told. Neither spoke to the other. Gerrit pulled the envelope filled with reichsmarks from his inside jacket pocket and handed it to the guard.

The short, stocky man fingered the bills while Gerrit watched, not daring to blink. The guard then turned and walked away.

Gerrit slumped against the rough bricks. His mission had just begun.

Bear warned him one guard watched the inside of the building at night. He made his rounds through the town hall every half hour. Gerrit's watch read a quarter to two. He had less than fifteen minutes to get in, grab the goods, and make his escape.

He slipped his hand in his pocket and fingered the key Bear

had given him. The local Resistance group had paid the guard a hefty sum of money some months ago to take possession of this key. His fingertips touched the cold metal and he shivered from head to toe. His hands shook as he reached for the doorknob. The key slid from his grasp and clattered to the pavement, the noise echoing down the narrow street.

Gerrit braced himself, waiting for hordes of soldiers to swoop down on him. Should he run or would that mean a bullet in the back? Not hearing any footsteps, he stood without moving, a mouse afraid he had been discovered by a hawk.

Five or more minutes passed before he dared to move again. No one heard, or if they had, they didn't investigate. He retrieved the key and held it tighter, not giving it a chance to slip through his fingers.

The slice of moonlight slid between the heavy clouds. Concentrating on the task at hand, but with one ear tuned for any noise behind him, he unlocked the door. Once he gained entrance, he shut the door behind him and slipped off his shoes, tying the laces together and slinging them over his shoulder.

Grasping the small flashlight Maarten had given him, he made his way down the hall. His heart thrummed in his ears and the beam of light bounced off the walls. He clutched the torch tighter, needing to keep the glow aimed at the floor, and licked the salty sweat from just above his lip.

The map Junior had drawn and then torn up was perfect, and Gerrit soon located the secretary's office. He extracted a pick from his jacket pocket and jimmied the lock to the door in short order. He had broken into his sisters' room numerous times during his boyhood. Trespassing sometimes paid off. God had a funny way of preparing him for this work.

He didn't dare smile at the idea.

He stood in the middle of the office, sure everyone in the

neighborhood heard the old, scratched floor creaking under his stocking feet.

Junior told him the secretary kept the ration cards in a sack locked in her large bottom desk drawer.

Every thump of his heart meant another second went by. The guard would head this way any minute.

He stepped around the gray metal desk, stopping every time the floor squeaked. The lock took a couple of precious minutes to open. He picked at it and jiggled it and at last, with a shaking hand, he pulled open the drawer. The cards sat in there, right where Junior said they would be.

He glanced around, his pulse throbbing throughout his body. He didn't waste time but grabbed packets of ration cards by the handful and stuffed them down his shirt—front and back—and into the pockets of his coat. He slid the drawer shut, scampered from the room, and closed the door with a soft click. The guard's boots clomped on the stairs above him, coming down.

Before he could move, the sentry shone a light in his eyes.

CHAPTER 27

Cornelia sat in a chair beside the window in her darkened room, daring to lift the blackout shade and watch the street below. A narrow shaft of moonlight fell across her lap, illuminating the thin gold band on the third finger of her right hand. With the hard work she had done in the years she had worn the ring, some of the luster had worn away. She twisted it, remembering her utter joy when Hans slipped it over her knuckle.

In her daydream this time, though, when she looked up from her hand, she didn't see Hans's boyish, loving face smiling at her.

She saw Gerrit's.

Because she loved Gerrit. Truly loved him. His gentle, caring manner. His loyalty and sense of duty. His strength and his conviction.

The realization startled her in one sense but not in the other. Long ago her heart had known it. Convincing her mind had taken more doing. Without him, she would be lost.

She had changed in the years since she had been married to

Hans. The war had altered her. He would always be a wide-eyed twenty-one-year-old youth. She could no longer claim to be that innocent twenty-year-old girl he had married.

Now her life had intersected with Gerrit's and these shared experiences bound them together.

She clasped her chest, a physical pain clawing at her ribs. She might lose him tonight or tomorrow or at any moment as long as this war lasted.

She wiped her eyes with the sleeve of her ratty pink robe and pressed her forehead onto the cool windowpane, gazing on the scene below. A black-and-yellow cat slunk down the street, in and out of the slice of moonlight. Nothing else moved about. Creatures of the morning wouldn't stir for another hour or more. Creatures of the night had finished their hunt and returned to their lairs to sleep.

The person she longed to see step out of the shadows never did. If this mission carried so much danger, why did he decide to go through with it?

What had been his assignment? To him, deliveries were second nature. He wouldn't characterize those as dangerous, even if that was how she thought of them. Rumors swirled about some of those low-flying English planes. The conjecture was that the English coordinated with the Resistance through secret messages on Radio Oranje. These planes would then drop weapons at times and spots designated in the coded messages.

Was that Gerrit's undertaking tonight? He had refused to tell her, insisting it would be better that she not know.

Her stomach churned. She prayed not. Most of these ended in tragedy. All the Germans had to do was watch the planes and they could then catch those involved. Few came out alive.

She strained to hear the sounds of planes.

She pulled down the shade and kneeled by her bed, trying to

pray. The words refused to come. More than anything, she wanted release from these years of paralyzing fear.

GERRIT STIFFENED HIS spine, his knees weak, his heart racing as fast as his mind. The beam from the sentry's flashlight stung his eyes and gave him a headache. The musty smell of the old building assailed him.

The night watchman took a step closer. "Who are you?"

Gerrit's mind whirled and in seconds he devised a plan. Or part of one. He would make up the rest as he went along.

His aunt married a German, so he learned the language at a young age. He prayed he sounded enough like a native speaker to deceive the man. He couldn't click his boots together as they still hung over his shoulder, but he gave a hearty, "Heil, Hitler."

"Heil, Hitler. I ask again, who are you? And why are your shoes off?"

"Are you the guard?"

"Why do you want to know?"

Gerrit swallowed to keep the trembling from his voice. "I am Inspector von Kaiser. Turn off the torch." He made his voice as official sounding as possible.

The man complied. So far, so good. God needed to keep feeding him these ideas.

The sentry approached him. "Inspector von Kaiser, I wasn't expecting you. No one told me you would be here. How did you get in?" An edge of worry crept into the man's words.

Gerrit didn't offer his hand. He couldn't allow the watchman to get a good look at him. Or touch his sweaty palm. When the secretary discovered the theft in the morning, the man would be grilled about any strange happenings and asked for a good description of "Inspector von Kaiser."

"How did I enter without you detecting me? That is a very good question." He cleared his throat. "Um, I am here to test your security measures, and you have failed. I entered through the front door, which was unlocked." He hoped he didn't cause the outside guard any trouble. "I removed my shoes because I wanted to see how far I got before you discovered me."

"But I checked the door less than half an hour ago. I don't understand. I tried the knob and it was secured. I assure you, sir, it was locked. I followed all of the procedures to the letter."

"You lie," Gerrit thundered. "What is your name?"

"Georg Heitzl."

"And your rank?"

"*Unteroffizier.*"

"The inspector general will be most disappointed to hear this. I expect that in the next day or two you will be removed from your position. The best you can hope for is to be sent back to the Fatherland, to protect our boundaries. But for so grievous a breach of protocol, I should think you will be reassigned to the front."

"I can't go to the front. I was shot on the beach at Normandy and still have trouble with my leg. That is why I was assigned here."

"That may have been then, but now the Canadians are advancing ever closer. Every man is needed to defend the Reich."

"I won't let it happen again. Please, sir, don't send me back."

"That is up to the inspector general. I will file my report with him in the morning and see what he has to say. That is all." Gerrit put on his shoes, gave a last "Heil, Hitler," though the words tasted bitter on his tongue, and marched out of the town hall.

The pale moon rose higher in the night sky and cast light across Gerrit's path as the clouds scuttled away. He needed to stay hidden in the shadows. He scraped along the brick buildings.

He had gone a few blocks, picking his way, turning and weaving through town, when his back prickled. Sure he heard footsteps behind him, he dove around a corner, turned, and listened. Utter silence. Not even a dog barked. He had become paranoid.

He decided to continue down the side street but hadn't gone more than a dozen steps when the sensation of being followed occurred again. He heard the whisper of someone's arms swishing as they walked. His heart picked up its already frantic pace.

Much as he wanted to, if he ran, he would call too much attention to himself. The best thing to do might be to keep walking in circles until whoever followed him decided to either make his move or break off his pursuit. Gerrit strolled down the walk as casually as if there were no curfew and he wandered the town every night, passing the bakery, the tsjerke, the milk plant, the butcher, and numerous tidy houses, all slumbering. His legs shook the entire way.

He tried to avoid the canal, not wanting to draw his stalker anywhere near Cornelia. So he walked the streets of this unfamiliar town, the exercise warming him, though a clammy chill hung in the air. Sweat poured down his face and dampened his shirt, which now clung to his back. No matter his intentions, from time to time he caught the glint of moonlight off the canal.

After an eternity of this hunter and hunted game, he dared to peek over his shoulder. A shadow disappeared around the side of what had once been the dress shop. A giddy rush of excitement pulsed through him. His opportunity to shake his tail presented itself.

He plunged around the side of a different building, slithering down the narrow space, deep into the darkness, unable to be seen from the street. He waited and waited, ears pricked, eyes scanning the road, body tense.

Five, ten, fifteen minutes passed—he couldn't tell how long— before steps echoed on the road. They paused every so often, then continued a little farther before stopping again.

The footfalls drew nearer and paused in front of him. *Be merciful to me, my God, for my enemies are in hot pursuit.*

He flattened himself against the wall and stood suspended. He didn't dare draw in a breath or exhale.

CORNELIA SAT ON the old blue sofa, her feet curled under her so they would stay warm in the predawn chill, a cup of hot water in her hand. She blew the steam from her face and watched it swirl on a current. She had not slept. She had expected Gerrit long ago.

She set her cup on the small coffee table and wandered to the window, peeking out, hoping to catch a glimpse of him in the moonlight. For several minutes she stood peering into the darkness, seeing nothing.

She wandered back to the chair and sat for a minute, her feet curled under her as before. Then she shifted, folding her legs so she could set her chin on her knees.

Had she heard footsteps? She sat straight.

Wrapping her robe so it hugged her, she went to the front, sneaking a look out the window. A dark shadow appeared on the bridge, crossing the canal.

She recognized him, knowing his tall and thin but muscular build, the nod of his head as he walked, the way his left shoulder drooped just a little lower than the right. And that's the figure that made its way toward the house.

She slung open the door and stood on the threshold waiting for him. He quickened his step and reached her in a minute, pulling her into the house. She took him into her arms, burying her head in the crook of his shoulder. Again, she was amazed how she fit in his arms so differently than in Hans's. He smelled like fresh air and ink and she heard the crumple of papers as she embraced him.

So that's where he had been.

He nestled his head against her neck, his breath warm. She trailed the tips of her fingers up and down his spine. He shivered and she held him tighter.

"Leafde," he whispered. "My love."

A quiver passed through her and he rubbed her arms, the gesture heating her from the outside in.

Together they stood for a long time. This moment could last forever.

Then Johan descended the stairs, stood at the landing, and cleared his throat. They jumped apart like children caught behind the schoolhouse.

"Sorry. I heard the door and wanted to see if you were still in one piece. Corrie sure has been worried about you all night, but I guess you figured that out."

Gerrit laughed. "Yes, they didn't get ahold of me. Not yet, anyway."

Her breath hitched. "Did something happen?"

They moved to the kitchen where she sliced the tiny loaf of bread for breakfast, though only the first beams of sunlight streaked the sky with pink. He had impersonated a German inspector—was there even a position like that?—and gotten away with it. She marveled at his composure as he related how he had been followed. If that had been her, she would have been too petrified to move. They would have had to chip her from the pavement come the end of the war.

Then the creases in his forehead deepened and his smile turned. "At first I thought I might have been imagining things. But I am sure now I was followed."

Johan leaned forward in his chair. "Followed? By whom?"

"I don't know. I only glimpsed a shadow disappearing around a building."

Cornelia picked at her slice of bread. "Then you could be mistaken." *Let him be mistaken.*

"I sensed his presence and heard his footsteps. He followed me for a long time before I managed to shake him. But he might know who I am and that I am here."

Johan shook his head. "I mean, you always have the best adventures. Where did you lose him?"

"I got turned around, so I don't know exactly. Somewhere near the canal. Maybe I led him too close to you. I think I need to leave."

CHAPTER 28

Gerrit sat next to Cornelia at the kitchen table in the early morning light, dark circles ringing his tranquil blue eyes. He was the man she loved, and the idea of being parted from him caused her throat to constrict. "Please don't go. You imagined being followed. And if you were followed, you said you lost him. Then why would he know where you are hiding?"

He searched her face. "I tried to stay away from the canal, but I kept happening upon it. I have endangered both of you, and you will be safer if I'm gone."

Johan licked his finger and dabbed the bread crumbs from his plate. "I agree with Corrie. You don't need to go anywhere. Maybe I can even work with you—help you out with deliveries and such."

"Nee. You stay here with your sister."

Cornelia pushed back her chair. "But if you are in danger, isn't Johan?"

Gerrit's brow folded into a crease. He scrubbed his stubbly chin. "If they come looking for me here, I suppose he is."

She could have turned off the lamps because her brother's eyes

SNOW ON THE TULIPS

would have lit the room. "Then I will have to move with you too. Where will we stay?"

Gerrit's shoulders drooped. "I didn't mean to endanger you. Perhaps it would have been better if I had left awhile ago."

Cornelia squeezed herself. Both of them would be gone.

Gerrit shook his head. "Bear will help us find a place. Perhaps with a farmer away from town some distance since I am a wanted man here. I will be able to work more freely in the country."

The country. She clapped her hands. "What about Frou de Bruin's? She has that house and big barn all to herself. You could hide there and every day I could still see you."

Gerrit smiled, his two dimples deepening in the creases of his cheeks. "That might work." He stroked her loose hair. "I would have missed you so much."

Johan groaned. "I have had to go through this mush with my sisters twice already. Don't tell me I am in for it again."

Cornelia chuckled but didn't say anything while Gerrit smiled at her, turning her knees to hutspot.

Gerrit pushed his chair back from the table and stood, smoothing out the creases in his wrinkled black pants. "You might have to, Johan. If I have my say, you will."

The new yet old quivering all the way to her toes didn't leave Cornelia until she arrived at Frou de Bruin's house.

Moving Gerrit somewhere else might be the best thing. Not only did her life stand in peril, but so did her heart.

THE ALWAYS-REGAL FROU de Bruin held court that morning, blue sapphire-like earrings dangling from her lobes, Cornelia her trembling subject waiting for her verdict. The old woman tapped her claw-like fingers on the worn surface of the table.

"Well, Cornelia, I must say, I never thought of you to be one hiding a Resistance worker."

If only she could decipher if that was good or not.

"You astound me, you really do."

Cornelia bowed on one knee before her majesty. Actually, she sat in the chair because her legs shook. Had she been wrong to trust her employer? She thought she might be sympathetic because she had fed starving women from the south during the *hongerwinter*. Maybe she had been wrong.

"I will have to give your request my full consideration and will let you know what I decide before you go home today. The crystal is covered with dust, so I think you had best wash it all. You never know when we will have guests."

She should have known that Frou de Bruin would make her suffer all day long, wondering what her answer would be. She went to the cabinet in the corner of the kitchen and removed a fluted water glass. The piece shook in her hands and she set it straight back in the cupboard before it crashed to the floor. No one ever visited here, so Cornelia didn't see why she needed the crystal cleaned. "Maybe I could wash the windows instead. I just . . . It is such nice weather to be outside, you know."

Frou de Bruin tsked. "Ja, maybe that is best. I don't want my beppe's good crystal to be nothing but shards. You are a clumsy girl." She dismissed Cornelia with a wave of her many-ringed fingers.

All day, as Cornelia cleaned and cooked, she jumped every time she heard a noise. Didn't her employer have any compassion? The clock's hands shuffled along slower than the old lady herself. Finally, midafternoon, Frou de Bruin ran out of tasks and prepared to send Cornelia home. "Don't be late tomorrow morning."

Cornelia stared at the elderly woman, perched as always in her chair. "Do you have an answer to my question?"

Frou de Bruin scratched her chin. "Question? What did you ask me?"

Cornelia bit the inside of her cheek. "About my brother and another man hiding here for a while."

"Ach, I answered you already."

"Nee, I am sorry, you didn't."

"You need to listen better, girl. Of course they may come here. I have had people in and out of here all war long, so having them will be nothing. There's a hiding place in the hayloft all prepared. Whenever they are ready, bring them by. And goodness, shut your mouth. It is most uncouth the way you are standing there with your tongue hanging out."

But she couldn't have been more surprised than if Frou de Bruin had announced she had been coroneted queen.

GERRIT SAT ACROSS from Frou de Bruin in the pale lamplight, her rings, necklaces, and bracelets sparkling. Dressed in a black flapper frock from twenty years ago, she didn't garb herself as if she belonged in this old, rather primitive farmhouse in the middle of a war. If she hadn't been so kind as to take them in, he would have laughed.

Gerrit ached for Cornelia. He didn't imagine he would miss her this much. She had invaded his thoughts, his heart, his life. She had been here all day today, since he and Johan had come before first light this morning, but they agreed it would be best for her to continue her usual routine, and she left once supper sat on the table.

While he may have questioned the extent of his feelings before, he knew for sure he loved that woman. More every day.

Frou de Bruin nodded at him, her drop earrings dangling from her lobes. "So, you are Frou de Vries's new beau. I had been wondering who put the spark back in that girl's step. Good for you. She has suffered much. Don't you forget that."

He wouldn't dare. Not if he had to answer to this formidable woman. "No, Frou."

Johan snickered under his breath.

"And you . . ." She turned her attention to Johan. "You had best not give her any grief either."

Johan sobered and Gerrit chuckled this time. They wouldn't get away with anything in this house.

JOHAN STARED AT the ceiling of the hayloft, the single cow snorting below them in the barn. Gerrit stirred on the mattress next to him. "I don't understand why she's making us sleep out here."

"Decorum. It wouldn't be right for two unmarried men to sleep in the same house with an unmarried woman."

Johan huffed. "She is old enough to be my beppe. She could have been kind enough to offer us a place in the house. It's not like she is using any of those bedrooms."

"During the war I have slept in worse places, so don't complain. The roof doesn't leak and it's not the depths of winter."

When Johan had lived on Umpka Kees's farm, he had been allowed to sleep in the house unless they feared a raid, but Gerrit didn't appear ready to give him any sympathy. Johan had something more important to speak to him about, anyway. "Now that I'm out from under Corrie's eye, do you think I can work with you? I mean, I know you have those ration cards to deliver and that you're still recovering. I could be a big help." He wished he could see Gerrit's face so he could read the other man's thoughts.

"Cornelia wants me to watch over you."

"Did she tell you that?"

He heard Gerrit shrug. "Nee, she didn't have to. She doesn't want anything to happen to you."

"Or to you either. Do you think you will marry her?"

Another shrug. "Do you think she still loves Hans?"

"Of course she does. She always will. But that doesn't mean she doesn't love you or couldn't love you. Anyway, do you think I can help? Is there something you can find for me?"

"Things are getting more dangerous as the Nazis get desperate. Bear told me they know their defeat is imminent, but they don't intend to surrender without a fight. Each day they round up more men and shoot them without much cause."

"Doesn't that mean the Resistance needs to be more active than before? Don't they need more men?"

This time Gerrit sighed. "I will have to think about it."

Why did everyone insist on treating him like a child? At twenty years old, he should be allowed to make his own decisions. He didn't need permission from Gerrit or Cornelia or anyone.

If Gerrit wouldn't give him a job to do, Johan would have to find one on his own.

CHAPTER 29

Cornelia scrubbed her face well with cold water from the sink in her bedroom and put on her best work dress, an old red number with yellow, white, and blue daisies. She made sure each hair fell into its proper place as she rolled the sides and pulled the back into a ponytail. Biting her lips to get some color in them, she wished for a tube of lipstick. Well, Gerrit had seen her looking much worse.

She had never dressed for work with such care. Then again, she had never seen Gerrit at Frou de Bruin's before. She couldn't keep away the smile that alighted on her face.

Before she left, instead of making a lunch for just herself, she included enough food for two. How fun for her and Gerrit to have a picnic—just the two of them. The March weather wouldn't allow them to sit outside, but they could spread a blanket on the hay and eat in the *deel* with the one remaining cow.

She remembered her excitement the first time Hans had asked her to go on a bike ride with him. Today her stomach fluttered in much the same way. As she placed the bread and small hunk of cheese in an old picnic hamper that had belonged to her parents when they courted, she thought about the things she and Gerrit would say to each other.

Courted.

She and Gerrit were courting, she supposed. The thought struck her as strange. Hans had courted her for two years. They had wonderful times together, taking picnics and going to tsjerke. Once they went to the nearby city of Franeker and saw the beautiful Eisinga Planetarium with the working model of the solar system on the bright blue ceiling. When he had held her hand that day, she had fallen in love with him.

She thought she would never be courted again, yet the prospect of calling Gerrit her beau thrilled her. She tried hard not to think of the danger he faced, instead turning her mind to the picnic they would share.

As she biked to Frou de Bruin's, planes hummed high overhead, hidden by the dark clouds that scurried across the sky. A chill wind blew, but she sang a song to herself as she bumped over the road on her bicycle with its rag-wrapped rims. All the while, the distance between herself and Gerrit shortened.

No sooner had she spied the farm than the cloud dropped its promised payload. Within seconds, the deluge drenched her.

Now cold and shivering, she cranked the pedals hard the rest of the way, her meticulously done hair falling into her eyes. What would Gerrit think of her looking wet and miserable?

Once she stepped inside, Frou de Bruin clucked over her. "Ach, don't you have the good sense to come in out of the rain? Stay on the rug and drip there. I will get you a towel." The old woman shuffled away.

Cornelia, much like a ten-year-old would, stood on the mat, pulling in her coat so it didn't dribble on the floor. Her employer returned with two large green towels a few moments later. Cornelia gave herself a vigorous rub. The old lady waggled her finger once Cornelia stopped dripping. "Come to the kitchen and make yourself a cup of tea."

Frou de Bruin had been one of the few who took Hitler seriously. For years prior to the invasion, she had stockpiled tea bags. "My sister lived in Belgium during the Great War," she had said. "She told me about the hardships and privations of war, and I vowed that when the conflict came here, I would have my tea."

And so she did. Of course, she reused the tea bags until they hardly colored the water. Dutch frugality at its finest.

Cornelia washed the breakfast dishes as her water came to a boil. Gerrit didn't come to say good morning and she wondered where he might be. Every few minutes she eyed the picnic basket but didn't ask Frou de Bruin about him. She couldn't give a reason for not asking, but she didn't.

She had finished half of her cup of very weak tea and had begun chopping vegetables for dinner when Johan discovered her. He came in from the hall smelling like hay and cows and placed a kiss on her cheek. "At least I won't miss your cooking. It is like it was before, just in a different house."

She landed a light punch on his arm. "Ja, and will you continue to complain that we have the same thing over and over again?"

"Of course." He jumped out of range of her swipe.

"Where is Gerrit?"

"Right after breakfast he rushed off. We had our Bible reading and he disappeared. I know he went to make deliveries, but he refused to take me with him." Johan thrust out his lower lip. "When he returned, Frou de Bruin put him to work on his chores. I'm finished with mine, but he's back in the deel."

"That's good." Her shoulders relaxed. Out there, he wouldn't have heard her arrive.

She puttered around sweeping the floors this morning. The

rain stopped and she shook the rugs outside. Gerrit didn't come to the house at all. Noontime arrived and she poured *snert*—pea soup—in bowls for Frou de Bruin and Johan. Those were the only two places she set.

The wizened woman took her position at the head of the table and fluffed her old black crepe skirt. "You may set places for the men. Because you know about them, they will eat with me."

That made Cornelia wonder. She had ever only made enough food for Frou de Bruin. What did those she hid eat? They must have had their secret store of rations hidden somewhere. Perhaps they kept it in the deel. She rarely went in there.

"Nee, those places are for you and Johan." She picked up the hamper and held it high. "I am going to have a picnic with Gerrit." Blood rushed to her cheeks and the tips of her ears.

A scowl deepened the wrinkles on the old lady's forehead. "You will be out there all alone with a man? That is not appropriate."

Cornelia stood with her feet apart. "It is nothing more than an innocent picnic. Couples have them all the time, out in the country where no one can see them. I went on many picnics with my husband before we married. We will be in the deel, and since it is attached to the house, it is as good as being in here."

Johan came to the table then and slid into a chair beside the woman in black. "You two behave out there or you'll have to answer to us."

If she were closer she would have knocked her brother on the back of his head. Instead, she turned and left for the deel before anyone raised more objections.

Animal smells assailed her. Beppe Kooistra told her if you breathed in that smell, you would live to be one hundred. It hadn't worked for Beppe, but Cornelia did it anyway. What could it hurt?

More than the odors, though, Gerrit's song greeted her. He worked in a stall where she couldn't see him, but she heard him.

In his deep bass voice, he quietly sang a traditional Frisian tune. She leaned against the door frame, enjoying the rollicking folk music.

Then he switched songs and began to sing the Frisian Provincial Anthem. Her heart stirred when she heard the third verse.

Unused to bowing, they stayed by the old folk in honor,
their name and language, their sense of freedom.
Their word was law, right, humble and true they teach,
and opposed to coercion from whomever it might come.

Sound loud then and thunder far in a round:
Your old honor, O Friesian ground!
Sound loud then and thunder far in a round:
Your old honor, O Friesian ground!

She neither moved nor announced her presence but listened to every note. His smooth, mellow voice reminded her of the well-worn, beeswax-oiled pews in the tsjerke.

The melody hung in the air for a while before she broke into applause. He peered around the corner of the stall, his grin lighting the dim expanse.

"Bravo! Bravo! I would call for an encore, but you need to be careful. You never heard me arrive over your racket in here. If I'd been the Gestapo or the NSB . . ."

He trotted to her, picked her up, and swung her around until she laughed. "That's better. Out here no one will find me."

She had to admit that she had been selfish wanting him to continue hiding with her in town. Fewer eyes lived in the country. "Not until the war ends will you be completely safe."

"But it will be soon. The farmer I made a delivery to this morning has a wireless set. We sat and listened to the Radio Oranje broadcast. Our daring Prince Bernhard has arrived and is organizing the Resistance so we are better prepared for this final push. If we work together, we will be able to rid ourselves of the Nazis in no time."

They may push the Germans back over the border, but at what cost? The same as when they crossed it?

For a little while, she wished the war away. She took him by the hand and led him to the middle of the enormous room. The lowing of the one black-and-white Frisian milk cow echoed off the walls. "The rain started just as I arrived. That's why I look like I've had an unsuccessful *fierljeppen* pole vault across the canal."

"You're beautiful."

"You know the right things to say."

He tipped his head.

"I brought a picnic, but we will have to eat it in here."

"Wait. I have an idea." He disappeared up the ladder into the hayloft and returned a moment later with a green-and-white blanket in his hands, spreading it over the floor.

She set out the bread, ham, and cheese, and a little bit of yogurt. "We can pretend it is a feast."

He said grace and they ate. All of the things she planned to talk about flew out of her mind. She suddenly became shy around him. "How are things here?" What a stupid question. He must think her incapable of intelligent conversation.

He smiled, flashing his dimples as deep as the sloten filled with water around the farm fields. "Frou de Bruin is quite the character. I admire you for working here for as many years as you have."

"Don't let her fool you. She may be all pomp and circumstance on the outside, but she's a dear, compassionate soul on the inside."

"I will try to remember that the next time she scolds me for leaning my elbows on the table when I eat."

"A capital offense, you know."

"So I found out. Johan and I were condemned to the deel for it." He smiled, his grin warm enough to melt an icy canal.

She laughed. Hans was sweet but serious. More of a gallant gentleman than a flirt. "Oh dear. Does she let you in the house at all?"

"From time to time, if I behave myself and get all of my chores done."

She stood. "Then maybe I had better let you get to your work."

He grabbed her wrist and pulled her to the blanket. "Nee, you are not going to get away from me that fast." He held her gaze for a long moment. "I missed you this morning." He had this uncanny way of saying the most disconcerting things. "But I still get to eat your cooking. That I wish I could miss."

She gazed at him through her lashes. Was he joking with her again? "I never poisoned you. Though if you don't stop teasing me, I might consider it. You just wait until the war is over and I can cook a proper meal for you."

He laughed. "So long as you promise not to poison me." A bolt of something—longing? desire?—flashed across his face, then vanished. It sent a shiver through her.

"Maybe I already have."

He held away the thin slice of bread spread with a sheen of butter and examined it. "Did you poison this?"

"Maybe. Maybe not. There is only one way to tell. Eat it."

"Nee, there is another way. You taste it." He held the slice to her mouth and she took a bite.

"Well, you haven't keeled over, but now you have butter on your face." Using his finger instead of the napkin from the hamper, he swiped the bit of butter from the corner of her mouth. The brush of his finger against her lips set her insides on fire. His blue eyes burned.

She didn't have time to think before he leaned in for a kiss. Gentle and innocent at first, it intensified and flared into passion.

She reciprocated, running her fingers through the short curls at the base of his neck.

"What is going on in here?"

Frou de Bruin stood in the entrance, hands on her hips and a scowl on her face.

The beautiful moment lay shattered at their feet.

CHAPTER 30

Under Frou de Bruin's glare, Gerrit shrank in size until he stood no taller than the Christmas figurines his mother displayed every year. The old woman, feet askance, hands on her hips, stared at him and Cornelia. The wind and rain slashed against the walls of the deel. Neither he nor Cornelia said anything.

The old woman waggled her gnarled finger. "I asked you, what is going on in here?"

Cornelia sat frozen, her mouth slightly parted. He refused to apologize when he had done nothing wrong. "Cornelia and I are courting and we shared a kiss."

"In my house, I will not tolerate such displays of affection."

He rose, a half meter taller than her, but didn't quite know what to say. "I . . . I am sorry."

Frou de Bruin shook her gray head. "Frou de Vries, come inside with me."

Cornelia rose to follow her employer. He touched her elbow and spoke to her so the old lady wouldn't hear. "Don't feel guilty about that kiss. I don't. Not at all."

She stared at the ground.

"Cornelia, I love you and that kiss was meant to express that love to you. We did nothing immoral."

She twisted the thin gold band around her finger. "I know."

"Do you?"

A small light flickered in her eyes as she glanced at him. "Yes, I do. But I have to go now and smooth things over with her."

"Good luck."

Frou de Bruin tapped her shoe on the barn floor. "Frou de Vries, come right now, girl."

Cornelia turned back to him. "I am not the one who needs luck. You have to live with her for the rest of the war."

He had forgotten that fact. No doubt the elderly lady would deal with him later.

CORNELIA FOLLOWED FROU de Bruin through the deel, through the enclosed breezeway where the vehicles were kept and the butter and cheese made, and into the house, all while never stepping foot outside.

The woman drew herself to stand as tall as possible. "What was the meaning of that?"

She didn't like being scolded by her employer. She also didn't care for being spoken to like a five-year-old who dumped the flour all over the kitchen. Gerrit was right. They hadn't committed any crime. "You stumbled onto an innocent kiss." But had it been innocent? The passion behind it had been real. Gerrit opened his heart to her and she let him see a little of hers.

"Really? It didn't look like it." There she went, tapping her long fingernails on the table again.

"Don't you remember your first kiss? Where was it? Let me guess. Behind the tsjerke after Sunday services?"

"Nee, it was behind this very deel." The woman's puckered face relaxed. "He was the handsomest man I had ever seen and I couldn't believe that he loved me. I will never forget the way he leaned over and kissed me."

"Then you understand."

Frou de Bruin slammed back to the present. "I remember the fervor of the kiss and how difficult it was to put an end to it. Trust me, girl, I am saving you from yourself."

"It is not like I have never been through this before. I was married once."

"And you still wear the wedding band on your finger."

Cornelia touched the ring. "You still wear yours."

"I am not being courted by anyone. Don't play with that young man's heart, girl. I like him." That was high praise from her. "You can't kiss him that way and still wear your late husband's ring."

Truth rang from Frou de Bruin's words. A truth Cornelia didn't want to admit.

THE DOWNPOUR DISSIPATED into a drizzle as Cornelia biked home. No one else dared to venture out on such a miserable day. Not so much as a rabbit crossed her path.

She hadn't seen Gerrit again. He must have been hiding in the deel. Sooner or later he would have to face the dour old woman.

She pondered what Frou de Bruin said all the way home. Peering at her finger, she wondered why she had yet to remove the band. That brief moment in her life happened long ago. So much had happened. So much had changed— both in the world and in herself. If Hans came back today, he would not recognize either.

She still bore his name. Was that much different from wearing his ring? Both declared her connection to him.

Mud splashed her feet and legs with each turn of the wheel, dirtying her socks. She wished she had worn her klompen. At least her feet would be dry and warm.

Did she have the courage to let go of the past and embrace the future? One that might include Gerrit?

She arrived home, kicked off her muddy shoes, peeled away her wet clothing, and dressed in her badly pilled pink robe.

Hans's photo sat on her nightstand, and she lay on her bed for a long time, staring at him. He posed erect, tall, and broad in his straight-collared army uniform. The black-and-white picture didn't reveal that the uniform had been dark olive. His creased cap sat not quite centered on his head. The eyes she remembered as emerald green peered through wire-rimmed glasses. He had a round baby face so different from Gerrit's angular profile.

"I loved you, Hans, with all my heart." Her tears fell in a steady stream. "When I vowed to be faithful to you until death parted us, I didn't believe it would come so soon. I never dreamed it would be that very night. When I lost you, I lost my very self."

She slid from the bed, grasped his picture, and, holding it close, sank to the floor. "Why were you so noble? You could have stayed with me and no one would have blamed you. It was our wedding night. Our army on bicycles didn't stand a chance against the blitz-krieg. Why, Hans, why did you choose your country over me?"

She keened, rocking back and forth. Hans had been in an impossible situation. She had begged him not to go, but his loyalty was one reason she loved him. He faced the task before him with courage and determination and that made her love him even more.

"I love you, Hans. I will always love you and cherish all of those precious memories. You were my first love. Forever you will hold an honored place in my life. No one will take that from you. Ever."

She wiggled the band Hans had placed on her finger almost

five years ago. Slipping it from her hand felt like ripping a scab from a wound.

Her vows to Hans had ended.

Her ribs became like tight corsets, crushing her lungs, cutting off her breathing as she placed her wedding ring in her jewelry box beside Mem's peach cameo. The gold band glinted in the pale light. Her hand felt weightless, Hans's place in her heart vacant. For a long time she stood and sobbed as she rubbed the empty place on her finger.

"Good-bye, Hans. The future is no longer ours."

Still weeping, she closed the lid of the jewelry box and left the room.

ANKI SAT AT her kitchen table, three sheets of paper filled with news for Piet. She had covered the front and back of each page, including the margins, writing in her tiniest script. She didn't know where he was, so she couldn't mail it, but someday he would read it and know what had happened while he was gone.

She wanted to share everything with him, every detail of every day he missed with her. Their baby continued to grow. The one pair of pants she owned had gotten tight, though her loosest dress still hid the slight bulge in her stomach.

She placed her hand over where their child slept and said a prayer for his father. Every night she heard the planes on their way to Germany. How that country could remain standing with all the bombs the Allies dropped, she didn't know. Each time she heard that now-familiar drone, she woke and prayed for Piet, that none of those bombs would rain on him.

He might still be in the Netherlands, though, building defense works, but the German defenses were falling. Every day Allied troops marched ever deeper into Dutch territory. Perhaps he would come home tomorrow and take her into his arms and this all would end.

Without her husband to care for, her days were empty. She didn't have his clothes to mend or his food to cook or his company to anticipate. The nights were the hardest. Many hours she lay awake, listening to the planes or to her own breathing, unable to sleep, distracted by the cold spot in the bed next to her.

She rubbed her belly, then collected the paper, lined up the edges, and folded the letter. She slipped it into an envelope and placed it in a box with the others she had written, carefully replacing the cardboard lid.

A cup of coffee sounded good, but a knock at the door interrupted her plans. A man she didn't recognize stood on her front stoop. A layer of dirt covered him where his tattered clothes didn't. What rags he wore hung on his emaciated frame. "May I help you?"

He held out his hand and she shook it, touching him as little as possible. "I'm Dirk Tjaarda. I labored with your husband, Piet Dykstra, on the defense works in the south."

This man had word from Piet? She flung the door open. "Please sit and I'll make you some ersatz coffee and slice some bread and cheese. Perhaps a little ham?"

He waved her away. "Nee, I won't stay long. I am from Achlum, just a few kilometers away, and I'm anxious to get home to see my wife and children. I escaped, and I promised Piet I would stop and see you on my way home."

"Is he coming too?"

Dirk's face sunk farther, if that was possible. "Piet won't be coming."

Her breathing grew shallow and she locked her lips to keep the words from exploding. "That stubborn man. He will stay to the bitter end. Wait until he gets home." She balled her fists.

"Frou Dykstra, I don't know how to tell you this, but the conditions we lived under were terrible. Piet got sick and there was nothing we could do for him. He died last week of dysentery. I'm so sorry."

Her ears buzzed. "He got sick?"

"Ja, very sick. We did all we could, but we didn't have much medical care available."

"You didn't take him to the doktor?"

Dirk's thin hands shook. "We did, but the doktor didn't have the medicine he needed. I stayed with him until the end." His voice cracked and he cleared his throat. "He could talk about nothing other than you and the baby. He told me . . ."

Her throat squeezed shut. Dirk spoke madness.

"He told me to tell you he loved you and that he was sorry."

Dirk's image blurred in front of her and everything took on a dream-like haze.

The man touched her shoulder. "Will you be fine?"

How could he ask that? Those two words—Piet died—crushed every hope and dream she ever had. She would never be fine again.

"Is there anyone I should contact? Parents? Siblings?"

"Nee, I'll let them know." She needed to be alone. This couldn't be real. "Bedankt. I am sure you are anxious to get back to your family."

He handed her a folded piece of paper. "Piet wanted me to give this to you. I've included my address if you ever want to contact me." His rough hand brushed hers and she recoiled.

"Are you sure you don't need anything?"

She couldn't breathe. He had to leave. "I am sure. Have a good day."

Dirk left, looking over his shoulder several times as he ambled down the street.

She shut the door and leaned against it. She tried to draw a deep breath but couldn't get it around the rock in her throat. "Piet. Piet. Piet! Don't leave me. Please don't leave me. Let this be a mistake. Come back to me. Please."

How could this happen? How could he leave her? She gasped for air.

She opened her hands to brace herself as she slid to the floor and the paper fell. With trembling fingers, she unfolded it. The handwriting didn't look like his. He wrote with big, bold letters, each formed the way they had been taught in school. The person who wrote this threw the words across the page, the lines slanting downward.

Dearest Anki,

My Lord is calling me home, but before I leave, I wanted to speak to you for the last time. Please don't be sad. I am not, because soon I will be in heaven with my Savior. I can't tell you how I am looking forward to that. The hardest thing is knowing I won't be there to see the birth of our child. Tell him that I love him. Raise him to know and love the Lord. That is my greatest prayer.

I will miss not growing old with you. Do you remember the plans we made together, the children we would have, where we would live, what our lives would be like? The Lord had different plans for me. I trust Him and know He always does what is best. I pray you will trust that too.

I'm so grateful the Lord gave me this chance to be married to you these four years. You are my precious gift, my treasure, my pearl. I love you more than the air I breathe. I don't regret anything I did. Following the Lord's commands is always right. This is His will for us. My time is short, but I wanted to say I love you one last time. I love you, darling. I love you. Farewell.

Your devoted husband,
Piet

The signature was his. She touched the page where his fingers had brushed it.

She stared at the other words on the paper, their meaning not penetrating her brain. She read it again. And again. And again.

Then she understood what it said.

She crumpled the paper and threw it across the room.

CHAPTER 31

The many thoughts whizzing through Cornelia's mind had held sleep at bay last night. She touched the base of her ring finger, the bareness of it.

The trouble was, her heart had gone and fallen in love with another without asking her.

She needed someone to talk to, someone to help her put things into perspective. Johan was only twenty and had never been in love—not that she knew, anyway—and he wouldn't understand like a woman. She couldn't speak to Frou de Bruin and certainly not to Gerrit, so she made the short trek to Anki's house. This being Saturday, it was the perfect time. Cornelia had gone too long without visiting her sister, having been caught up in moving the men and getting them settled.

And angering her employer. Such feistiness contained in such a dainty package. For the rest of the war, she and Gerrit wouldn't be allowed out of the woman's sight. They would have to sneak around like teenagers.

A warm breeze brushed her face as she made her way to her sister's house. At her feet, the daffodils readied themselves to burst in color with the first balmy day.

She knocked at Anki's door, the third one down in a row of neat houses, but no one answered. Strange, her blackout shades covered the long front windows, though it was ten o'clock in the morning. Cornelia paced on the small step and rubbed her hands together.

She knocked again, but no one stirred inside. Nausea rode a wave across her stomach. She pushed the door open and stepped inside where cold and darkness greeted her.

"Anki?"

No answer. Cornelia struggled to remain calm.

"Anki!"

After a minute or two, her eyes adjusted to the dimness of the front room. Her sister sat in the brown overstuffed chair across from her, curled in a ball, not moving. Her limp, shoulder-length auburn hair hung in strings across her face.

Cornelia rushed to her. "What is wrong?"

Anki withdrew farther, hugging herself tighter, her back buried into the chair. Tear tracks etched paths down her cheeks.

"Is it Piet?" Cornelia shook.

Anki nodded.

"Tell me."

Her sister pointed to a balled piece of paper across the room. Cornelia retrieved it and smoothed the page. Then she read the awful words.

Dear God, this cannot be happening. Not to Anki. Please, Lord, please, don't let it be true.

Memories assaulted her—the pop of gunfire, the sweetness of Hans's kiss, the smell of death.

She knelt beside Anki and held her hands, rubbing them between her own. "Oh, Anki."

Anki looked at her with sunken, bloodshot eyes. "Do you think it is true?"

"Do you?"

"I don't want to believe it."

"So long I waited for Hans to return. He never did." Was this what it meant to love a man of honor? Could she bear the grief if this happened to Gerrit? "Piet sent you this letter?"

"Nee, a man brought it. He said that . . ." She raised her shoulders and swallowed hard. "He said he was with Piet when . . ." Fresh tears raced down her face.

Recollections of those awful first hours of the war slammed into Cornelia. Even when she went home, for months afterward, she expected Hans to walk through the door, sweep her off her feet, and make her laugh. Anki needed time.

"When did this happen?"

Her sister shook her head. "I forgot to ask." Anki bolted upright and grabbed Cornelia's wrist, her eyes large in her sallow face. "Oh, Corrie, I forgot to ask."

She patted her sister's hand. "Don't worry. I saw the man's address. When you are stronger, you can write to him and find out. When did you get the letter?"

Anki slumped back in the chair. "I don't know. A day or two ago. I can't remember."

"Have you had anything to eat?"

Anki shook her head, lost and alone in the big seat.

"You have to eat for the baby. I will make you something." Cornelia rummaged through the kitchen cupboards and found a small and somewhat stale loaf of bread. Later she would have to take Anki's ration cards and get more food. She started the kettle for ersatz coffee.

When she had everything prepared, she brought it on a tray to Anki and sat beside her on the armrest as she ate. She nibbled the bread but did drink all the coffee.

"You have to eat more than that. Think of the baby."

"Piet will never know his son or daughter. This child will grow up without a father." She closed her eyes.

"You will be a wonderful mother and you will tell your child about his father. We will help you." Cornelia rubbed her sister's shoulder.

After she cleared the plate and cup and washed the dishes, Cornelia snuggled her way next to Anki in the chair. They had both lost weight during the war and managed to fit. She wrapped herself around her sister.

For hours, they sat together and grieved.

ANKI WOKE THE next morning and rolled over, wanting to snuggle in bed with Piet before they had to get up. She reached for him, but his side was empty. She maneuvered on the mattress, lumps in the wrong places. This wasn't her bed at all.

On the opposite wall, she spotted the grainy photograph of her, Cornelia, and Johan as children. She and her sister wore huge bows in their short, curly hair and Johan sported knickers. That picture had always been in Mem and Heit's room.

That is where she had spent last night—in the large featherbed in their room. In Johan and Cornelia's house.

Why?

And like the whoosh of air out of a balloon, she remembered everything. The letter. The pain. The emptiness.

She rolled with her face to the wall, coiled in the fetal position, wanting to shut it all out. She didn't want to remember. She didn't want to feel.

Piet hadn't been perfect. They disagreed from time to time, including the last time they had been together. If only she had done things differently. She should have done everything in her power to keep him from going away. Even if he didn't want her help. Even if he left of his own accord.

She sat up with a jerk.

All of this could have been avoided. They could be sitting at home right now, planning for their coming child. Their world should be filled with joy, not this unimaginable pain.

Many righteous men had chosen to dive underground, onderduikers not willing to surrender to the authorities. She didn't believe they would burn for disobeying an evil regime. Piet could have done that too. He chose to leave her alone, knowing he might never come back.

She pounded the pillow. He didn't have to do this. He didn't have to go. He didn't have to leave her a widow.

Soft footsteps entered the room. Arms encircled her. "Let it out," Cornelia whispered. "Be angry. You should be. Let him know how upset you are that he left you."

Anki turned and grasped her sister's thin arms, shaking her. "Why didn't you stop him? Gerrit could have helped. With all we did for him, he owed us that much. He got Johan out of custody. He should have done the same for Piet. I saved his life."

"Piet went freely. If he wouldn't listen to you, Gerrit couldn't have done anything."

"We should have done more. I should have done more."

"Don't blame yourself."

"I should have told him about the baby sooner. Maybe if he had time to get used to the idea, he would have been more excited. And he would have understood his responsibilities better. He wouldn't have left then."

"We can't change the past."

Anki sank back against the covers, spent.

"I'm frying a little ham now. Come and have some breakfast."

Her stomach lurched at the mention of food. "I can't eat."

"Think of your baby."

Through the fog of grief, the light pierced. Forever she would have this part of Piet. She had lost her husband, but she wouldn't lose her child.

Corrie handed her a dark purple housedress she had packed from home. She slipped it over her head, and her sister brushed her hair and pulled it back with a clip. The gentle pressure on her scalp soothed her.

Ten minutes later she descended the stairs, ready to face the day.

Her first day as a widow.

CORNELIA WANTED TO close the gap between Gerrit and herself as soon as possible, so she pedaled her bicycle hard. She and Anki had spoken to the dominee about a memorial service for Piet, and then Cornelia convinced her sister to lie down for a while. She didn't want to be gone long but did want to tell Johan the news. And find some comfort with Gerrit.

German soldiers crawled over the countryside like ants, scurrying this way and that, though mostly east. She shivered and quickened her pace.

Just a short distance from the farm, a dull green truck, caked with mud on the lower half, pulled beside her, blocking her way forward. She braked, but her heart continued to pump as fast as her legs had. A young kid, younger than Johan by a few years at least, climbed out of the driver's seat and pointed his rifle at her. Her knees became as soft as the Frisian sand and she worked at straddling the bike and not falling to the ground.

"Where are you going?"

She shrugged, pretending not to understand.

He motioned for her to produce her identification. Her hands shook as she dismounted and gave it to him. He rubbed his chin as he examined it. His baby face showed no signs of stubble. The kid wasn't even old enough to shave. If she wasn't trembling so much, she might laugh.

He, however, took his job seriously. After handing back her papers, the boy spit at her feet, then shoved her off her bike and onto the road. He jumped into the truck and gunned it, splattering mud all over her.

She sat in the muck, dumbfounded. Mud splattered her pink flowered dress, the vibrancy of the colors long since washed away.

Cold outside and numb inside, she picked up her bicycle and continued to Frou de Bruin's house. As she knocked, she hoped the older woman would stop watching her every move as she had for the past week.

Her cheeks burned as she thought of Gerrit's and her kiss, and a tingle pulsed in her heart, like fingers thawing near the warmth of a fire after an extended skate on the canal. Just as with defrosting fingers, it hurt sometimes. But in the end, the numbness passes and feeling returns.

Frou de Bruin's still-sharp blue eyes narrowed when she saw Cornelia. "Why are you here? It is Saturday. And look at you. What have you been doing? A pig is cleaner than you, girl."

She slipped her hand into her sweater's pocket. "I'm sorry about the dirt. A German truck splattered mud all over me. Please, may I come in? I have to see Johan and Gerrit. Something has happened they need to know about."

The gray-haired woman opened the door a little farther, just enough for Cornelia to slip into the house. She led the way to the kitchen. "Gerrit is in here. Your brother is in the deel."

Gerrit rose from his chair at the table when she entered the warm room. His mouth opened into an O, then his brows furrowed. "What happened?"

Cornelia had difficulty forming the words, as if saying them made the reality truer. "A man who worked with Piet in the south visited Anki yesterday. Piet died of dysentery."

"Oh no."

She nodded, her throat clogged like a busy canal.

"How is she doing?"

"She is angry and grieving. All that is to be expected, you know." She pushed the painful memories aside.

Gerrit came to her and held her hands. She wished he would take her in his arms, but with Frou de Bruin perched on her chair, that might not be a good idea. He leaned toward her and spoke in a low, soothing voice. "And you. What happened?"

"A German soldier in a truck stopped me. He was no more than a boy. When he left, he spun his tires and splashed me."

"You need a hot bath." He rubbed her fingers. "How are you coping with the news?"

"I am fine."

He released one hand, stroked her cheek, then turned to speak to the old woman. "If you will excuse us, we're going into the front room. Alone. I promise not to kiss her." He pursed his lips.

Frou de Bruin hardened her face. "I will be in here. And I will be checking on you."

Gerrit and Cornelia stood on the frayed rug in the front room, facing each other but with plenty of daylight between them.

He caressed her with his eyes. "Now tell me how you really are."

How did you tell someone you loved about your feelings for your husband? "Alone. In the past few hours, I have thought so much about you. And about Hans."

Tears began to roll down her cheeks unchecked, and she didn't know if she would ever be able to stop them.

He came to her, but she pushed him away.

CHAPTER 32

Gerrit stared at Cornelia as tears moistened her pink cheeks. She had pushed him away, but he wasn't deterred. He stepped a little closer to her and wiped away the tears with his thumb, then rubbed her arm. "You can tell me about Hans. He is part of who you are. Never would I ask you to act as if he hadn't been part of your life."

She worried the hem of her gray sweater, not looking him in the eye. "The pain was so intense that my lungs refused to draw in air. It was like my world had stopped. Everyone else rushed ahead, but I stood still, unable to move."

"I wish I could take this from you."

"You have." She touched his hand and exhilaration zinged through him. "I don't want the world to leave me behind anymore. I want to move ahead."

"I am not going anywhere."

She shook her head, her little pearl drop earrings swaying with the motion. "You can't make that promise. Hans told me he would be back. He never came. We don't know what tomorrow holds. Look at what happened to Piet."

He didn't know how to reassure her. "What happened to Piet won't necessarily happen to me."

"But it could. How many executions are you going to survive?"

"Ja, war brings uncertainty."

"Not just war. Life is uncertain. Fragile. Fleeting."

"We don't know how much time God has ordained for us, but He has blessed us with life. And it is worth living. Are you really living now?"

"I am trying to move on. You have given me this gift. Before you, I didn't want to try."

"For however long it takes I will wait for you." He couldn't imagine any future that didn't include her.

"Someday, maybe there will be something special between us."

His throat tightened. "There already is."

She closed the gap between them and nestled in his arms, her head on his shoulder. He held her close, her heart beating against his.

They stood there for a long time, grateful Frou de Bruin didn't interrupt them. He held her and rubbed her back until she relaxed, then for a long time afterward. Only with reluctance did he release her.

"Will you have a service?"

She dabbed her red-rimmed eyes and nodded. "Tuesday morning."

"I will see you then."

She frowned and shook her head. "You can't come. Whoever followed you the other night might be waiting for you to return. You need to stay where it is safe."

"I want to be there for you."

"You will be here for me longer if you stay put. I am begging you, don't come." She wrung her hankie.

He heard the pleading in her voice but experienced an overwhelming pull toward her. "I will only come if it is safe."

She sighed. "Why do the Dutch have to be so stubborn?"

He brushed his lips across her cheek, not caring what Frou de Bruin thought. "It is what makes us survivors."

"I wish you wouldn't come."

"I promise to stay safe."

"Don't make promises you can't keep."

THAT OLD BAT Frou de Bruin told Johan that he needed to feed the black-and-white Frisian cow and clean her stall. People never grew tired of telling him what to do. Johan, go here. Johan, go there. Johan, do this.

So far, not even Gerrit had supported him or his idea to work for the Resistance. If they needed so much help, then they should be clamoring for him to join them. Cornelia stood in the way. All of this was her fault.

Mumbling under his breath, he grabbed the pitchfork from its perch on a nail in the wall. "It is not fair. It is really not fair. Why can't anyone see I have grown into an adult?" He huffed as he flung the dirty straw from the stall.

"Hey there, don't hit me with that stuff."

Johan swung around and spied Gerrit behind him. "Sorry."

"So what is not fair?"

Johan leaned against the stall's wooden wall. "Let's keep Cornelia out of the equation. If I were any other twenty-year-old begging to help you, would you let me?"

Fine lines radiated from Gerrit's pursed lips.

"I want an honest answer."

"I probably would."

"Then put me to work."

"That is out of the question. Cornelia would never speak to me again. I got her to forgive me once for putting you in harm's way. She will never forgive me a second time."

"You are afraid of your girlfriend."

"Don't taunt me. You are like my little brother. I can't do it." Gerrit turned to walk away.

"Wait."

Without looking back, Gerrit waved his hand.

Johan picked up his pitchfork.

"It is not fair. It is just not fair."

"ARE YOU READY to go?" Cornelia stood at the front door with her hand on the knob.

Anki stared at her sister. Were you ever ready to go to your husband's funeral? Or memorial service, as they called it, because Piet's body remained in the south. She would never have the comfort of going to the churchyard and seeing his headstone. This child was the only thing she had left of him.

She nodded, smoothing her black skirt and adjusting the fitted button-down collared jacket. The outfit didn't fall well because of the baby, but there wasn't a dress or fabric to be found. She had to make do with what she had worn to Mem and Heit's funeral.

That was the theme of her life now. Making do. She straightened her shoulders. She would be brave today and strong. Piet would want it that way.

She put on her brimmed hat and pulled the black veil over her face, then tugged on her black kid gloves. "Let's go."

Cornelia looped her arm around her sister's and together they walked the few blocks to the tsjerke. The wind swirled last fall's leaves around their feet, and Anki drew her threadbare coat across her shoulders to shut out the chill.

Already a few people waited for them.

Anki almost didn't recognize Nell without her four children attached to her. "How are you doing? I could not believe it when I heard the news. That is the most awful thing. Your poor family, to have to endure another tragedy. You have my deepest sympathies, and Luuk's too. If there is anything I can do, anything at all, you please let me know. Any time of the day or night, well, night might be hard because of the curfew, but any time of the day you need me, you give me a holler. How are you holding up?"

How could she be? *Fine and wonderful, bedankt. Couldn't be better. It's a perfect day for a funeral. I have been looking forward to this.*

Instead, she nodded. "I appreciate your coming today." The words sounded stiff and mechanical to her. She attempted a small smile to soften them, but the corners of her mouth refused to curve upward. How would she survive the next hour or two?

She pushed herself toward the front of the tsjerke. Several other old acquaintances and family friends offered their sympathies. As before, she nodded and thanked them but didn't say much else.

A few minutes later they stood in the front of the sanctuary. So far, she had made it without crying. Massive gold-adorned organ pipes covered the front wall. The intricately carved pulpit floated above the congregation to the left, almost suspended in air, the large sounding board above it. Her family's pew was located in the middle of the sanctuary and it was strange to be in front, all eyes on her.

She slid across the hard wood bench, smooth from centuries of use. Cornelia, her strength, sat beside her. Five years ago she had buried her own husband. She wouldn't ask unanswerable questions.

The dominee intoned the service, but Anki heard little of it. A fog surrounded her, as if this were happening to someone else. She sang the songs at the appropriate times and bowed her head to pray when instructed. Everything and everyone faded into the distance.

Her baby, the only good left in her life, fluttered inside her.

GERRIT SLIPPED INTO the cool stone tsjerke as the service started. With help from Frou de Bruin, he dressed in baggy, moth-eaten clothes and hunched over the late Hear de Bruin's cane. None of the busy soldiers bothered to stop an old man shuffling along the road.

Not wanting to draw attention to himself, he climbed the steps to the choir loft overlooking the small congregation. He spotted Cornelia's auburn head in the front row. Then he slunk into the darkness. Maybe she would be able to sense his presence.

He watched Anki's grief. She sat straight in the pew, her shoulders back, her head held high. She had pinched her lips together and clasped her hands in her lap. Her black veil blew in and out with each breath.

Beside Anki sat Cornelia, her arms clutched around her middle. She bowed her head, her shoulders rounded. Every now and again she wiped her eyes.

Somber music flowed from the organ. The dominee led the service. Women wept.

The service concluded, but Gerrit stayed in the shadows. He watched the congregants surround Cornelia and Anki, wanting to be there himself. Person by person, the tsjerke emptied until the two women stood alone with the dominee. After a while, he walked away. Gerrit skipped down the stairs and into the sanctuary. Cornelia spied him and her eyes sparked with fire.

He touched her shoulder. "How are you doing today?"

"I told you not to come."

He thought she would be happy to see him. He turned his

attention to Anki. "I am sorry about Piet. I wish I could have done something."

"Bedankt." She dabbed her eyes with her pink lace-trimmed handkerchief. "Piet wouldn't have wanted it. He believed this was God's will for his life."

Cornelia pulled him to the side, not allowing him to finish his conversation with her sister. "What are you doing here?"

"I thought you might need me."

"I would rather know you are safe."

He lowered his voice. "Yesterday I distributed ration cards. Coming here is far less dangerous. And Frou de Bruin concocted a brilliant disguise. No one stopped me."

"What is the use of a hiding place if you don't stay there?" Her words seeped out through her teeth, a strangled whisper.

"I'll be careful."

"I am tired of promises that can't be kept." Her shoulders slumped.

He took her into his arms. "I won't let my fear prevent me from doing what I feel is necessary."

"This wasn't it."

"Life is about risks."

She touched his chest with balled fists. "Life is about survival."

"Sometimes, without risks, you will only survive. You won't live. I don't want to argue with you."

"Then why did you come?"

"Because when a man loves a woman, he will do anything to be with her when she needs him the most."

She relaxed. "You should go."

"Trying to get rid of me?"

She shook her head, apparently not in the mood for flirting and teasing. It had been a bad attempt in a place and time that called for solemnity. "Tomorrow you will come by?"

"Ja. Don't you go anywhere."

"I have deliveries to make."

"Don't they realize the price on your head? Bear shouldn't be sending you out."

"Let's not start again. It was my idea to get back to work. If I get caught, one man dies. If those cards aren't delivered, many die."

She cringed. He inhaled to tell her he would be careful but blew out the breath.

The drone of planes broke the quiet of the sanctuary. She stiffened as she always did at the sound, gripping the back of the pew.

"Come here and sit with me." He pulled her to the front bench. She moved like a Nazi soldier marching in a parade—arms and legs rigid, never shifting her eyes to the right or left.

He drew her close and held her trembling body to his. "Why are you so afraid?"

"If that older woman died while hanging laundry on the line, none of us are safe."

"There is more to it than that."

She shook all over.

"Tell me about the night Hans died."

Her shivering calmed as she transported back to that time. "It was our wedding night."

He knew Hans died soon after their marriage. He didn't realize it happened that soon.

"We were in Nijmegen on the German border. About four or five o'clock in the morning, we heard the planes overhead and an explosion as our men blew up the bridge. Gunfire crackled in the air. Hitler had broken his promise."

She paused and studied the multicolored stained-glass windows running the length of the tsjerke. "Hans was in the army, such as it was. He told me he had an obligation, that he had to leave to fight the Germans."

A lone tear scuttled across her cheek. Gerrit barely heard her next words. "I begged him not to go. I pleaded with him to stay. They would give him an exemption for being a newlywed. He chose the queen over me."

Gerrit drew her in and held her close. Anki tugged on her jacket and made a move for her to come, but he shook his head to keep her away. He wanted to hear the rest of the story. Cornelia needed to tell it.

"He didn't choose her over you. He went to fight for you, to keep you safe."

She didn't reply.

"What happened next?"

"All day I stayed in the room, listening to the fighting. All night I cowered in the corner, a young girl alone in a hotel in a strange town, not knowing where my husband had gone or when he planned to return. Explosions shook the little hotel, the air alive with the reverberations. German voices shouted on the street below. What would they do if they discovered me?"

He rubbed her arms as she shivered.

"I prayed and prayed, for myself and for my husband. Then there was silence. Hans would be back soon and I had survived. But the door to the room never opened. I sat on the bed and watched it, hour after hour, not daring to fall asleep."

"He never came."

She bowed her head and cried. Gerrit rubbed her back until the tears dissolved and she hiccupped.

"I was young, so young then, caught in a war zone without my husband. Anything could have happened to me."

"But nothing did. God in His mercy preserved you."

"God took Hans from me." Her eyes pleaded with him to help her understand why God did such a thing. He didn't know what to say. "After a long while, I went to look for him. If he had been injured, he would need me to nurse him. I didn't want him to be as alone as I was. I went to the hospitals, but he wasn't at either. No one had seen him. They sent me to the morgue.

"Dampness and mold seeped through the mortar in the morgue. The place reeked of chemicals I hadn't smelled before. Death hung in the air. No one steadied me as I stumbled down the hallway. I don't know how I got the strength to open the door.

"There were a handful of bodies, and the coroner led me to a sheet-covered form across the room. Before he showed me the corpse, I ran to the bathroom to lose the contents of my empty stomach."

He wanted to stop his ears so he couldn't hear another word.

She gripped the edge of the pew, her fingernails digging into the soft, centuries-old wood. Her breath came in ragged gasps as she closed her eyes.

"I lifted the sheet. Under it was my husband's body, riddled with bullet holes, covered in blood."

CHAPTER 33

errit sat in stunned silence, light streaming through the stained-glass tsjerke windows coloring the dark pew blue and red and green. The whine of the planes' engines faded and the twittering of birds on the trees in the churchyard filled the hush.

He clenched and unclenched his jaw, trying to measure his words. "Those Nazis. Those murderous, vicious, bloodthirsty beasts." He balled his fists and sat straight on the hard pew. "I hate that you had to go through such a terrible experience. You shouldn't have had to live through that. Not you." She raised her hand to touch his shoulder, but he caught her wrist and kissed her palm.

She quivered. "Why are you angry?"

He scrubbed his face. "No one—absolutely no one—should have to see the things you saw. Trained soldiers break when they encounter death like that. How much more a fragile young woman."

"Every night when I closed my eyes, I used to see Hans again. When I was little and had trouble falling asleep because I was afraid of things lurking in the dark, Mem would tell me to think nice thoughts to chase away the bad. Do you know what I think of now to soothe myself?"

He shook his head.

"You. I still have nightmares, but in the night when I wake up frightened, I think about you and about that psalm you taught me."

"You don't want to fight back?"

"I want them all to go home. There would be no more killing then. No more women would lose their husbands or mothers lose their sons."

He rose, hands in his pockets, and gazed at the soaring buttresses. He sighed. "Wishing it will not make it happen."

"We cannot all be Resistance workers."

"Why not? Our country would have been freed years ago if more joined the fight."

"We aren't all like you. Some of us don't have the courage."

He faced her. "You are the bravest woman I have ever met."

"I am?"

How could he make her understand? "It takes strength to get out of bed every day, to live with what you have had to live with."

"But I don't put myself in danger every day like you do. I cook and clean and do laundry. Nothing very grand. Nothing for our country and our queen."

"Look at the way you handled the soldiers who came to the house. You couldn't have done any better. You even saved my life when I coughed. You did what you needed to do when you needed to do it." And wasn't that what the Resistance was all about?

"Inside, my stomach quivered."

"Courage is not a feeling. Courage is an action."

Anki came and stood beside her. "Are you ready to go?"

"Ja." Cornelia came to him and brushed her lips across his stubbly cheek. "I need to take Anki home, but tomorrow I will see you when I come to work."

He rose and returned her kiss, her cheek soft and warm. "I can't wait."

ANKI HELD CORNELIA'S hand as the two of them ambled through the streets of town. She had been strong throughout the entire service, not crying once. Piet would have been so proud of her for not breaking down. She heard his voice in her head. "I am in a better, happier place, Anki. Don't cry. This should be a joyous day as I feast with our Savior."

But he had left her alone. His absence created a bomb-crater-sized hole in her life. Did this pain ever go away? Part of her wanted to hang on to Piet forever, always mourning his absence.

She studied her sister, remembering the conversation between Corrie and Gerrit. She had observed her sister's shoulders heave as she sobbed. "What were you and Gerrit discussing?"

Cornelia tightened her grip on Anki's hand. "Hans."

"What did he say that made you cry?"

"Nothing." She paused. "Actually, he asked about the night Hans died. I told him everything."

"All of it?"

Cornelia nodded. "He knows I identified Hans's body."

"He loves you."

Cornelia pressed her free hand to her chest. "He told me so."

"Do you love him?" She couldn't imagine ever loving anyone other than Piet.

"Ja. But it's different this time, you know? It's not like it was with Hans. Maybe I have changed, maybe the war has changed things. It is confusing and complicated."

"In what way?"

"I am not the innocent young woman I was when I married Hans. I have been through things and have seen things that have made me feel older. Love is a wonderful thing, a gift from God, but a gift He can snatch away at any time."

"So you are still afraid?"

"Not afraid of love, but of loss."

Anki paused in front of the dressmaker's window and pressed her forehead against the glass. The forms the seamstress used to display her creations boasted remade dresses, some from men's suits. "I don't know what I am going to do."

Cornelia stood beside her and wrapped her arm around her sister. "You are going to do the same thing I am."

Anki's breath steamed the cool glass. "What are we going to do?"

"Live life."

"How do you do that?" Anki's voice rose.

"I am trying to figure that out."

THE MUSTY OLD farmhouse sat quiet and Johan spied his long-awaited opportunity. Gerrit had gone against Corrie's wishes and went to Piet's funeral and the old monarch Frou de Bruin had lain down for a nap. Now he could sneak from the house without anyone stopping him.

He snatched his klompen from the breezeway between the barn and the house and sat on a barrel to put them on. His thoughts drowned out everything else and he didn't hear Maarten enter until he saw klompen in his line of sight.

"Is Gerrit here?"

"Nee." Johan had to crane his neck to look at the man's thin face. "He went to Piet's funeral."

"I hoped that he would reconsider." What a stubborn man. "Where are you headed?"

Would a little lie hurt? "Gerrit agreed to speak to Bear about an assignment for me. I am on my way to get to work."

"That is a surprise. Last time we talked, Gerrit had no intention of ever allowing you to help. I take back my old Dutchman comment. So he has agreed to let you help Bear and Junior on the rail line today."

"Ja, ja." Perfect. The information he needed.

"I'll wait in the barn for Gerrit to return. Be careful. You are rather exposed on the dike."

With that detail, Johan had a strong idea of where to look for Bear and Junior.

Keeping his eyes and ears at attention, he slogged across the muddy farm fields. His heart throbbed in his throat and blood whooshed through his ears. He controlled himself to keep from skipping. He passed some sheep grazing on tender new shoots of grass and a black-and-white cow flicking her tail back and forth, head down against the wind.

At the precise place he expected to see Bear and Junior, Johan spied their figures advancing toward him. He quickened his pace as they dropped to the ground. Following suit, he cased the area. Nothing else moved, not even a fly dancing on the wind.

Of course. They didn't plan on meeting him here. They must have mistaken him for the NSB or something, walking across the field in his klompen. He crouched low and approached. They lay on their bellies, faces mashed into the soft ground.

He hissed at them, "Bear, Junior, it's me, Johan Kooistra. I want to help you."

Bear lifted his face from the dirt. "What on earth are you doing here? How did you know about this? You could ruin the entire operation."

Johan hadn't thought about that. "Maarten told me. Don't be upset with him—I tricked him into thinking you had given your approval. I just want to do something noble for our country and our queen."

He thought he heard Bear mumble something like, "Stupid, impulsive child."

Before he could ponder what the big man meant, Bear pulled Johan down farther. "Since you are here, you can stay. If you leave, you might draw unwanted attention. You can be our lookout. Warn us if you notice anyone coming."

"But . . ."

Bear narrowed his eyes and glared at him. The withering look caused Johan to clamp his mouth shut. If Bear said he would be a watchman, he would be a watchman. Next time, though, he would be the one planting the explosives.

While Bear and Junior worked their way down the line, placing the bombs in several locations, Johan kept a vigilant eye on the surrounding farmland. If he did this job well, perhaps he would earn a promotion and Bear's trust. No one, however, passed through this drowsy area of the countryside. Only by guessing at what Bear's wrath might be like if Johan fell asleep on the job did he manage to stay awake. Just once in his life had he ever been so bored—in the dominee's catechism class. He rubbed his hands together in an attempt to remain alert.

Then from the corner of his eye, Johan spotted green trucks moving along the road in their direction.

He sprinted to where the men were planting the explosives. His movement must have tipped off the Nazis, because as he ran, he spied them pouring from their trucks, racing toward them.

"Bear, Junior," he hissed. "I think some soldiers have seen us."

The great man looked up, his eyes wide, his mouth gaping. A moment later he regained his composure. "Run." Bear shooed him. "The Germans will be here any moment. Run."

His quaking legs found life and he skimmed over the fields faster than he had ever run, his pulse keeping perfect time.

Behind him, he heard gunshots and the soft thud of a body hitting the ground.

CHAPTER 34

April 1945

Johan's feet flew over the damp farm fields, his klompen collecting mud until they were almost too heavy to lift. He had run for a very long time and, unable to draw a deep breath, his chest heaving, he allowed himself to slow.

All around him fell silent. Good, he must have outrun those Nazis. He tried not to think about the sounds he heard as he fled—the zing of bullets and the thunk of deadweight.

A grinding of gears alerted him to trucks on the road. German military trucks. Many of them. All, he assumed, searching for him. He spun around, assessing his situation, standing in the middle of a flat farm field, no cover to be found.

A few sheep grazed at his feet and about five meters from him, a heavily pregnant ewe lay in a furrow. While he would have preferred the cover of trees or his own hiding place in Corrie's house, he didn't have any other options. He curled up behind the sheep, thankful for his lean build. Not wanting the Huns to get a good shot, he lowered his head against the sheep's side, burrowing against her, breathing in dirt and damp wool. What seemed like a few short minutes later, he heard the soldiers' throaty voices.

"We can't go back to headquarters empty-handed. We killed the one, but I know I saw two escape. They don't have that many places to hide. We have to find at least one of them." As he spoke, the man's voice grew louder. He approached.

Johan thought he might wet himself. He couldn't control the trembling in his legs. The odor of damp wool made him want to vomit.

He sure had wanted adventure, but Corrie would be right in calling him foolish and headstrong. This wasn't adventure. This was life and death.

He lay there behind the sheep, quivering like a plucked string. *Father, deliver me, I beseech You. Send Your angels to watch over me and protect me. Turn those soldiers away from me, I beg You.*

The dominee had been right when he told the group of uninterested teens in his catechism class that someday they would be grateful for his instruction. Johan clung to those precious truths now—that God was sovereign and He had everything in His control.

The ewe stirred. For half a second, he thought she would move and he would lie exposed. His heart stopped beating and his breathing ceased. *Lord, keep me from harm.* The sheep settled into the same spot.

A few moments later the soldiers' voices quieted as they moved away.

"No one here. I don't know where they have gone, but we won't give up. Come, let's go a little farther."

Johan's tears mixed with the mud. God gave Abraham a ram and Johan a ewe.

CORNELIA STOOD AND arched her back, lavishing in the sun streaming on her face. She pushed her red paisley kerchief farther back on her hair. April had arrived two weeks ago in all its glory. She had neglected to care for the flower bed in front of Frou de Bruin's house for too long, and now the weeds threatened to take over. She hadn't done much but already her knees and shoulders ached.

A bird twittered in the bush at the corner of the house, but German trucks rumbling down the road almost drowned out its song. Allied planes buzzed overhead, the noise so constant she had learned to block out the hum.

With all the kinks out of her shoulders, she returned to her job, working carefully around the leaves poking their heads above the ground. Frou de Bruin wouldn't be pleased if she pulled out a wanted plant by accident.

Tulip buds rested in the cup of leaves, their showy colors ready to burst. She touched one of the blossoms. She couldn't wait for their riotous display.

"Oh, there you are."

Cornelia startled, then turned to the voice. Gerrit stood in the doorway of the house, handsome as ever. "Don't you hear the trucks? Don't get reckless."

"Don't worry. I'll be careful. I promise."

"How long have you been watching me?"

"Long enough to know you are the most beautiful woman I ever met."

"'Beauty is but dross if honesty be lost.' The German traffic here has been heavy the past few days, you know. You shouldn't be in the open." She waved her hand shovel at him.

He shrugged his wide shoulders. "Fine. I will sit on the threshold, with the door ajar just enough to see you and speak to you." He plopped down most of the way inside, only his feet peeking out. If Frou de Bruin caught him with the door open, she would scold him for letting in the cold air and the bugs. If the Germans caught him, they would make the old woman look softhearted.

"As soon as we see those trucks coming anywhere near at all, I will close the door."

His dimples appeared and she wanted to break into song. He sat without saying a word for a few minutes while she tugged a stubborn weed from the dirt, watching him from the corner of her eye.

He inhaled deeply and let his breath trickle out. "I can almost taste spring."

She rubbed her gloved hand across her mouth. "I can taste it."

"And you have it smeared on your cheek. Come here."

Shovel still in hand, she obeyed, crouching in front of him. With his palm, he wiped the dirt away. The brush of his skin against hers awakened a long-forgotten passion, her mouth aching for his. More brazen than she had been even with Hans, she placed her lips over his. He returned her ardor and cupped her face in his hands, pulling her closer.

Light and warmth washed over her. Time didn't matter anymore—not the past nor the future, only this precious moment with the man she loved. The spring flowers would fade, but she would always have this memory.

From behind Gerrit, someone cleared his throat. Gerrit released his hold on her and she tottered, landing on her backside.

"Well, well, well, what do we have here?"

Cornelia glared at her brother. "Don't you have anything better to do than to spy on us?"

He held up his hands and smiled—something that had been missing the past couple of weeks. "I wasn't snooping. It is getting chilly in here and I came to close the door. Never did I think I would find the two of you out here kissing like a couple of teenagers."

Gerrit stood, brushing dust from his creased pants, grinning like a child who had gotten away with raiding the cookie jar. "If that is how teenagers kiss, I want to be eighteen forever."

"Go back where you came from, Johan. Why don't you muck out the cow's stall?" The heat in her face had not a thing to do with sunburn.

Trucks thundered as they approached. The glow of the moment fled. "You both need to get inside the house. Now."

"Come on, Johan. We will see if we can get Frou de Bruin to part with some of her precious tea."

Frou de Bruin picked that very moment to appear. Today she sported a jaunty red velvet hat with a large diamond-looking pin and a red feather. "Do we always sit and have coffee in the doorway? Be sensible and come inside." The trucks approached as the drone of planes increased. "Gracious, you are letting the heat escape and we will all catch cold. Have you finished weeding the flower bed?"

Cornelia shook her head. "I will be done here in a few minutes and then I'll start dinner."

"See that you don't dillydally anymore. I hate it when my dinner is late. It upsets my schedule for the entire day." The old woman shooed the men inside and shut the door.

Just before it clicked, Gerrit turned, smiled, and winked.

She told her heart to slow its furious beating.

CORNELIA COMPLETED HER day's work. She wished she could stay at the de Bruin farm for the duration. Allied planes shot at anything that moved along the road, not wanting the Germans to retreat and regroup or to escape the country with the loot they gathered. Yesterday they had come so close to her, she could see the shadow of the pilot in the cockpit. Frou de Bruin, however, hadn't made the offer and she hadn't asked. Tonight she would cut through the fields, feeling safer. Hopefully the bombers kept their eyes trained on the roads and railroads and not on farm fields.

Before she left, she wanted to see Gerrit one last time. No matter how often she looked at him, it wasn't enough to satisfy her longing.

Last she saw, he had gone to the deel, so she looked for him there, the smell of fresh hay welcoming her. The rafters creaked from the heating of the day, and not another sound reached her ears. Not wanting to disturb the peace, she didn't call to Gerrit but walked farther back searching for him.

Most of the stalls stood vacant, their tenants confiscated by the Germans years ago. She went a little way until she heard the low drone of men's voices.

Urgency laced Gerrit's words. "I will do it, but I was followed again, a few weeks ago."

Cornelia leaned against the wooden post. He hadn't told her.

"And you waited until now to tell me? Did they follow you out here?" She recognized Maarten's voice. He hadn't come through the main part of the house, which made her wonder how many other times he and Gerrit had held meetings in the deel.

"Nee, in town."

"For Piet's funeral." Frustration edged Maarten's voice.

"I had to be there for her."

Maarten sighed. "With the Canadians now in Friesland, the Nazis are getting desperate."

"So I have heard."

Maarten's voice sounded muffled, as if he covered his mouth. "Two or three days ago I got the feeling of being followed too. I never saw the man, but it took me awhile to shake whoever tailed me."

"Exactly the same in my case."

The Gestapo or NSB must have discovered Gerrit's Resistance network. In a matter of hours, they may well be arrested.

"Even if liberation comes in the next few days, these people are going to need these cards. Food isn't going to appear on the market shelves by magic just because of surrender."

She imagined Gerrit nodding at this. "I understand. I will make sure these cards get delivered. I have taken risks before, and this is no different."

"We don't have much choice. With the way Johan botched the rail-line operation, I don't trust him at all."

"I will go."

She had to keep Gerrit from making these deliveries—especially if the alternative meant Johan would be exposed. She didn't understand what Maarten referred to with the rail-line operation, though she meant to find out.

"We don't have an alternative."

Nee, Gerrit could be followed again and perhaps arrested this time. She couldn't let him take this risk. Not with their freedom so close. Not when mere days from now they could go about their work in the open. Not when he had survived for five years.

She closed her eyes and willed her legs to stop shaking, then rounded the corner and stood in front of them. "I will make the deliveries."

GERRIT BLINKED SEVERAL times, not sure Cornelia had truly appeared in front of him. He clapped his ear, convinced he hadn't heard her say she would deliver the ration cards. "Where did you come from?"

A sparkle lit her eyes, but she swallowed hard. "If you want to have clandestine meetings, you need to pick a better place. Here people snoop too much."

He shifted on the little milking stool and rubbed his chin. "I don't want you to."

She squared her shoulders but her hands shook. "When you first came, you wanted me to contact the local Resistance cell for you. Even at Piet's memorial service, you didn't like it when I talked about waiting for freedom."

"Ja, I did. But things have changed." His stomach flipped. He had fallen in love with her. The thought of her out there, in danger, perhaps never coming back . . .

In that moment, he understood. He understood why Maria's husband refused to let him stay. He understood why Cornelia wouldn't allow Johan to join the work.

Love meant you did whatever you had to do to protect those you loved. In his case, that meant working with the Resistance. In Maria's husband's case, it meant getting rid of him. In Cornelia's case, it meant keeping Johan from the Underground.

She huffed. "The only difference between now and then is you're in more danger than ever."

"How much of our conversation did you hear?"

"Enough to know that Johan has been involved. Did you think I wouldn't find out?"

"I can't explain right now. And please, don't speak to Johan about it. I'll tell you later. Trust me when I say I had no involvement whatsoever."

"That doesn't change the fact that you were followed after Piet's service. The one I told you not to attend."

"I didn't want you to worry." He stood and turned to Maarten. "But this confuses me. Whoever followed me had plenty of opportunity to harm me. I can't be sure, but I don't think I am in any more danger than before."

Maarten mussed his dark hair. "We can't take unnecessary risks. Junior is dead, and I am being followed too, but we will find someone to deliver these." He also rose.

Cornelia stood with her feet askance. "You don't need to find anyone else, because I have volunteered."

"You don't have to do this. You don't need to prove your courage to me or anyone else." Gerrit went to her and held her. They both trembled as they nestled together. "Please, leafde, don't do this."

He breathed in her hair's clean scent. "In the past I have pushed you to do things that frightened you, but now the thought of some awful thing happening to you terrifies me."

She kissed his cheek and this simple gesture caused him to go cold all over. "Cornelia, please don't go. I will do it."

She pushed against his chest and took a step back. "Nee, I am not going to let you. And I am not doing it to show you or Johan or even myself how brave I am. I am not courageous at all. But you said courage is an action, not a feeling. There are people depending on these cards, aren't there?"

Maarten stood beside him. "Ja, several families."

He wanted to sock his friend. "But Maarten said he could find someone else."

"Why should he when I am available?" She rubbed his upper arm. "I want to do this because people need these cards and I can deliver them. It is that simple. Because I am a woman, I can move around without raising suspicion. That is another reason to allow me to go. Tomorrow morning I will leave first thing and be home in time to make dinner. Gerrit, please understand."

Why, why had he ever pushed her to work for him in the past? "It is dangerous on the roads."

"The planes are in the air when I come and go from here. I will be careful. I promise."

She gazed at him with her gorgeous hazel eyes and wore away his opposition. "Don't make promises you can't keep."

She stepped back into his arms where she belonged. "You will pray for me?"

"From now until you return." Their hearts beat in unison. His life would be nothing without her.

Then Maarten handed her the cards she would deliver.

CHAPTER 35

ornelia clutched the frayed edge of the pink blanket to her chest. Her stomach churned and she shook all over. The haze of the nightmare hung over her—dreams of rat-infested, wardrobe-sized cells and bitterly cold work camps. She forced herself to take deep breaths.

A warm breeze blew through the trees on this Lord's Day. The delightful spring smells called all the world to wake. The tulips would soon bob their heads in the wind.

She wished she could hop checker-like over today and land on tomorrow.

Knowing what she had to do, she pulled back the covers and slid out of bed. For a few minutes, she stood still, not thinking much, not praying much. Then she squared her shoulders.

She chose the simple, dark-colored dress she had worn to Piet's funeral. The frock showed its age, worn and faded. One of the matching buttons was as loose as a child's tooth. She pulled the black patent leather belt around her midsection.

It was strange not to be getting ready for services at the tsjerke. The few other times she had missed in her entire life had been

SNOW ON THE TULIPS

because of illness. For this act of mercy, however, the Lord would forgive her.

Yesterday she had pretended to be brave in front of Gerrit. She had even talked back to him. Her bravado fooled him. She would give the rest of this month's ration cards for some of that daring and confidence now.

GERRIT STAYED IN the deel while Cornelia finished making breakfast for Frou de Bruin. She would leave to make her deliveries as soon as the older woman settled in for the day. Her gout prevented her from attending services.

For some reason, he didn't hurry to go to Cornelia.

Maybe he didn't want to see the fear in her face.

Maybe he didn't want her to see the fear in his.

While she worked in the house, he stayed in the loft, playing a game of dominoes with Johan. Frou de Bruin would frown on them playing games on the Lord's Day, so they stayed here, out of her eyesight.

"I beat you again." The younger man laid down his last domino, but he didn't take his usual pleasure in winning. His eyes were bloodshot. Then he shook his head. "I don't understand. I have never beaten you before and now I can't lose. Is something going on?"

Gerrit knocked over his remaining pieces, then turned them upside down. "I have something on my mind."

Johan shuffled the dominoes. "Is there a big operation taking place?"

"If there was, would you want to be part of it?"

The young man shrugged his narrow shoulders. "I have to tell you something."

Gerrit leaned forward on the table. "What?"

"I killed Junior." His blue eyes widened.

"I don't understand. The Germans shot Junior."

"Didn't Maarten or Bear tell you I was there?"

"Ja, they did."

Johan mussed his sandy hair. "I tricked Maarten into giving me the information."

"Go on. I know the story, but I want to hear it from you."

"I met Bear and Junior at the spot and they weren't happy about seeing me, but Bear put me to work as a sentry. I sure wasn't a very good one. If I had alerted them sooner or if I had not run to them when I saw the convoy, none of us would have been spotted."

Gerrit inhaled a lungful of air and released it little by little. "Not all operations are completed without a glitch. In fact, most aren't. You have to be careful and quick-witted so you don't get yourself or someone else killed."

"I mean, I just wanted to help." Johan's shoulders drooped.

"And did you?"

"Nee. My actions caused Junior's death."

"How do you know you were to blame? Perhaps those soldiers saw Bear and Junior first. When you alerted them, instead of killing Junior, you might have saved Bear."

The boy lifted his head. "I never thought of it that way. So I did help?"

Gerrit didn't know the answer to that question. Maybe there wasn't one, because the full truth of the incident would never be known. "Yes, it is very possible you did."

"Bedankt, Gerrit. I have wanted to tell you these past couple of weeks, but the time never was right."

"I'm glad you did. Now let's shake and pick our dominoes for a new game."

In the pause that followed, Gerrit heard Cornelia's soft footfalls in the hay below. "I'll be right back." He scrambled down the ladder and landed in front of her.

She raised her brows, her hazel eyes wide, her back straight.

"Are you ready?"

She nodded.

Dear Lord, please don't let anything happen to her. Don't take her from me. "I can go instead if you have changed your mind."

"Nee, I will do this. Please hold me."

He took her in his arms and granted her request.

She nestled her head against his neck, a perfect fit. Her breath brushed his skin. He couldn't tell if she trembled or if he did. Perhaps they both did.

He breathed in her scent. "I'm praying for you."

"Lord willing, I will be back for supper." She loosened her hold and kissed him long and hard. Moments later she broke the kiss. "I have to go."

He understood all she meant by that statement and released her.

He memorized the curl of her hair at her neck, the graceful arch of her back, the soft sway of her dark dress as she walked out the door.

CORNELIA BICYCLED OVER the bumpy roads back into town, past her sweet little house and out once more into the wide expanse of the Frisian countryside. Her rag-wrapped rims did not provide much shock absorption. A few peeks of warm sun massaged her shoulders, but they were not able to unknot the kinks in her neck. Black-and-white cows grazed in the fields, chewing their cud, and sheep bleated to each other. A gust blew across the open land and the windmill in the far field spun round and round.

Her heart pounded faster than her legs pedaled. Perspiration dotted her forehead and her breath grew short, but she didn't stop riding. She had to finish her job. Tonight she wanted to sleep safely in her own bed, all of this behind her.

She and Hans had ridden bicycles together in this area, picnicking in the fields. One evening, soon before their wedding, they lay on a blanket in the grass, admiring the stars dotting the sky. He held her hand and they whispered to each other, not wanting to break the stillness of the night. They spoke about everything and nothing at all. For a long while they lay in silence.

No matter how many years rolled by, she would always remember that day. And that was as it should be. She had a set of memories of Hans.

If she knew then how life would turn out, would she have walked away from him and missed the one beautiful night she had as his wife? Would she give away all those memories to avoid the pain?

Never.

What memories would she miss making with Gerrit if she turned her back on their future? She would miss out on all the joy the Lord had prepared for them if she was afraid of the sorrow.

Cornelia looked up and saw the first of the two farms on her itinerary in the distance. They should be back from the tsjerke by now. Neither Gerrit nor Maarten told her anything other than the name of the person living there, not whether they harbored Juden or onderduikers nor how many of them. Judging by the bulging envelope of ration cards strapped to her chest, there must be a good number in hiding.

Looking ahead on the road, three German military trucks headed her way.

Oh Lord, oh Lord, keep them from stopping me.

She moved to the right side of the road, her head down, not wanting to make eye contact with the soldiers in the trucks. Her muscles went weak, but she forced herself to keep pedaling. The first one zoomed past, as did the second.

The third truck slowed and then stopped.

So did Cornelia's heart.

Two men dressed in gray uniforms, eagle insignias on their chests, hopped out, toting guns. One—tall, lean, and young—towered over the other, his complete opposite—short, squat, and graying. They reminded her of Lyts and Grut, the little man and the big man from the bedtime stories her father used to tell her.

The soldiers stepped into the road in her path. She had no choice but to brake and come to a stop in front of them.

Her hands shook and she grasped the bicycle's handlebars tighter to keep the soldiers from noticing.

The older one she thought of as Lyts stretched himself to his full height. "We need to see your papers."

He spoke German and Cornelia shook her head and shrugged.

"Identification," the big one, Grut, said in Dutch. "Schnell, schnell."

With shaking hands, she handed Grut the card. The two Nazis examined it carefully, glancing between the card and Cornelia, no doubt wanting to make sure the picture matched the woman on the bicycle.

They handed it back to her. Her heart began to beat again, slow and timid.

"Ask her where she is headed," Lyts said to Grut. The short one had to be the leader and the tall one the interpreter.

He asked.

She had practiced in her head through the long night just what to say, but her voice squeaked. "To Roos's house." Gerrit had told her to keep her answers short and to the point. Give the barest of information. If they wanted to know more, they would ask.

"Who is this Roos?"

"My friend."

"Why are you going there?"

"For dinner."

Lyts leaned forward, his hands on his hips. "You would come out today of all days for dinner?"

"I don't work on Sundays." Cornelia's legs trembled and she sat on the seat of the bicycle for support.

Grut snatched her purse from the bicycle's basket and rummaged through it. She gripped the handlebars, her fingers growing numb. Let them search it all they wanted. Just so long as they didn't search her person. The ration cards poked her each time she took a breath. Thankfully her coat, buttoned to her throat, helped to hide them. As long as they didn't ask why she wore a long jacket on such a mild day.

Grut shook his head. "Nothing in here," he told his superior. "I don't think she is up to anything."

Lyts flashed a sinister smile. "Let us escort you to your friend's house. It is dangerous for a woman to be out here alone."

She papered a bewildered look to her face until Grut spoke to her in Dutch.

"Nee, that won't be necessary. See, it is right there." She pointed to the farmhouse about half a kilometer on the left—single story, thatched roof, barn attached to the house. Her finger quivered and she withdrew it with haste.

The stout man grabbed her elbow and dug in his fingers. "But we insist. We want to make sure you get there safely."

Lyts's smile sent a shiver down Cornelia's spine. They pretended to be helpful, but they didn't care about her safety. They wanted to make sure she told them the truth.

She tipped her head and grinned, digging her fingernails into her palms. "I don't want to inconvenience you. It's not far, and I will be fine."

Lyts pulled her off the bicycle. "It is not a problem at all. We are happy to offer our services." His flashed his yellow, half-rotten teeth again.

Grut grabbed Hans's bicycle by the handlebars and slung it in the back of the truck. She wanted to mourn over its loss.

Lyts still held her elbow, now yanking on her arm and steering her toward the truck. Her heart pulsed at an alarming rate. Were they arresting her? What would happen to her when they searched her person?

The older soldier opened the passenger door and shoved her into the seat before settling in next to her. She quivered, hoping he didn't hear the crinkling of the ration cards as her breath shot out in short spurts. He smiled at her, and his leer sent another tremor racing through her body.

Grut climbed in and turned the ignition key. The truck's engine roared to life. Petrol fumes infiltrated the cab. Cornelia gagged. She allowed herself to relax only a minute amount when Grut turned the truck and headed for the farm where she was to make her first delivery.

In reality, it took mere seconds before they screeched to a halt in front of the neat home. To Cornelia, a lifetime passed as they traversed the short distance. Lyts once more seized her now-bruised elbow, and both of the soldiers accompanied her to the door. Cornelia focused on breathing and walking, not sure she could do both at the same time.

Without giving away the true reason for her visit, she had to get whoever opened the door to play along with her game.

CHAPTER 36

Cornelia rapped a timid knock on the old wooden farmhouse door. There were people inside who needed time to hide. No matter how much she wanted these Germans to go away, she had to give the Juden and onderduikers a chance to get out of sight. No one answered the door.

Grut, his massive hairy hands clutching his rifle, got her attention with the butt of his gun. "Knock louder."

She did.

A young woman, an infant on her hip, pulled in the door.

Cornelia didn't give her a chance to say anything that might put either one of them in jeopardy. She crossed the threshold and wrapped the woman and child in a warm I've-known-you-forever-and-it's-so-good-to-see-you-again hug. "After all this time, it is wonderful to be here, my dear friend. Bedankt for the invitation to dinner."

Cornelia stepped back and motioned toward the soldiers with her eyes, giving a small nod to convey the message that the woman needed to play along. "I am a terrible cook, you know. It will be such a pleasure to eat something that is not burned."

"I'm just sorry we couldn't make it work earlier."

Cornelia exhaled. "And look at Derk, how big he's grown since the last time I saw him." She took the baby in her arms and buried her nose in the blond fuzz at the top of his head. He didn't cry for his mother, and Cornelia thanked the Lord for that.

The woman turned her attention to Lyts and Grut. "Who are these gentlemen with you?"

"They stopped by the side of the road and offered to escort me here. Wasn't that kind of them?" Cornelia jiggled the infant, ridding herself of some nervous energy. Now if they would only go away.

Grut peered down at Lyts and Lyts craned his neck to see his comrade. They nodded to each other, then to the women. "We'll be going." Lyts glared at Cornelia. "Be careful in the country all by yourself." As she shivered at his icy words, they turned and walked the path to their waiting truck.

The woman, her leathery face and hands telling the story of years of hard farmwork, shut the door. The Bible passage came to Cornelia's mind where God told the apostles they wouldn't need to be afraid when they appeared before men to give their testimony because He would give them the words to say.

Ja, God had given her the words to say.

The infant fussed and Cornelia handed him back to his mother. "Heel hartelijk bedankt for going along with my ruse. Those soldiers stopped me on the road and insisted they escort me here. Nothing I said would dissuade them." Her stomach flip-flopped as the realization hit her of how close she had come to being arrested. Only by God's grace had the Germans turned that truck and brought her to the farm.

"I'm Karin."

"Anna."

Karin took her by the hand. "Come in and sit at the table. You look warm. I will get you a cold drink."

Cornelia declined the offer and stayed on the rug, though she did slip off her klompen. "A drink would be wonderful, but I can't stay. I have a delivery for you, so if you will show me to the restroom, I will be on my way."

Karin nodded and smiled, the grin softening her worn features. Cornelia scooped up her klompen as Karin led her through the house so similar to Frou de Bruin's, then through the deel to the very back stall that served as an outhouse.

Once inside with the door shut, she pulled a packet of ration cards from under her skirt, leaving a second one hidden in her clothing for the next house.

Another house. Another delivery. Another chance for something to go wrong.

As she put herself back together and prepared to leave, her leg jiggled.

GERRIT PACED THE floor in Frou de Bruin's kitchen, the one Cornelia had scrubbed yesterday. He was a caged dog, longing to be out there working, doing anything but sitting here. Twice he went to the door and almost turned the knob to release himself.

Only because of Cornelia did he stay inside. When his heart belonged to him alone, he hadn't given a second thought to taking crazy chances. Now he had given his heart to Cornelia and that fact kept him indoors.

He had made his umpteenth circuit of the front room and kitchen when someone knocked. Cornelia must be back. He wilted with relief and sprinted to peek out the window.

His stomach took a dive from under his ribs to his feet when he saw a young woman waiting. This woman matched Cornelia in height, but not in coloring. She was fair and blond, with cold blue eyes. She wrung her neatly manicured hands and licked her lips. He went to admit her.

"Good afternoon." Her words were precise and her enunciation impeccable.

"How can I help you?"

"I have come from Polder's Edge Farm, about five kilometers to the east of here. We have six Juden hiding with us. Four days ago we ran out of ration cards. The man who supplied us didn't show up when we had expected him. Our food stores are almost exhausted." She spoke flawless, almost cultured Dutch.

"What does this have to do with me? We have no food to spare, no cards we could give you."

Without an invitation, she stepped across the threshold and shut the door. Gerrit's skin itched. She leaned toward him, her hot breath making the back of his hands prickle. "I heard there was a Resistance member hiding here. Word is all over the place. I know you are him. You have that look."

Where did she get that information? "I am not him."

She grasped his arm, her rounded nails digging into his flesh. "But you are, and you have to help me. We are desperate."

"I can't help you."

"You must. A Christian man like you wouldn't let women and children starve to death. Not with peace coming in a few days."

A picture of his mother and his sister Dorathee flashed in front of his eyes. If they were in such a situation, he would want someone to help them.

"You have to go to Bear and get more for us."

How did she know the leader of the local cell? Perhaps Bear, long ago, had delivered the cards himself. "Who was your regular delivery person?"

She studied her dusty shoes. Under the dirt, he could tell they weren't worn in the least. "We have had several. I suppose they keep getting arrested, or maybe they rotate. None of them told us their names."

"How do you know Bear?"

The woman stood up straight and glared at him. "Will you help us or not?"

How could he turn down a woman in need? "Tell me where the farm is. I will get the cards for you, and this afternoon or tomorrow morning will deliver them."

Her eyes widened and she shook her head with vigor. "Today. It must be today."

"Fine. Today I will bring them."

"No need. I will be by later to get them." With that, she clicked her heels and disappeared.

A cold shot raced down his spine.

A LONG LINE of German trucks had rumbled past Karin's farmhouse as Cornelia prepared to leave, so Karin had persuaded her to stay and have a little to eat while she waited for the trucks to pass. If the Germans stopped her again, they might discover her contraband.

Cornelia sat at the big farmer's table, large enough to hold the family and any hired hands. She leaned against the high back of the chair, a cup of cool water in her hand, while Karin sat across from her and bounced baby Arie on her knee.

"It's been awhile since we heard any trucks, hasn't it?"

Karin nodded. "It sounds like they are gone for now. They remind me of the locust plague in Egypt. When the Lord turned the wind to the west, the locusts were caught up and drowned in the Red Sea."

The analogy made Cornelia smile. "The Lord is removing the plague of the Germans from us."

"Maybe I won't need these cards much longer, but bedankt for bringing them. We appreciate all of you risking your lives to save those of others. I can't believe someone would be willing to give his life that others would live."

The way Karin articulated the thought made Cornelia stop and consider what she said. "That's what Jesus did for us, you know." If Christ could do that for the worst of sinners, shouldn't they be willing to do that for their fellow man? Did Hans leave her on their wedding night because he had an idea how many would die if the German blitzkrieg succeeded?

"Greater love hath no man than this, that a man lay down his life for his friends."

The words from the gospel of John took her breath away. What else had John said? She couldn't remember the exact verse, but the words spoke about it being better for one man to die than to have the entire nation perish.

Hans, is that what you did for me? For our country?

She put the thought aside for later, set her cup on the table, and pushed her chair away. "I should be going. I have another delivery to make yet today."

Karin's forehead wrinkled. "What if more trucks come?"

The thought of them stopping her again cut off her breath, but Gerrit's saying that courage had more to do with actions than with feelings drove her forward.

When I am afraid, I will trust in You.

She gathered in a deep breath and took her coat from the peg. "The Lord is with me and I will be fine. *Vriendelijk* bedankt for everything."

Karin swept her into a hug. "May the Lord watch over you."

Yes, Lord, be with me. Danger hadn't passed by, and it wouldn't until not a Nazi boot remained on Dutch soil.

She walked back to the road. Clouds, though they didn't threaten rain, scuttled across the sky. Her thoughts turned to Hans. Out of habit, she went to twist the gold band on her finger only to find it empty. She loved him more than ever. He had had the courage to sacrifice everything for her, to give her a chance at life.

Bedankt, Hans, bedankt.

She had taken the first step toward that new life by saying a final farewell to her husband. That dance had come to an end, and now she needed the courage to start a new one with Gerrit.

She paused her hurried pace and stopped a minute to listen. Off in the distance, she heard a low, deep sound she couldn't identify and prayed it wouldn't be more Nazi trucks. Wishing she had her bicycle to speed her trip, she continued on her way.

Gerrit wanted her whole heart and he deserved someone who could give him that. If she gave her entire self to him, she would be giving herself the greatest gift—life without fear.

Up ahead, along the straight road, another column of German trucks bore down on her in a hurry to make it across the border. She hopped to the side of the road.

The distant noise she had heard before grew to a low drone.

Like a swarm of summer mosquitoes, Allied planes burst through the clouds and filled the metallic gray sky. The crackle of machine guns resounded across the countryside as the trucks accelerated and soon were almost upon her.

And so were the planes. They strafed the road. One of the dozen or so trucks in the convoy exploded into a ball of flames.

Cornelia jumped. The stench of burning fuel and flesh churned her stomach.

She stood dazed on the side of the road, her legs locked, unable to move. She had nowhere to hide.

Hans had left her in the opening days of the war.

And in the closing days, she would join him.

CHAPTER 37

Gerrit pulled the hood of his jacket over his head, wearing the old man disguise he had used in the past. He called to Frou de Bruin, "I am going out for a while."

She emerged from her bedroom as fresh as if she had slept for ten years. She narrowed her eyes in the annoying habit she had and glared at him, hands on her hips. "Where do you think you might be going?"

How could he explain when he didn't understand himself? "A woman came to me for help. I have to go into town."

"I hid ten English pilots during the course of the war, and none of them were as stubborn as you. You are incapable of staying in one place. What about when Frou de Vries comes and wonders where you are? What should I tell your girlfriend?"

Gerrit couldn't help but smile at the term. If you asked him, he liked the word *wife* better. Ah, maybe someday. "I shouldn't be gone long. Tell her to wait if she gets here before me and I will be back soon." He planted a kiss on her wrinkled cheek. A wide-eyed look of surprise crossed her faded face. "My mother always called me a rogue."

"Young and reckless is what you are. One of these days you will settle down. When you have a wife and a family of your own, you will think twice about taking these kinds of chances."

"When I have a wife and family of my own, I promise to settle down." He slipped out before she could open her mouth again.

He hadn't gone more than half a kilometer before he got the feeling of being followed once more. He kept his head down and leaned on Hear de Bruin's cane. A fleet of eastbound German trucks passed him but paid little attention to him. His old man disguise fooled them at least. But with each passing second, a sense of impending doom bore down on him.

DIRT SPRAYED AT Cornelia's feet.

Bullets whizzed past her ears.

Airplanes swooped so low she saw the pilots in the cockpits.

They were trying to kill her!

She came alive. She swiveled her head in both directions and dove for a ditch on the left side of the road. The pilots continued to shoot, rocks stinging the backs of her legs. As the pain grew worse, she prayed they weren't bullets.

Her heart leaped to her mouth and pounded there. This had to be happening to someone else. She wanted to scream but bit her hand. Funny, really, because the planes made so much noise, no one would hear her.

She lay there, her face in the grass, the tender young blades tickling her nose. She worked for each breath she drew.

She was going to die.

In a matter of moments, she would stand in the Lord's presence.

Her entire body shook. Would it hurt much? Her screams erupted then, a flow she couldn't stop. "God, help me! Help me!"

Planes swooped low. She pressed her body against the ground. An eternity passed as she lay there. Any moment she expected brilliant, shining light.

She closed her eyes. An explosion shook the ground. She had never been in an earthquake, but she imagined it must be like this.

Oh, that the end might come quickly. Her heart had already stopped beating. "God, where are You?"

"When I cry unto thee, then shall mine enemies turn back: this I know; for God is for me." There was more she couldn't remember. Then a snippet came to her mind. *"I will not be afraid what man can do unto me."*

The planes continued to screech overhead.

"I am crying to You, Lord. Please, please help me. Turn back those who are trying to take my life. I trust You, Lord. Please save me. I beseech You, Father, may it be Your will that I live. I praise You for the way You have cared for me."

All the fear drained from her body.

No matter what happened, God had this situation in His control. If she died, she would be with her Lord forever. If she lived . . .

Well, if she lived, she would live. Truly, fully, completely.

The planes climbed in the sky. Another explosion rocked the ground around her. One less German truck now, she supposed. She didn't dare look.

Time passed. No more men shouted or screamed. Perhaps they were all dead.

If she lived, she would take whatever time she had with Gerrit. She refused to let fear rob her of the days or months or years the Lord might give them.

As the acrid smell of burning tires stung her nostrils, she cried.

Not in sorrow.

Not in fear.

In joy.

ANKI LONGED TO hear another voice in the house besides her own. The emptiness echoed around her. Her child fluttered like the brush of fish fins inside her stomach. She cupped her hand over the swelling in her belly. Hunger reminded her it was time to eat. Only because of her child did she even try to force a little food down her throat.

The depth of her loneliness surprised her. She had spent most days alone while Piet had been working. She thought life would continue much as it did at those times. Maybe knowing he wouldn't come home for dinner and wouldn't share her bed at night made things different. She hated sitting in her chair hour after hour. Because of morning sickness, she didn't feel well enough to do much cleaning, and one person alone didn't create much dirt.

She needed to get out of the house and be among people. Services on Sunday and the brief social time they afforded only increased her loneliness. The other six days of the week stretched into infinity in front of her.

After a quick lunch, she combed her hair, not caring much how it looked, and slipped a fresh dress over her head. The thin cotton material strained across her middle. With the war ending, she hoped she would be able to buy new clothes soon.

Stepping onto the front stoop, she raised her head and let the wind flow over her, lifting her spirits. She had eaten the last of her bread and needed to stop at the bakery tomorrow. Today she decided to go see Johan. Perhaps he would know why Cornelia hadn't been in tsjerke this morning.

Against the horizon, Allied planes swooped and rose like eagles in the sky. Today they flocked in the opposite direction of Frou de Bruin's house. Cornelia would be glad they stayed far away.

The fresh, balmy air revived her so much that she decided to take the long way through town. The expectant tulip buds would burst open any day now, and she wanted to see if any early comers had bloomed in the window boxes. Nothing was more beautiful than the bright flowers bobbing their heads in all the window boxes up and down the streets. The town came alive then.

She wandered, not paying much attention to where she was going. She couldn't get lost. The exercise and fresh air helped her feel better than she had in days.

She turned one corner and ran into a crowd. A drab green Nazi truck with a canvas top idled in front of a house. People milled about while soldiers shouted. Through a gap in the crowd, she saw a man being led from the house, the long barrel of a gun in his back.

She knew that man, the hunch of his shoulders, his dark head. Not many men in Friesland had hair that color.

Maarten.

Gerrit's friend in the Resistance. He had been at Corrie's house once when she had stopped by. She wasn't supposed to know the man's identity, but Corrie slipped and made her vow never to tell who he was.

The Gestapo dragged him to the street, kicked him, and threw him into the back of the truck.

The baby inside of her fluttered wildly and she placed her hand over him, trying to calm him. She watched a moment more. A tall soldier shook his head as he spoke with another. "Nein, there are more inside. We are not leaving until we have them all. Keep searching. And there is one more coming."

One more coming. Gerrit didn't stay at this house. Could they be speaking of him?

She had to talk to Cornelia.

Anki turned and jogged past brick houses and silent businesses to her sister's house, all the while her blood pounding in her ears. Corrie couldn't stand another loss. She had been crazy to urge her sister to fall in love again. If something happened to Gerrit, her sister would not survive.

She spied the cheery house on the other side of the canal and trotted across the bridge. Breathless, she pounded on the door. No one answered. Her heart raced like a skater across a frozen canal.

SILENCE ROARED IN Cornelia's ears. No more planes cased the sky. No more trucks or tanks thundered down the road. No more men screamed.

She dared to lift her head. Nothing moved.

She sat up and scanned her surroundings. About thirty meters behind her lay the skeletons of trucks, blackened and smoking.

The back of her leg throbbed and pain shot up to her thigh and down to her foot as she stood and attempted to brush the mud from her damp dress. She bent to examine the cause and discovered a large gash in her calf. A rock or a bullet had struck her and the injury burned. A trickle of blood seeped down her leg.

She could do nothing about it at this time but ignore the discomfort. The crinkle of the ration cards under her shirt reminded her of her mission. No matter what happened to her, people still depended on these. She had to get them where they needed to go. Besides, she couldn't sit along the side of the road waiting for help. The next people past might be more Germans or another squadron of Allied planes. She scanned the area to get her bearings and remember which way she needed to go.

A groan from the side of the road stopped her. She must have imagined it. She took a step toward her next destination, but the groan came again.

The planes hadn't killed all of the soldiers.

One of them, dressed in a gray uniform, writhed and moaned.

He tried to move and moaned again. Blood spattered his chest. "Help."

She touched her midsection, the ration cards crinkling under her fingers.

Off in the distance, planes whined.

Her legs urged her to run. Her heart urged her to stay.

CHAPTER 38

The pungent odor of burning petrol and charred flesh sent bile racing up Cornelia's throat.

She bit it back and picked her way through chunks of metal and around the smoldering remains of trucks, trying not to look at the bodies, twisted and broken. The stench caused her to gag. She drew her handkerchief from her pocket and placed it over her nose.

The man who had groaned—a boy really . . . he couldn't have been more than seventeen—quieted when he saw her. "Help me."

Wishing she possessed Anki's nursing knowledge, she knelt in the dirt beside the towheaded boy.

"What is your name?" She spoke in German.

"Rolf."

For his sake, she removed the hankie from her face and smiled. What she had so feared now lay helpless and harmless. Just a boy sent to a foreign country to fight. If situations were reversed, this might be Johan.

She sent the thought away. "This might hurt, Rolf, but I am going to move your shirt to look at your wounds."

He nodded and she swallowed hard, willing her stomach not to heave as she peeled away the mangled fabric. Every move reminded her of the day Gerrit stepped into her life.

Once she saw the damage to the boy's body, his shredded flesh, she turned away and coughed, trying not to vomit. Even if she had a medical degree, she doubted she would be able to help the young man.

"*Fräulein?*"

She turned back to him.

"I am going to die, aren't I?"

What would be the right thing to tell this boy? She held his hand. "I think you might meet Jesus today, but don't be afraid. I will stay with you." Her own calm in the situation surprised her.

"*Danke.*" Already his breathing grew shallower.

"Do you know Jesus?"

"*Mutti* took me to church a long time ago. She told me He loved me."

"He does. Do you love Him?"

"I did once." He struggled for breath. "I remember praying to Him."

She smoothed his hair from his sooty, sweaty brow. "God doesn't forget you. Do you want me to pray with you?"

He nodded, crying.

Peace flooded her as she spoke to the Lord. "Dear Father in heaven, please be near Rolf now. Ease his pain and suffering. Help him remember that You love him and help him recall that love he once had for You. Cover his sins with the blood of Your Son. Wash him clean and clothe him in the white robes of righteousness. Prepare him to meet You and spend eternity in Your holy presence. Amen."

Rolf's eyelids fluttered. "I have done lots of bad things. I lied about my age. I shot and killed people."

"If you are truly repentant for your sins, there is nothing God can't forgive."

"I am. I wish . . ." He sucked in air. "I wouldn't have done those things."

"Then He will forgive you."

Rolf lay still for several minutes, his eyes closed, his breathing irregular. Then he inhaled deeply. "What will heaven be like?"

"Beautiful beyond our wildest dreams. More beautiful than a sunset over the North Sea or the sun shimmering on a canal."

"Or the trees of the Black Forest?"

"Ja, more beautiful than that." She couldn't stop the tears flowing down her face.

"I think I see it."

Rolf's features relaxed. Cornelia had never seen such tranquillity on a person's face. His chest rattled, then stilled.

She sat in the blood-soaked dirt for a long time, soot mixing with her tears. She didn't know quite what to make of what had happened. She had been a part of something terrible and wonderful at the same time.

"Hans, was someone with you when you died? Or were you alone and afraid?" That part bothered her the most. "Did it happen so fast you didn't even feel anything?" She wished she knew. She never would.

But Rolf's family could.

She bit her lip and searched his pockets until she found his *soldbuch*, his pay book, in his tunic pocket. With shaking hands, she flipped the pages until she found his parents' names and their address. She would write to them and tell them all they might want to know.

Her legs fell asleep, the injured calf throbbing, and she shifted into a more comfortable position, the ration cards poking her skin. She closed Rolf's eyes, kissed his forehead, and limped away.

Death, life, trouble, peace, fear, calm—all this tumbled inside her.

As she reached the next farm, a large, rotund old man met her at the door.

"I have something you need."

He smiled and nodded. "Come in, child, come in. You look like you have been through it."

She limped over the threshold.

"You are hurt." He spun her around and examined her leg. "Come into the kitchen and sit while I get some things to doctor you. What happened?"

"The planes shot at me. I don't know if I got hit by a rock or by a bullet."

The old man shook his head, his jowls following along. "The planes? I heard all that commotion. How did you manage to escape?"

"God."

"Ah yes." His blue eyes danced. "You are good to come out in all this chaos. Or foolish."

She laughed. "One or the other."

"God bless you, child. Bedankt for the cards. Even if the war ends tomorrow, we will need these."

His gratitude embarrassed her. "I am just a frightened woman doing what God would have me do."

AFTER THE KIND older gentleman cleaned Cornelia's wound and sent her on her way, she walked as fast as her injury would allow to Frou de Bruin's house. She was dirty and exhausted and hoped the elderly woman would make her a cup of real tea. That would taste better than a beef roast right now.

And she couldn't wait to see Gerrit, to have his arms around her, for this entire terrible day to be over.

All the way there, she kept vigil, scanning the horizon at all times, waiting for more swooping planes or green trucks to halt her progress. None came. For now, all lay quiet.

She admitted herself to the farmhouse, kicked off her klompen, and made her way to the kitchen where the elderly lady sat enthroned on a chair next to the table, a steaming cup of something in her hand. She waved a bony finger at Cornelia. "I told him you would come."

By *him*, she assumed Frou de Bruin meant Gerrit. "Was he worried?" The thought made her smile all over.

"Not worried enough to stay put."

Cornelia stared at the woman. "He's not here? What are you talking about? Is he out back?"

Her employer shook her head, her cut-glass earrings sparkling in the pale light. "Someone came to him, begging for help, and Gerrit said he would go. I told him he was a fool."

"He went into town? Why would he do something like that?"

"He left not long ago, but told me to have you wait for him." She put on her spectacles and took a good look at Cornelia. "What happened to you?"

Exhaustion overwhelmed her and she shook her head, unable to speak.

"There, there. Heat up some water for yourself and enjoy a bath. It's the least I can do for you."

"That's kind of you—"

Someone knocked at the door.

"Please answer that. My arthritis is bothering me today."

Cornelia hobbled to the door and was shocked to see her sister's pale face. "What's wrong?"

Anki stepped inside but didn't remove her klompen. "Is Gerrit here?"

"Nee. Frou de Bruin said he had to go out for a while."

What little color remained surged from Anki's face.

A cold band constricted around Cornelia's stomach. "What is it?"

"There was a raid at Bear's house. I saw them take away Maarten. They said they were waiting for one more person to arrive. Could that be Gerrit? Corrie, he could be walking into a trap."

"Nee, nee. Not Gerrit." *Please, Lord, don't let this be a trap.* Her prayer didn't dissolve the cold lump in the depths of her stomach.

Johan stepped in front of her. She hadn't heard him enter the room. "I'll find him."

Cornelia pulled herself together. Courage wasn't a word. Courage was an action. "I'll go. It's not safe for you on the streets. I don't need to lose both of you."

Her brother grabbed her arm. "Corrie, let me go this time. I want to do this."

"I need to do this."

Anki touched her hand. "Are you sure?"

"Never more sure of anything in my entire life."

Sure she needed him. Sure she loved him. Sure she had to tell him everything in her heart.

GERRIT ENTERED THE little town he had come to think of as home. This game, a combination of hide-and-seek and cat and mouse, had him paranoid. He believed eyes stared at him from every alley. He convinced himself he heard footfalls behind him. Someone's breath, and not the wind, tickled the back of his neck.

He had to lose the tail before he got to Bear's. If he wasn't a wanted man, he would guide them straight to the police station. Or maybe to the tsjerke.

The tsjerke. Perfect. He could slip in one way and slide out another and perhaps shake himself of his follower. Morning services had let out and afternoon services had yet to start. He zigzagged through town, down backstreets and alleys, until he came to the centuries-old tsjerke. He thought of the last time he had been here, when Cornelia had bared her heart to him.

Perhaps someday soon she would pledge herself to him in this same place.

He pulled open the heavy carved doors and entered the cool interior, the ancient wood floors creaking beneath his feet. Good. That would alert him to anyone coming behind him. He crossed into the sanctuary, flying buttresses soaring like eagles overhead. Massive pipes from the organ anchored the front.

Taking just a moment, he rested on the edge of the pew and prayed. Prayed for Cornelia's safety as she made those deliveries, for the possibility of a future with her, for the success and safety of his mission, and for a speedy end to this long, bloody struggle.

"What time I am afraid, I will trust in thee."

His taut shoulders relaxed.

"Amen, so be it, Lord."

He walked down the long center aisle with much more peace than he had when he entered. No longer did he feel like someone pursued him because he remembered Someone walked beside him.

He stood and debated for a while, not knowing through which door to exit. The wrong choice might have him walking straight into the arms of the Gestapo or the NSB. The right choice would mean he could complete his mission and get the ration cards to that woman without incident.

He chose the door on his right, the one leading to the cemetery. Before opening it all the way, he peered out, turning his head in either direction. He didn't see anyone. Only a little brown-and-black bird hopped on the ground near one of the gravestones. He startled it and it flew away when he approached.

He wandered for a few minutes between the headstones, some

weathered and tottering sideways, husbands and wives buried on top of each other to save precious land in this country where it was a greater commodity than gold. Dead leaves from last autumn carpeted the ground, crunching under his feet with each step. He stopped suddenly, but no leaves crunched behind him.

He had lost whoever had been trailing him from the countryside. He wouldn't be surprised if it was nothing more than his imagination.

Whatever the case, he needed to get to Bear's.

CORNELIA ARRIVED BREATHLESS on the outskirts of town. Though she had run so hard her leg screamed in pain, she never caught up with Gerrit. Either he had been too far in front of her, or he cut through the farm fields and she missed him on the road.

Her leg throbbed, but she didn't have the luxury to sit and rest. She had to find Gerrit.

Fast.

CHAPTER 39

Cornelia traced a direct route to Bear's house, alternating between a brisk walk, jogging, and all-out running, whichever her injured leg and burning lungs allowed. She forced her breath through her constricted throat. Gerrit had been ahead of her.

If he made it that far. Their small village teemed with German soldiers, more than she had seen the entire course of the war. She pushed and shoved her way through a group of them, all noisy and raucous, like a group of teens at a soccer game.

Her heart threatened to explode. *"Be merciful unto me, O God: for man would swallow me up."*

She turned onto Prince William Street where Bear's house stood. From Anki's description, Cornelia expected to find the way clogged with soldiers and trucks, but all sat quiet, in stark contrast to the main streets. They had come, collected who they wanted, and left.

She gasped, drawing in short, ragged breaths.

Too late. She had arrived too late.

She didn't know what else to do other than to stand in the middle of the street. For weeks she had been too afraid to act on love. When she had, it turned out to be too late.

Because the Germans wouldn't show mercy to their prisoners. Gerrit wouldn't escape execution a second time.

GERRIT, HUNCHED OVER his cane, neared Prince William Street. The way he had his hood drawn over his head blocked his peripheral vision. He had been wary, careful to the extreme, because the main streets teemed with German soldiers, men he had bumped against but who paid him little attention. His gut twisted. The Nazis should be leaving, not congregating.

He turned the corner and lifted his head, seeing Bear's place down the street. A strange sight met his eyes. A young, lithe woman stood in the middle of the road, her shoulders hunched. The curve of her body in the baggy black dress looked familiar, but what would Cornelia be doing here? Had something gone wrong with her deliveries?

He took half a dozen steps toward the woman. Even with her head bent, the pale light ignited the auburn color in her hair.

Cornelia.

His breath hitched. She was so beautiful, so vulnerable. Needing to keep up his disguise, he couldn't run to her as he wanted, but he went to her. His fingers tingled as he touched her shoulder.

She jumped and turned. As she did so, he lifted his head and pushed back his hood, and her mouth became as round as a wagon wheel.

"HUSH. DON'T SAY anything." Gerrit placed his finger over Cornelia's lips. It tasted salty from sweat. "What are you doing here?"

She hugged him, pulling him close, relishing the feel of him. "I found you. I can't believe I found you. Here I stood, thinking they had taken you."

"What's going on?"

"You can't go there." She tipped her head in the direction of Bear's house but didn't release her hold.

"I have to get some ration cards."

"It's a trap. Anki saw Maarten being taken from here. She overheard the Gestapo say they were waiting for one more person. We think that person is you."

His hand on her cheek trembled with the news, and she covered it with her own. "I can't believe I found you. You are safe."

She closed her eyes and tilted forward to kiss him, to let her heart speak directly to him. Before her lips could touch his, a dirty hand reached around from behind and covered her mouth. A matching hand covered Gerrit's lips and someone pulled both of them from the street, around the corner of a brick building, and deep into a dark, dank alley.

"DON'T MOVE." A low German-tinged voice growled in Gerrit's ear. "I am going to help you."

Gerrit struggled and kicked, trying to wriggle free. The Nazi kept a tight hold on both Cornelia and him. Gerrit had to get her released. Even if he couldn't get away, he had to make sure she stayed safe, as he had always protected Dorathee. He twisted and turned, but the man strengthened his grasp. His hot breath warmed Gerrit's neck.

"I'm going to help you, Gerrit Laninga, like I helped you before."

Gerrit stilled. The voice sounded familiar. He tried to think. He had heard it before, but where? How did this Nazi know his true identity?

"I could have killed you, but I missed on purpose."

His heart careened into his ribs.

"More than once I could have turned you in to the Gestapo. I never bought your flimsy story about your drinking problem. Your little girlfriend is daring, but not a very good actress."

It must be.

"If I uncover your mouths, do you promise not to scream? I can't save you if you do something that stupid."

Gerrit glanced at Cornelia, telling her without words to promise. They nodded in unison. The dirty hand slid from his lips.

Gerrit reached for Cornelia's hand and squeezed it before they turned. Even in the dim alley, those unmistakable blue eyes pierced the darkness. "Who are you?"

"My name is Neumann, but that's not important."

"Will you let us go?"

The soldier grasped his wrist. "You can't."

Gerrit clung to Cornelia's hand, sure they would soon be separated. "Are you arresting us?"

"Nein. But it's too dangerous for you to be on the street. They are waiting to take you into detention, like they did the others. Eyes are watching all over for you. If you had stood in the street a moment more, it wouldn't have been me who grabbed you."

Cornelia gasped. "It was a trap."

"I couldn't keep up the charade any longer, so I had to tell them where you were. Instead of taking you into custody on the spot, though, I talked them into this orchestrated razzia. They had already uncovered the location of your headquarters, so they sent that woman to flush you into the open and lure you here to make the arrest. I wouldn't have let you get any closer to the house, but your girlfriend got to you first."

Gerrit nodded. "Why did you miss? Why are you helping us?" He kept his voice low, but he needed to know more.

"The way you stared at me as I lined you up to execute you, pleading with me for your life. I thought I could do it, but I couldn't."

"There's more."

"The Gestapo found that my brother in Munich was hiding Juden. Right before the incident here, we received word from a friend of his released from the same camp as my brother. Helmut died there. Over the last five years, I have arrested men and women for saving Juden, men and women just like my brother. And he died."

The soldier cleared his throat. "You have the same eyes as my brother. I wasn't able to inflict grief on another family the way it has fallen on mine."

"You didn't kill me."

The German shook his head.

Boots clacked on the street in front of them and a few trucks rumbled past. The soldier pulled them farther into the darkness.

Realization dawned on Gerrit. "You are the one who has been following me."

"Ever since I found you at the house beside the canal." He rubbed his cheek. "I volunteered to be the one to hunt you down. Your brazenness almost got you into trouble more than once."

"All this time, you have been the one watching over me." Thoughts buzzed in Gerrit's head as he tried to comprehend. He didn't know what to say. Even when he had faced a firing squad, God sent the most unlikely of people, a German Gestapo officer, to watch over him.

Cornelia trembled beside him.

He stroked her hair.

Neumann touched her arm. "You aren't safe yet, not until liberation comes. We're not going to give up this town without a fight. All these extra soldiers you see are here to defend the village—one of the few villages in Friesland they have decided to defend. The Canadians will be here by nightfall and we expect a firefight. You can't go back to the farm because it's too dangerous there now."

Gerrit's mouth went dry and he swallowed hard. Liberation. The word brought tears to his eyes. Cornelia rested her head on his shoulder. This long struggle had almost come to an end.

The Gestapo officer pulled his metal helmet lower over his eyes. "I have to go back to the house where they're waiting for you or they will grow suspicious. I'll tell them I found you and shot you on the spot. That will give you time to get to safety. Stick to the back roads and keep the hood over your face. I'm sorry about your friends. I will do my best to hold off their executions." He took a step forward.

"Wait."

But the blue-eyed soldier darted away, either not hearing Gerrit's soft call or not answering it.

Gerrit leaned against the rough brick of the building. Cornelia fell into his arms. "I can't believe it."

"Neither can I."

He held her, reveling in her heart pounding against his, which hadn't slowed in hours. By all rights, both of them should be dead. "Are you okay?"

"Better than okay. Better than anything, you know. I have something to tell you."

He kissed her forehead as voices floated from the street. "That will have to wait." He held his breath, not wanting to make a sound until whoever passed had long gone on their way.

She rested her head on his shoulder. The tickle of her breath made him glad for the building's support.

All fell very, very quiet, like when the birds and the trees were still before thunder breaks.

A boom crashed in the distance and a fireball lit up the dusk.

Cornelia startled. "What was that?"

His pulse raced. "It's the Canadians." Their liberation appeared on the horizon. "We have to get out of here so we don't get caught in the fighting." He grabbed her hand, pushed the hood over his head, and pulled her to the street, praying they would make it across the bridge.

In between his prayers, he wondered what she had been about to tell him.

CORNELIA GRASPED GERRIT'S hand and struggled to keep up as he dragged her through the streets. Pain shot up her leg with every step. She gasped for breath, having run so far today and having eaten so little. "Please slow down."

He turned toward her and slackened his pace until they walked side by side. "You're limping. Are you hurt?"

She shook her head, unable to summon the breath needed to answer him. After a few more steps, the burning pain become worse than ever and buzzing filled her ears.

Gerrit swooped her into his arms. A few hundred meters and they would be home. Halfway across the bridge, a shell whizzed past them and exploded in the canal, showering them with cool water.

Her heart accelerated like a speed skater at the start of a race. "They're shooting at us!"

Gerrit's legs turned as fast as a bicycle's wheels and they flew over the ground between them and the house.

They fell inside and shut the door, breathless and shaking. Gerrit drew her toward him, quivering as much as she did.

It was like the beginning of the war all over again.

CHAPTER 40

For a minute or two, Cornelia and Gerrit sat together in her front hall. He gazed at her beautiful heart-shaped face, dirt and tear-stained. He brushed her leg and discovered the filthy bandage. "You are hurt."

"As I was on my way to the second delivery, a convoy of German trucks appeared, chased by Allied planes. Either a bullet grazed me or I was scraped by some debris."

"You were shot at?" A ripple of shock streaked across his chest.

"I ran for the ditch and flattened myself as much as possible. I didn't dare move. I have never been so frightened in all my life." She shivered.

He rubbed her arms. "I'm sorry you had to go through that."

"I'm not."

He shook his head. "You're glad Allied planes shot at you?"

"Ja."

"Why?"

"I lay there in the ditch, unable to move or think. But I could pray, and I prayed more than I did that first night in Nijmegen. I had never been in so much danger. Psalm 56, the one you taught me, came to mind. And do you know what?"

He desperately wanted to know.

"God gave me this incredible calmness and serenity. He took away my fear. All of it. Whether I lived or I died, God's will would be done, and I was at peace."

"You weren't afraid?"

"I wasn't. All those soldiers died on the road there. I held the hand of one as he passed into glory."

Gerrit wrapped her in his arms. "I want to make this nightmare end for you. For all of us."

She traced the outline of his lips with the tip of her thumb. "I learned something else out there today."

All rational thought fled. "What?"

Just as she opened her mouth to tell him, someone thundered down the stairs.

"ANKI." CORNELIA STOOD, her hand over her heart.

Her sister flew the rest of the way down the hall. "Gerrit! Corrie found you."

"I hear I have you to thank for the tip."

"I stopped by to tell you that Johan joined the Canadian troops when they went past on the road. The shelling prevented me from going farther."

"Johan did what?" Cornelia swayed on her feet.

Gerrit's strong arms supported her. "Let's have Anki look at your leg and then we will get you something to eat. Johan needs to do this."

She let him lead her to the kitchen while Anki drew the black-out curtains. The explosions continued in the distance. Each one reminded her of Johan, fighting their oppressors.

Gerrit slid her into a chair and kissed her forehead. "You look like you've had a tough day."

The surge of energy that kept her going from first thing this morning tapped out and she sank against the chair's back. "I can't believe all that happened." She had been interrogated by two soldiers, was shot at by the Allies, held a boy's hand as he died . . .

She drew Rolf's soldbuch from her pocket. "Look at this."

Gerrit took it and examined it. Anki leaned over his shoulder. "Where did you get it?"

"This belongs to the boy whose hand I held as he died. And that's all he was. Like Johan, just a boy." She pinched the bridge of her nose.

A closer burst shook the little house. She clasped her hands to prevent them from shaking.

Gerrit rubbed her knee.

"I reminded him of his childhood faith. He told me he saw heaven."

"What a beautiful sight that must have been." Anki wept beside them.

"I took this so I could write and tell his parents about his final moments. They will want to know." Would someone do that for them if Johan died?

Her sister wiped her tears. "That's a good thing to do."

They all fell silent while the air around them buzzed. Gerrit sat beside her, not quite touching her. She felt his presence nonetheless.

"I'm proud of you."

She studied his strong, square jaw. "God turned back my enemies, just as He promised. He gave me the courage of Daniel and his three friends combined. I don't know how else to explain where my bravery came from."

"Because there is no other explanation."

"You're right. I acted not in my own strength, but in the Lord's. That is how I want to live my life." She looked between her sister and the man she loved.

Gerrit smiled at her and the warmth of it drove away the chill. "That's how we all need to live."

Anki nodded. "I want to clean you up and examine your leg. Gerrit, can you move her to the chair in the front room?"

Again he scooped her into his capable arms. She nestled against him, listening to the steady beat of his heart. Ach, did she love him.

He remained next to her as Anki cleaned and dressed her wound, then went to the kitchen to prepare a small meal. The percussion of explosives continued every few minutes, drawing closer and closer.

When Anki left them alone, Gerrit pulled Cornelia against his side and rested his head on top of hers. "I love you, Cornelia."

Her body relaxed at his words. She had come home.

Anki entered the room with some bread and coffee.

Cornelia ate the food, Gerrit beside her the entire time. The weight of fatigue fell heavy on her, and she had a difficult time finishing. She set her empty cup on the floor and rested her head on his shoulder.

The last thing she remembered was the smell of his line-dried shirt.

CORNELIA'S BREATHING TURNED soft and even. Gerrit didn't dare move, not wanting to wake her. The fine lines caused by hard years of war faded and serenity softened her face.

This is what he wanted, every day for the rest of his life. How could he convince her that she could trust him with all of her heart? That he wanted her fully and wholly?

When Anki came down the stairs, Cornelia had been about to tell him something she had learned today. He wondered what that might be.

Could she have been about to utter the words he longed to hear from her?

His emotions agitated inside of him. Mostly he, too, was worn out. Five years of war had taken their toll. More than anything, he wanted it all to be over. All the fighting, all the loss, all the uncertainty.

He leaned back on the davenport and drifted off. He dreamed that Cornelia picked him a sunset-red, fully opened tulip. She handed it to him.

A loud detonation jolted him awake. Cornelia sat up with a start. "What was that?"

He missed the warmth of her against him. A succession of explosions answered. "Freedom." The house shook and the windows vibrated from the force. Another burst and they shook even more, threatening to shatter. "Get to the hall. Away from the windows."

They picked up davenport pillows to cover their heads from any debris that might fall and hurried to safety. Anki raced down the stairs. Together the three of them sat on the floor, huddled under pillows, their knees drawn to their chests.

And waited.

Cornelia scooted closer to him. "At least this time I'm not waiting alone."

He grasped her cold hand. "You don't ever have to be alone again."

The *rat-a-tat-tat* of machine-gun fire pierced the air. The smell of smoke drifted under the door.

They sat without speaking while the battle for the bridge continued outside the door.

He wondered about Bear and Maarten and prayed for their safety. With the Allies closing in, Gerrit hated to think about what the Gestapo would do to their prisoners.

He prayed for Johan, too, in the midst of the fighting. Cornelia needed him to return alive.

A burst of light illuminated the gloom, filtering around the edges of the blackout curtains. Immediately, a gigantic boom followed, rattling the dishes in the cupboards, glass crashing to the floor as the entire house shook. He gripped his pillow tighter over his head while Cornelia cowered lower beside him, Pepper on her lap. Plaster rained around them.

She squeezed his hand. "What was that?"

"I think someone tried to blow up the bridge. Either the Germans are trying to prevent the Canadians from getting into town, or the Canadians are trying to prevent the Germans from escaping."

A few more rounds of gunfire popped.

Then came silence.

Gerrit held his breath. Judging by Cornelia's stillness, she must be holding hers too.

Several minutes of quiet passed. Then several more. They sat for a long time before vehicles rumbled past.

Cornelia leaned over, her breath tickling his neck. "Do you think it's over?"

"Stay here. Keep the pillow over your head."

She didn't follow as he made his way to the front window, the one that overlooked the canal. He lifted the corner of the shade, bright sunlight illuminating the scene.

Smoke rose near the bridge, but it remained intact. Whoever had tried to blow it up had been unsuccessful.

And then he saw the most glorious sight of his entire life.

"Cornelia! Anki! Come quickly."

"WHAT'S WRONG?" CORNELIA fought off a wave of panic, having held an entire ocean of fear at bay during the battle. But Gerrit's words held an almost euphoric tone.

Could it be?

Anki ran to another window while Cornelia limped to his side. He had thrown the blackout curtain open. "Look."

Tanks processed across the bridge and down the narrow street.

Tanks bearing a white flag with a red maple leaf.

But this wasn't like the opening days of the war. Everywhere, people poured out of their homes. These victorious soldiers sat high above their vehicles, the covers hanging open, their guns held over their heads.

Cheers arose. She had to see this up close, had to be a part of it to believe it. "Let's go."

Hand in hand, Gerrit and Cornelia crossed the bridge, Anki behind them, the peaceful water not stirring. Men who hadn't seen the light of day in years emerged from their homes, blinking in the morning's bright sunlight. Women cried and boys chased each other on the clogged sidewalks.

They continued following their liberators into the heart of town. Orange flags, red, white, and blue Dutch flags, and lily-speckled Frisian flags flapped in the breeze, publicly displayed again after a long absence.

Couples kissed on their doorsteps.

Perched on top of one of the tanks, surrounded by Canadian soldiers, Johan waved to them. Cornelia jumped up and down and waved to her brother.

A thin man, half a head taller than the rest of the crowd, pushed through the throng toward them. Neumann had been true to his word. Maarten had survived.

They stopped in front of the deserted bookseller's shop, the man who owned it taken long ago, a reminder that things would never be the same as they once were. She studied Gerrit's strong profile, his distinctive Dutch nose.

For each of them, the war had changed their lives forever.

Life could be good again.

Nee, life could be wonderful.

She pulled Gerrit away from the street and the cheering throng, back against the stone of the building. The time had come. The time to let go of the past, of the fear and the darkness.

A time for the snow to melt from the tulips.

"I didn't finish telling you what I learned yesterday."

He gazed down at her. His deep blue eyes told her all she needed to know.

THE CHEERS AND merriment of the crowd faded from Gerrit's consciousness. He saw and heard only Cornelia, even though she didn't say a word.

His heart slowed. "What did you want to tell me?"

"This." She stood on her tiptoes, leaned forward, and kissed him. Her soft, yielding lips spoke to him with fervor and passion, holding nothing back.

In that moment, it happened.

She gave him her whole heart.

"I love you, Gerrit."

In the shop's flower box, a single deep crimson tulip had raised its head.

THE STORY BEHIND THE STORY

M y father's cousin, Kay vander Meer, was married on May 9, 1940, in the Netherlands. She and her new husband spent their wedding night in a town on the German border. When the Germans invaded in the early hours of May 10 and the fighting broke out, her groom, a member of the ill-equipped Dutch military, left her to join the battle. He never returned.

On April 11, 1945, in the town of Dronrijp, Friesland, Netherlands, the Nazis marched fourteen men along the streets to the edge of the Van Harinxma Canal. Twelve of these men were Resistance workers. The other two were suspected collaborators. They had been arrested in Leeuwarden, a larger city farther north, and transported to Dronrijp. In groups of three, the men were brought to the water's edge and executed. They were shot in retaliation for the Dutch Resistance sabotaging railroad lines farther north near Leeuwarden, causing a Wehrmacht train to derail cars. The Germans were very nervous because Allied planes were in the air when they arrived in Dronrijp. Gerard de Jong, though wounded, survived by playing dead. Later, some of the town's men, including Ynse Poslma and my dad's cousin Johan Feitsma, found

Gerard and took him to my Aunt Hiltje's house where she nursed him. Dronrijp was liberated only days later. Every year while my aunt lived, Gerard visited her on her birthday. Even after she passed away, he brought flowers to her grave.

Days after Gerard's rescue, the Germans fled most of the Frisian towns without a battle as the Canadians closed in. However, they congregated in and chose to fight for Pingjum. I fictionalized the battle for the bridge there that took place on April 15–16, 1945.

Nijmegen, Franeker, Leeuwarden, and Achlum are all real towns. Franeker does boast the famous Eisinga Planetarium.

The story of the execution became legend in our family. My father visited the site in 1978. As he showed us the slides he took, he told us the story. We couldn't believe our family endured such trials during the war. Nor could we believe their bravery. I wrote this book to preserve the stories of people like Gerard, Ynse, Hiltje, Johan, and the many, many others who labored and gave their lives without fanfare so this generation could enjoy freedom. May we treasure it.

The author and Hillie Feitsma, the granddaughter of the woman who was the inspiration for *Snow on the Tulips*.

READING GROUP GUIDE

1. What was Cornelia's greatest fear, and how did she deal with it? What is your greatest fear? How do you handle it?
2. What were the three different types of responses to the Nazi authorities? Which characters embodied these responses? What does the Bible have to say about submission to authorities? (See Romans 13:5; Hebrews 13:17; 1 Peter 2:13–3:2.)
3. Why does Anki go behind her husband's back to help Gerrit and the Jewish woman? Did she handle these situations the right way?
4. Gerrit took great comfort in Psalm 56:11, which says, "I will not be afraid what man can do unto me." What can man do to you? Why should we not fear?
5. What was Gerrit's motivation for joining the Resistance? Was it the proper motivation?
6. According to Gerrit, what is courage? Would you agree or disagree with that statement?
7. At the beginning of the book, Gerrit was faced with death. How did he respond? At the end of the book, Cornelia was faced with death. How did she respond?

8. The last line of the first stanza of the old Dutch hymn "We Gather Together" says this of the Lord: "He forgets not His own." In what way did the Lord remember Gerrit and Cornelia throughout the story?

9. Near the beginning, Johan calls Gerrit a hero and Gerrit answers, "Not a hero, just a man doing what I have to do." What is your definition of a hero? Would you call Gerrit a hero? What about Cornelia?

10. The snow-covered tulip is a metaphor throughout the story. What does it symbolize?

ACKNOWLEDGMENTS

This book would not have been possible without the contributions of many, many people. Heel hartelijk bedankt and deepest appreciation to Newton vander Woude, Jack de Jagers, and Jacob Geertsema (who has since gone to be with the Lord) for sharing with me the stories of your lives during World War II. At times it was painful, but the world will now know of your incredible courage and faith.

Thank you to my amazing agent, Tamela Hancock Murray, for all of your support and hard work through the years, for believing in me when I stopped believing in myself. Thank you to Andrea Boeshaar, the first author I ever met and my longtime mentor. You started me down this crazy road to publication. Thank you to Hillie Feitsma for filling in some of the blanks in the family story that became this book.

I owe a debt of gratitude to the folks at the Verzets Museum in Leeuwarden, Friesland, Netherlands, for help with some of the aspects of Resistance work in Friesland at the end of the war. Bedankt to the historian of the city of Nijmegen, Netherlands, for help with details about the first night of the war.

My wonderful critique partners, Diana, Laura, and Robin, were honest with me and helped me make this book the best it can be. I appreciate you all. Thank you to my dear friend Sabrina Tolbert for help with a subject I knew nothing about.

To Amanda Bostic, Natalie Hanemann, Julee Schwarzburg, Jodi Hughes, Daisy Hutton, Becky Monds, Becky Philpott, and the fabulous team at Thomas Nelson, thank you for stepping out in faith with this story and for your aid in fine-tuning it. I couldn't ask for a better group of people to work with.

My family—you are a precious gift from God. Thank you to my husband, Doug. It takes a certain kind of man to be married to an author often "living" in another era. You are the best, and I love you deeply. My deepest gratitude to my amazing children, Brian, Alyssa, and Jonalyn, for your help with the chores, with meals, and the oldest two, with caring for your sister. Without that, I wouldn't be able to write. My parents both instilled in me a love of reading, the written word, and the Lord. That combination produced this book. Thank you to them for loving me.

Now to Him who is able to do immeasurably more than all we ask or imagine, according to His power that is at work within us, to Him be glory in the church and in Christ Jesus throughout all generations, forever and ever! Amen.

AN EXCERPT FROM *DAISIES LAST FOREVER* BY LIZ TOLSMA, AVAILABLE MAY 2014

BRAUNSBERG, EAST PRUSSIA

February 8, 1945

B right red and orange explosions lit the dark, deep winter East Prussian evening. Gisela Cramer hugged herself to ward off the chill that shook her. Her warm breath frosted the window pane and with her finger she shaved a peep hole. She didn't know what she expected to see. Maybe the Russians surging over the hill.

An icy shudder racked her. She couldn't block out the sights and the sounds of the last time the Russians had found her.

Behind her, Ella's two small girls giggled as they played on the worn green and blue Persian rug which covered the hardwood floors.

A Russian mortar shell hit its target not far from them in the city and rocked the earth beneath her feet. The vibrations almost buckled her legs. Her heart throbbed in her chest. How much longer could the German army hold them off?

Almost at the same instant, an urgent pounding began at the door, accompanied by Dietrich Holtzmann's deep voice. "Gisela, Ella."

Gisela spun from the window, tip-toed over and around the children's dolls and blocks, and answered the door for their neighbor. "Come in out of the cold."

The breathless older man, once robust, now gaunt, stepped over the threshold. The wind had colored his cheeks red.

"Let me get you something hot to drink. Some ersatz coffee maybe?"

"I don't have time. We're leaving, Bettina and Katya and I. Tonight. Whoever is left in the city is going west, as far and as fast as possible. By morning, the Russians will be here. You and Ella need to come with us. Take the children and get out of here. It is safe no longer."

Gisela peered at the girls, who now clutched their dolls to their chests and stared at Herr Holtzmann with their big gray eyes. Gisela repressed a shudder. She knew all too well the danger they would be in if they didn't leave before the Red Army arrived.

Her cousin Ella stepped into the living room from the tiny kitchen, wiping her cracked hands on a faded dish towel, then tucking a strand of blond hair behind her ear. "We knew this time would come."

The cold wrapping around Gisela intensified. "They will be here by morning?"

Dietrich nodded. "You can't wait for daylight to flee. By then it will be too late. Pack whatever you can and get out of here. My sisters and I are leaving within the hour."

Gisela rubbed her arms. "Can we get to Berlin?" She needed to be with *Mutti*. Even though she was twenty-two, she needed her mother. And *Vater* would keep them all safe.

Dietrich pulled his red knit cap further over his ears. "Right now, go. Head west and worry about the final destination later."

Gisela turned to her cousin. "We should have left sooner. Weeks ago."

"The Red Cross needed me. Still refugees pour into the city."

"I am not concerned with them. I know what the Soviets do to women and children."

Ella stepped to Dietrich's side. "We will be ready in an hour."

She ushered their neighbor into the frigid night, then came and held Gisela's hand. Another nearby blast rocked the house, reverberating in her bones.

Closer. Closer. They were coming closer.

In her memory, she heard them kick in the door. Heard screams. Gunshots.

She clutched her chest, finding it hard to breathe.

They had to run.

An hour. They would leave in an hour. She drew in an unsteady breath and steeled herself. "We can't let them catch us."

Ella nodded, deep sadness and fear clouding her. "You leave."

Gisela let go of Ella's hand and took a step back. "What about you?"

"What about the refugees and those who can't leave? They will need the Red Cross and that means I must stay." She squared her shoulders and straightened her spine.

Gisela glanced at Annelies and Renate playing once more, now pulling a tin train on a string. "What about the girls? They can't stay."

"I want you to take them."

Had Ella lost her mind? She couldn't be responsible for a five- and a three-year-old. She couldn't leave her cousin here alone to face a horrible certain fate. Those young girl screams she had heard once rattled in her brain "*Nein*. I will not leave without you. Let's get packed."

As she stepped toward the kitchen, Ella grabbed her by the shoulder, her fingers digging into Gisela's flesh. "You are not listening to me. I'm not going." Annelies and Renate ran to their mother who lowered her voice. "I will help you get ready and give you whatever money I have, but you have to be the one to take my children. For now, I am needed here. And when the war is over, this is where Frederick will come looking for me. If I'm not here, he won't be able to locate me. *Bitte, bitte*, take my children to safety. I will join you as soon as possible."

Gisela dug her fingernails into her palm. The pleading, crying in Ella's voice pinched her heart. Should she take the girls and leave her cousin behind? "You know what happened the last time I was responsible for someone's life."

"Gisela, you have to do this. For my sake. Save my girls. Take them from here. It's their only chance."

The fluttering in Gisela's stomach meant she would never see Ella again. They both knew the fate which awaited Ella. "Think about this. Your girls need you. Their father is gone and you are all they have left. They need you. I'm not their mother. I'm not enough for them. You have a responsibility to them."

The color in Ella's fair face heightened. "And I have a responsibility to the people of this area and a vow to my husband. This isn't easy for me to send my children away, but remember, your parents did it. I am asking you—begging you—to do this for me."

Thoughts whirled like a snowstorm through Gisela's mind. How could she take care of the girls? Even if she got them to the west, what would happen to them after the war? Their father would never find them.

Ella drew Gisela's stiff body close and whispered in her ear. "I trust you. I have faith in you. *Bitte*, for my sake, for the girls' sake, take them."

"I won't separate them from their mother. If you don't come with us, I won't take them."

Ella released her hold and Gisela fled up the steep stairs to her second floor bedroom. The pictures of the East Prussian countryside on the wall rattled as another shell hit its mark. They had no time to waste.

The room was tiny, with little space not taken by the bed and the pine wardrobe. A small, round bedside table held her Bible and a picture of Mutti and Vater.

Without thinking much, she grabbed all of her underwear, a red and green plaid wool skirt, two blouses, and a gray sweater and stuffed them into a battered, well-traveled pea-green suitcase. From her nightstand, she took her leather-bound Bible. She opened the pages to the book of Psalms until she found a daisy pressed in between the pages. She touched the brown petals before she slapped the book shut and stuffed it into the suitcase as well.

Hurry, hurry, hurry. The words pounded in her head in time to the pounding of her heart.

A coffee tin hidden in the back of her wardrobe held all the money she had in the world. She withdrew it and removed the small wad of Reich marks, counting them three times to make sure she knew what she had. Or didn't have. Never would they get to Berlin on this.

She folded the cash and slipped it into a pocket sewn on the inside of her dress, much as she had two years ago when she traveled to East Prussia and to safety, away from the Allied bombs. The war had caught up with her when she stayed with her aunt farther east in the country.

And it had caught up again.

Lord, please keep us safe this time. Let us escape.

The story continues in *Daisies Last Forever*
by Liz Tolsma, available May 2014

ABOUT THE AUTHOR

Photo by Bentfield Photography

L iz Tolsma has lived in Wisconsin most of her life. She and her husband have a son and two daughters, all adopted internationally. When not busy putting words to paper, Liz enjoys reading, walking, working in her large perennial garden, kayaking, and camping with her family.

Visit www.LizTolsma.com